DATE DUE

DISCARD

THEODORA

BOOKS BY SAMUEL EDWARDS

Theodora
Barbary General
Daughter of Gascony
Fifty-five Days at Peking
Master of Castile
The White Plume
The Queen's Husband
The Naked Maja
That Randall Girl
Devil's Prize
The King's Messenger
The Scimitar

THEO

PRENTICE-HALL, INC

DORA A NOVEL

SAMUEL EDWARDS, *pseud.*

ENGLEWOOD CLIFFS, N.J.

For
Elizabeth Louise

There was none like her in all the world, from the beginning of time, whether for the doing of good or evil, there being some who swore she was an Angel, while others well knew she was possessed by the most dissolute and vicious of Demons.

—PROCOPIUS OF CAESAREA,
A.D. 548

THEODORA

ONE

❦ ❦ ❦

Gossip was more than an idle pastime in sixth-century Constantinople, the cosmopolitan capital of the shrunken Roman Empire. Even the most subtle shift in alliances within the household of the old Emperor Justin could mean starvation or plenty, the levying of new taxes or the outbreak of an insurrection, the persecution of minorities, the declaration of a new war or the proclamation of a new peace, so everyone had a vital stake in the trivia of daily Imperial existence.

Certainly there was ample cause for gossip, but the interpretations differed. The magisters, heads of bureaus in the government of Flavius Caesar Justin, breathed a sigh of relief, and privately told one another that the silent, long-nosed man whom they called "the Emperor's shadow" was, perhaps, human. Their wives merely sniffed.

Members of the nobility rejoiced, and claimed they had known all along that the fellow's zeal and industry were no more than a sham. Their luxury-loving ladies smiled discreetly and felt they had been given a new license to commit their adulteries. There were exceptions, of course: the patrician parents of eligible daughters were outraged.

No one knew what the hard-bitten soldier--Emperor who liked to pose as an untutored peasant thought. Justin, who relied on his nephew's intricate network of spies to tell him what people were thinking and saying, never discussed others and sternly discouraged loose talk in his presence. The Empress Euphemia, who still looked like an uneducated farmer's wife, was more broad-minded, or perhaps because of her femininity, was willing to listen to the whispers.

Single-minded young army officers like Belisarius, second in command of the Imperial Cavalry Guard, and Mundus, his infantry counterpart, wisely kept their mouths shut. Not until years later did it occur to anyone that they had passed no judgments in the matter; loyalty to the Crown was their consuming passion, and they had no interest in the private lives of those related to their master.

John of Cappadocia, the principal tax collector, was somewhat concerned. He had been cultivating the friendship of the earnest man who asked him endless questions and hoped that new distractions wouldn't weaken their budding association. Narses, President of the Imperial Secretariat, was disappointed. He had long admired the Emperor's devoted nephew and had dreamed in secret of establishing a relationship with him similar to others he enjoyed in the privacy of his own quarters. The only man in the palace who was openly pleased was Tribonian of Pamphylia, an assistant to the Quaestor, or Minister of Justice.

"No man can work eighteen to twenty hours a day, seven days a week," he said. "This will be good for him."

Anthemius, the brilliant and ambitious young architect, agreed. "You have no idea how often he's come to my house in the middle of the night and stayed until dawn, looking at sketches and questioning me until I've grown dizzy," he confided to his intimates. "He's been lonely beyond belief."

The merchants who dealt in woolen goods and grains and leather sat on the terraces of their houses overlooking Constantinople's spectacular harbor and wondered whether the unexpected development would be good for business. The crowds that filled the vast Hippodrome every Thursday to watch the chariot races decided the Emperor's nephew wasn't as remote and scholarly as they had thought, and cheered him in the streets. And passing soldiers saluted him, although they were not required by law to recognize civilians.

The Greek scholars who were in charge of the great library founded by Constantine himself sighed quietly and muttered that the man was as frivolous as everyone else who became wealthy. The Jews who taught languages and history and mathematics at the university kept their opinions to themselves; enjoying an unaccustomed respite from persecution, they took care to utter no careless word that would cause them to be oppressed anew.

Members of the Blue, the city's dominant political faction, gloated quietly, taking pains to make it clear that rumors claiming the Emperor's nephew was either celibate or a fancier of dancing boys were false. As was to be expected, the Green called him a profligate debaucher.

In the Mesé, Constantinople's principal thoroughfare, the vendors who sold brandied figs, Egyptian dates, and bits of garlic-flavored lamb roasted over charcoal repeated the story only because their customers bought more freely. Of all the residents of the teeming city, the vendors, the owners of public baths, and the proprietors of inns entertained no illusions about human nature.

The girls who were required by law to wear scarlet cloaks and stockings and who congregated nightly at the Square of Venus, near the taverns of the seamen's district overlooking the Golden Horn, were the least surprised. They could have told stories of their own about the man and his habits, but streetwalkers knew better than to speak out of turn about the man who, in the opinion of many, had acquired power second only to that of the Emperor himself.

As was to be expected, the wealthier courtesans were wildly jealous of the wench who had taken his fancy. Some, remembering her as an adolescent dancer in the dining halls near the Hippodrome, said she had always been a scrawny bitch, and that the fellow lacked taste. Others, who had heard of her travels to Alexandria and Pentapolis in Africa, to the great Imperial cities of Antioch, Beirut, and Edessa, said it was obvious she had learned arts of black magic and had bewitched her victim.

The reaction of the clergy was strange, even startling. When a stammering seminarian brought the news to the aged Patriarch of Constantinople, who was engaged in a bitter theological dispute with the bishops of the West, the old man merely smiled and sent for several monks. That same day ships set sail for the ports of the Inner Sea, later called the Mediterranean, and the monks carried the tidings to Ephesus and Caesarea and Beirut. The Patriarch Anthimus of Antioch summed up the feelings of his colleagues when he said fervently, "The Almighty, in His eternal wisdom, has chosen the best of all instruments, His humble daughter, to heal our schism and cause the priests of the West to perceive the Truth. Blessed be the Lord."

Merchant ships and official schooners brought the gossip to the far reaches of the Empire and the lands beyond its borders. Certainly no one was more upset than Hecebolus, the Imperial Governor of Pentapolis. If he had treated the girl more gently, if he had shown her greater kindness, she might be with him yet. Increasingly afraid each day that a messenger would arrive to deprive him of his post and place him under arrest, he could only hope that in the years that had passed since he had last seen the girl she had forgotten him.

In Rome, decaying and forgotten, once the seat of Empire but now held in loose bondage by the barbarian Ostrogoths, the Pope Silverius walked in the ruins of his Church of St. Peter and shrugged when he was told the story. Mankind was corrupt, his own title was an empty honor, and the man who was the probable successor of the Emperor Justin preferred the ways of the world to those of the spirit. The bishops of the West, like the Bishop of Rome himself, apparently could look for no help or relief from earth-bound creatures.

Only two people knew the real truth behind the whispers and rumors, the sly stories and tales of lust. They told it to no one, in part because it concerned no one but themselves, but, in the main, because the truth was so bizarre that no one would have believed them . . .

❀ ❀ ❀

Justinian, Caesar Praefect of the Roman Empire, still looked like the Macedonian peasant boy who had walked on the dusty roads from his native hills beyond Greece to enter the household of his uncle, then a general. Now forty years of age in the year A.D. 522, Justinian had the broad shoulders, sturdy legs, and thick arms of one who had spent his formative years behind the plow. He wore his blond hair cut very short in the manner of the Macedonian and Bulgar farmers, and he walked with the graceless, shambling gait of one who had spent his childhood avoiding rabbit snares, fox traps, and mounds of cow dung in the fields.

But there the resemblance to the youthful Justinian ended. His attire, oddly, was the shapeless gray robe of a secretary, carelessly ink-spotted and food-stained. His worn shoes of goatskin had been bought in the market stalls that stood between the Hippodrome and the Forum of Constantine, and the black cloak flung over one shoulder was as shabby as that worn by the most impoverished student at the university.

No sane man wandered through the streets of Constantinople unarmed after dark, and Justinian's sword, a short, double-edged blade of the type Roman soldiers had been using since the time of Scipio Africanus, revealed his true rank. Rubies, diamonds, and emeralds ornamented the hilt, all of them worth a magister's ransom, and if worn by anyone else, an irresistible temptation to the cutthroats of all classes who made the city unsafe for pedestrians at night.

It did not occur to Justinian to be concerned about his life, and he refused to permit a squad of Imperial guards to accompany him when he went abroad. He had acquired a measure of skill as a swordsman in his student days, when his uncle had insisted that he acquire a rounded education, but he continued to rely on the prodigious physical strength the Lord had given him at birth. The rumors that he could cut through a mature pine tree with a single stroke were only slightly exaggerated.

He depended on more than his physical prowess to insure his safety. His intensive study of the daily espionage summaries made him aware of the people's moods, and he knew that no man in Constantinople, drunk or sober, native or alien, friend or enemy, would dare lay a hand on the Caesar Praefect, nephew of the Emperor. No one could escape from the net of Imperial agents, retribution would be swift, and the tortures that would be inflicted on his murderers in the palace prisons were too ghastly to contemplate. Therefore he was free to go where he pleased, freer, in fact, than the ordinary citizens, who after dark usually traveled in groups for their mutual protection.

Justinian walked by the hour along the Mesé, on the great walls overlooking the harbor pockets on the Sea of Marmara, on the still-higher walls above the Golden Horn. Irritated because he was restless, angry because he was wasting precious time, he nevertheless could not force himself to return home and concentrate on the huge stacks of scrolls and papers that awaited his attention. His uncle's physicians had told him repeatedly that he was working too hard and needed a holiday, but the suggestion was absurd. He had thrived on work all his life, never requiring more than three or four hours of sleep in a single night, and able, when inclined, to labor for as long as seventy-two consecutive hours without a pause. Work was the sole reason for a man's existence, and without it he was a lost soul.

When Justinian had first come to Constantinople as a boy of seventeen, he had demonstrated his capacity for learning by taking virtually every course of instruction the university offered, completing a fourteen-year curriculum in a scant five years. And now, while continuing to study for the development of his own intellect, he read every document intended for his uncle's signature, scrutinized every bureau and ministry report, delved into every file.

Proud of his talents and capacity for work, he could not understand why the annoying sensation would not dissipate itself. The feeling was not new, but in the past he had conquered it by taking a daughter of Venus to a room in a public inn for an hour, and then he had been at peace for several weeks. During the past month, however, he had been unable to obtain relief, even though he had gone to the Square of Venus for a girl on an average of every other night.

Inevitably, his steps led him to the Sancta Sophia, the city's great cathedral, where he had gone every night of late to pray for Divine help. It disturbed him that he disliked the church, which he found cold, formal, and gloomy. The heavy odors of incense caused him to sneeze, and he knew, too, that other worshipers were aware of his identity. It was wrong that they should stare at him and whisper to one another in a house of God, and he wondered whether his discomfort was making it impossible for him to devote his entire being to his prayers for Divine assistance.

Entering the church by the one side door that remained open after sundown, he rubbed his red-rimmed eyes, then stood blinking until he became accustomed to the flickering glow of the burning candles that stood in long rows on a table beneath the altar. Ignoring the customary murmurs, he made his way to the front of the church, dropped to his knees before the icon of pure gold, and prayed earnestly, in silence.

"Thy will be done," he muttered, and pulled himself to his feet again, distressed because he had been aware of the cold stones of the inlaid mosaics beneath his knees.

Still reluctant to return home, he walked slowly toward the rear of the Sancta Sophia. Later, trying to remember, he couldn't recall the moment when he first became conscious of the girl.

Of the thirty to forty worshipers in the church, she alone seemed unaware of the presence of the Caesar Praefect. But it was impossible for him not to take notice of her. She was seated on a stone bench beneath a high bank of candles near the side door, and she was striking. Masses of blue-black hair that shone in the light of the tapers fell to her waist, and her profile was delicate, but there was strength in her chin and a piquant beauty in the line of her straight nose. She wore the saffron cloak and stockings of the higher-priced courtesan, which was mildly surprising, although it was not unknown for prostitutes who had wealthy protectors to be seen in church.

A wide girdle of tooled leather held the folds of her thin, silk gown of violet, and her waist was so tiny that Justinian could have encircled it with his hands. Her wrists, arms, and ankles were unusually small, too, and at first glance she looked no more than sixteen or seventeen years of age. Not until later did he learn that she was twenty-two.

What astonished him was that she was reading a leather-bound book by the candlelight. In all of his life Justinian had never known more than three or four women who had mastered the art of reading, and it was almost beyond belief that a courtesan should have learned. Although he rarely gave in to impulse, his curiosity impelled him to move toward her.

She looked up and regarded him soberly with violet eyes lightly fringed with kohl.

Nothing had prepared him for their impact, and for a moment he felt bewildered, like a man flung unexpectedly into a deep sea. "What are you reading?" he asked, not realizing he sounded rude.

If she found his manner too curt, she gave no sign of it. "Bishop Augustine of Hippo," she said, naming the most renowned of Church theologians, who had died a little less than a century earlier.

Justinian's sense of amazement increased. Most clergymen and university lecturers with whom he had tried to discuss the works of Augustine found the great bishop's erudition beyond their grasp. It was possible, of course, that the girl was reading his *Confessions*; portions of it, taken out of context, might have a salacious appeal to someone of her mentality. He held out his hand for the book.

Still solemn, she gave it to him.

His surprise was complete when he saw it was a collection of the bishop's works, published in Latin. Under no circumstances could he believe that a girl who spoke the easy Greek of Constantinople's streets was capable of reading and understanding Latin.

"I'd be very pleased to hear you read a few lines, if you would," he said.

A priest appeared suddenly, annoyed because of the loud, echoing voice he had heard, but his anger disappeared instantly and a sycophant's smile appeared on his face as he said, "We are honored by your presence, my lord."

"In this place we honor God's presence," Justinian said bluntly, and, turning his back to the priest, handed the book back to the girl. "Perhaps you'd step outside with me, so we won't disturb others."

She seemed willing enough to accompany him, and they halted in a beam of light cast through a window by the candles. "Is there anything in particular you'd like to hear, Lord Justinian?"

"You know me." He felt disappointed, although he didn't quite know why.

"Everyone in the Empire knows the Caesar Praefect."

"I doubt it." His likeness appeared on no coins, his portrait in mosaics ornamented the interior of no building, and not one statue of him had been erected anywhere. The suspicion, virtually a certainty, crossed his mind that the girl had been waiting for him, hoping to attract his attention. If so, she wasn't the first, although more clever than the others. Any number of his acquaintances knew he read Augustine for edification and pleasure, so it was likely she had chosen a shrewd stratagem to arouse his interest.

Again she extended the book toward him, a faint smile on her full, artfully rouged lips.

He opened the volume at random to a page from *De Ascensione* and thrust it at her.

Instantly recognizing the challenge, her eyes seemed to turn a somewhat paler shade of violet. *"De vitiis nostris scalem nobis facimus, si vitia ipsa calcamus,"* she began.

"Translate!" Justinian commanded, interrupting.

" 'We make a ladder of our vices, provided we stamp those same vices underfoot,' " she said easily. "The idea is rather obvious, don't you agree? It's one of those little moral truisms that no one can deny."

For the moment, he had no desire to be drawn into a discussion of the point. It was possible he had opened the book to a page she had memorized, and he decided to test her again, more thoroughly. "Here," he said, flipping the leaves of heavy parchment to Book Ten of the *Confessions*.

The girl was untroubled. *"Da quod jubes et jube quod vis. Imperas nobis continentiam."* Not waiting for his reaction, she translated immediately. " 'Give what thou order for us, and order what thou wilt. Thou imposest chastity upon us.' It might be better to use 'moderation' in place of 'chastity.' Depending on their use they can mean more or less the same thing, but not necessarily, and Augustine's intention isn't too clear here, at least to me. I'd need to read the whole chapter to be certain."

Justinian gaped at her, half-afraid she was a creature possessed by strange demons. In fact, his exhaustion made him wonder whether she was herself an apparition.

"Basically," she said, deliberately sounding a battle trumpet, "I think Augustine and the other bishops of the West are wrong."

He shook his head. "I beg your pardon?"

"They stress the duality of Christ—Jesus the man, and Christ the Son of God. That's a form of theological sophistry. Jesus was never less than the Christ."

She was attacking the very core of his beliefs, and her glibness annoyed him. "If we accept the Virgin Birth," he replied, starting to walk without realizing it, "He was the Son of God, naturally. But Jesus the man suffered for our sakes, to show us the way. If He didn't, the Crucifixion has no significance."

"But it does," she said vehemently. "He set no less of an example for us by being the Son of God." She realized they were heading in the general direction of the highest portion of the palace walls, at the crown of the hill overlooking the city, and struggled to match his long gait.

"You've been influenced by the Monophysites of the East," he said grimly. It was the fault of the Churchmen farthest removed from the feeble but persisting beliefs of old Rome that had caused the terrible, spreading schism in the ranks of Christians.

"The Patriarch Anthimus of Antioch was my tutor," she said, proudly raising her head. "The Senior Deacon of

Petra taught me to read and write, and I was introduced to works of theology and philosophy by the old Patriarch of Edessa."

"It's no wonder you have such warped ideas." He had almost forgotten she wore the courtesan's saffron. "Do you know Augustine's *City of God*?"

"I've tried reading it, but my mind wanders. I'd need long instruction from a bishop before it made sense to me."

"I don't claim I really understand him. I'm not that spiritual." Justinian led her away from the street and began to climb a long flight of smooth steps. "But I believe I could explain the fundamentals to you."

"I'm willing to try, but I don't think even the great Bishop of Hippo could change my convictions."

A pair of palace sentries making their rounds outside the walls stood aside on the steps and saluted.

The light of the torch carried by one of them picked up the soft yellow of the girl's cloak, reminding Justinian of her vocation. "Is your protector a supporter of the patriarchs?" he asked as they continued their climb.

"I have no protector."

His curiosity increased. "How does it happen that someone in your profession was taught to read theology by Churchmen, then?"

"They gave me food for my body when I was starving, and nourishment for my soul when I thought my spirit had died within me." She spoke with passionate intensity and unless she was a great actress, could not have been simulating.

Her expression confirmed her earnest words.

Justinian reached into his voluminous gown for a key, and unlocked a door of stone set in a wall so thickly covered with vines that, at a distance of just a few feet, it looked like an impenetrable row of bushes.

She knew they had arrived at his house, a miniature palace with a wall of its own, just outside the main walls of the Emperor's palace with, she presumed, a passageway that enabled him to enter the grounds of his uncle's inner realm.

"Who are you?" he demanded.

"I am called Theodora."

Waving her ahead and following her up a still-narrower flight of outdoor steps inside the door, he concentrated hard. As the Emperor's magisters and ministers well knew, he had the ability to recall to mind literally anything he had ever read. So, if someone called Theodora had been mentioned in the reports of spies within the city, those who kept him informed of developments in the patriarchate or those who kept wary eyes on strangers coming to the capital, he would remember her name. But he felt positive he had never seen it inscribed on parchment.

Intrigued, he couldn't help asking, "If you have no protector, Theodora, why do you wear that cloak?"

"Surely the Caesar Praefect knows the law," she said bitterly. "She who is the daughter of a harlot must wear the red of a harlot, and may exchange it for the saffron of a courtesan or actress only if she finds one protector who will himself support her. But even if he casts her out, she is condemned to wear saffron forever."

The innumerable, bewildering, and often contradictory laws that governed every phase of an individual's life from the moment he was born until he was laid to rest were a constant irritation to him, and he had often discussed with his friend Tribonian, the assistant Quaestor, the urgent need to codify, modernize, and unify them, a task that staggered the imagination. "Why, a daughter born to a harlot has no chance to become anything other than a harlot herself. I suppose the daughter of a courtesan must wear saffron?"

"Naturally." Her mouth twisted, and for a moment she looked ugly.

"Even if she isn't herself a courtesan?"

"Ah, but she is. She needs bread and wine to survive, and can earn money in only one way. Yes, and when men see the yellow or scarlet cloak she wears, they know she must come to them when they beckon."

"The law," said the man who might succeed his uncle as Emperor, "is unjust."

Theodora's silence was more eloquent than any reply she might have made.

He said nothing, either.

She did not know whether he was embarrassed or was angered by inequity, something that, as the well-informed knew, was a matter of unending concern to him.

Justinian led her onto a mosaic-tiled terrace that opened onto the great hall of the house.

It was Theodora's turn to be astonished. Weeds had pushed up between the tiles, and the foliage of the garden beyond the terrace was so thick it resembled a jungle. Feather stuffing was emerging from the covering of a brocaded divan, the arm of a delicately carved ivory chair was broken, and a layer of dust covered everything in sight. The great hall was in a shambles, too, and the scrolls, books, and boxes of papyrus that filled the top of an enormous teakwood table were the only signs of habitation.

"Is this where you live?" She could not conceal her amazement.

Justinian, searching absently for a lamp or taper, did not hear her tone. "Yes, I prefer seclusion. I can read and study here without being disturbed, and if I choose to spend a whole night working, the court doesn't know it the next day."

She watched him as he located a lamp, discovered it was empty, and finally filled it with oil from a jar that stood on the floor beneath a gold-inlaid table that unaccountably had a broken leg. When he tried clumsily to light the lamp with a flint that he struck again and again on a plate of rough metal, she became impatient.

"May I?" she asked, and lighted the lamp in a single, swift motion.

Justinian looked vaguely relieved as he went to the table, picked up a book, and, holding the lamp in his other hand, went back to the terrace. "It's a fine evening," he said. "We can sit out here." Apparently unaware that the divan was in a state of near-collapse, he sat at the end farthest from the split cushion.

Theodora took a chair opposite him, trying as best she could to conceal her saffron stockings with her full skirt.

"*The City of God*," he said, opening the book. "There's one thing in particular I want to read to you." He began to search, occasionally found a passage that caught his interest, and all but forgot the girl.

Theodora watched as his free hand repeatedly pawed an empty marble bowl. "How long since you've eaten?" she asked him quietly.

Justinian wrenched himself away from the book, blinked, and tried to remember. "I think I had some bread and cold mutton sent to my office at noon. Yes, I did. With a cup of goat's milk." He turned back to the book.

Theodora would have laughed if she hadn't felt a deep wave of pity for him. The civilized world thought that Flavius Caesar Justinian, Praefect, lived in magnificent splendor and dined on delicacies brought to his table from the far corners of the Empire. The truth was beyond credulity. "You haven't eaten in almost twelve hours," she said.

He did not look up. "Food doesn't mean much to me."

"Obviously, but you really should eat," the girl replied sternly. "Why don't you ring for a servant?"

"I prefer to live without any. They're always under foot, they steal—"

"Do you mean you have no food in the house?"

"Oh, someone from the palace brings something to the larder every morning."

"Where is the larder?"

He remembered his manners. "Of course. I've forgotten to get you something."

"Where is the larder?" Her voice became a trifle strained.

"Beyond the great hall. I—"

"Never mind, I'll find it." She vanished before he could heave himself from the divan.

Justinian watched her as she made her way toward the inner part of the house, and it occurred to him that he had never seen a woman's hips sway so enticingly. Then, remembering the book he held, he resumed his search in its pages.

It seemed like no more than a moment before Theodora returned with a silver platter on which were arrayed a grilled breast of swan, slices of pickled ox tongue, a mound of goose liver mixed with chopped olives, a huge bowl of honey, and several loaves of bread. It did not occur to him that she had cleaned the tray and had taken a considerable time to arrange the food artistically.

"There are all kinds of good things in the larder," she said, placing the tray on the table beside him.

"I suppose so. The people who bring me supplies every morning take away what they've left the previous day, and I dare say they eat it themselves. It never looks this appetizing."

She accepted the compliment with a slight smile. "I searched everywhere for wine, but couldn't find any."

"I never drink it myself, but I keep a few jars for my friends when they visit me. It's in my dressing room upstairs, so if you'll forgive me for a moment—"

"I don't care for any, thanks. I do wish you'd eat."

"Help yourself." In spite of his education and rise to the highest rank of nobility in the Roman Empire, his manners were still those of a barbarian farm boy.

"I'll wait, I think." It amused Theodora to see that he

was ravenous, and she had never known any human being to eat so much so quickly.

"I wish you'd take something," he said, spreading the last of the goose liver on what was left of the swan's breast.

Steeling herself so he wouldn't see she was hungry, too, she poured some honey on a chunk of bread she tore from a round loaf.

"You like it," he said, pleased.

"I've never tasted such fine wheat bread or pure honey," she told him truthfully.

His broad smile was unexpectedly boyish. "I've been eating this bread for so many years I've been taking it for granted. But I can remember my first meal at the palace —I sat at the commoners' table, with the secretaries and scribes—and I couldn't get enough of it. The reason it tastes so good is that all but the best of the wheat is sifted out by a kitchen slave who does nothing else, and they use hens' eggs and milk in the batter. It costs more than the bread sold on the Mesé, but it stays fresh an average of two and one-third days longer."

Not one of the scores of men she had ever encountered would have known the recipe, cared one way or the other, or have been able to cite such statistics. Apparently there was nothing that escaped his attention.

"Have another loaf," Justinian said, noting with surprise that her table manners were those of the high-born: after licking her fingers, she wiped them on a dampened cloth of linen that had been reposing on one side of the tray.

Theodora happily accepted the invitation.

Having known the extreme hunger of the poverty-stricken, he realized she had not eaten in many hours, either. There was little doubt in his mind now that she had contrived their meeting, but he did not condemn her for it. She had proved herself domestically helpful as well as intelligent and decorative, and he had never met any woman quite like her.

"You really should make this house more presentable," she told him, and decided to take a risk. "A man is judged by the way he lives, and I've heard it said there are scores of servants in the palace of the Consul Vitalian, that he lives in luxury almost as great as that of the Emperor himself."

Apparently she was capable of perpetrating endless surprises, but he should have guessed she would be familiar with the most important political question in the Empire. Vitalian, a handsome, energetic general who had fought with distinction against the Persians and now was commander of the forces that defended the capital, was Justinian's only rival to succeed the old man who now sat on the throne of Caesar Augustus. "You have friends among the Greens," he said, referring to the political faction that supported his rival.

"I know as many Blues as I do Greens," she replied quickly, "and now I know why the Blues worry about you."

He stroked his long jaw. "I could have as many slaves here as anyone might want, but how could I make sure they'd stay out of my way? And how could I be certain of their loyalty?"

"Someone who knows servants could select them for you and supervise their work." Theodora didn't dare say more.

He started to reply, but a door at the far end of the garden opened, and a centurion of the household infantry, in full uniform, approached and saluted.

The officer was startled by the presence of the girl in saffron, but after one swift glance in her direction, pretended she didn't exist. "I bring you a message from the magister of the Vaults, Caesar."

Justinian took the small scroll, unrolled it, and read quickly. "Tell him I'll join him at once."

The centurion saluted again and departed.

"A treasure galleon of the Vandals traveling to Carthage has fallen into our hands," Justinian said, "and the director of the treasury is afraid to announce its capture for fear it will weaken the price of gold. He wants me to join him at an emergency meeting of ministers." He stood, brushing crumbs from his robe onto the tiled floor.

Theodora rose, too.

"I wish you'd wait for me," he said quickly. "The conference shouldn't last too long, and I still haven't read you those passages from *The City of God*."

She seemed to hesitate for an instant before nodding in agreement.

Relieved, he went off through the garden.

Watching him, the girl sighed and told herself that for one night, at least, she would have a roof over her head.

TWO

❧ ❧ ❧

The first dirty light of dawn was breaking over the red-dish green hills of Asia Minor when Justinian returned from the palace. The problems raised at the meeting of ministers had been far more complicated than he had anticipated and were not yet solved. It would be necessary to present the Emperor with specific, clear-cut recommendations when he held his regular audience with his magisters and ministers, later in the morning, so the conference would be resumed as soon as the officials could change their clothes.

Pausing to draw some water from the well in the garden for washing and shaving, Justinian's mind was filled with the intricacies of higher finance, and he reached the terrace, slopping water from the bucket, before he suddenly became aware of the changes in his surroundings.

Broken and shabby pieces of furniture had been removed and were piled in a far corner of the garden. In their place, both on the terrace and in the great hall, were handsome pieces that had never shown off to good advantage in the cluttered rooms. A rug that, he vaguely recalled, had been presented to him the previous year by the Viceroy of

Syria, now covered the floor of the great hall, and a gem-encrusted table, its legs of elephant tusks, that had been presented to him by an Indian Maharajah after his elevation to Praefect, stood in its center. He had actually forgotten he owned such valuable items.

The furniture gleamed, there were no traces of dust anywhere, and even the oil lamps had been cleaned so their glass picked up the rays of the early morning light. Looking around slowly, he saw that some of the weeds choking the tiles of the terrace mosaics had been removed, too.

All at once he became aware of Theodora. She was stretched out on a divan of rich Oriental silk that she had managed to move from a corridor into a corner of the great hall, and was sound asleep. Her long hair was tousled, her gown was stained by perspiration, and smudges of dirt streaked her hands and bare arms.

Justinian stood for a time, staring down at her, but she was sleeping soundly and made no move. Half-smiling, he shook his head, then covered her with her saffron cloak and went upstairs to his bedchamber to shave.

❀ ❀ ❀

The bells in the dome of the Sancta Sophia were chiming the noon hour when Justinian returned from the magisters' audience with his uncle and walked hurriedly through the garden. Two slaves in the green and white tunics of the Imperial outdoor household were at work there, slashing at the overgrowth of foliage, pruning bushes and pulling weeds from flower beds. Three slave women were busily cleaning and polishing, too, one on the terrace and two in the great hall, and the changes were even more marked than they had been early in the morning.

Books and scrolls that had been piled beneath the staircase now filled shelves that lined one wall of the huge room, and an ornamental lamp of pure gold, a gift from the citizens of Hierapolis, stood on an ebony and ivory table behind a cedarwood chair laden with cushions. Everything was different, everything sparkled, and Justinian found it difficult to realize this was his home.

Theodora materialized from the rear of the little palace, a feather dusting mop in one hand. "I'm so glad you're here," she said calmly.

"I—ah—I came because I was afraid you might have gone."

"I've been far too busy." She led him toward the dining hall, which he had neglected for years.

A monks' refectory table of polished oak gleamed in the center of the chamber, a rich rug from Cathay covered the floor, and plates, urns, and jars of silver, gold, and fragile porcelain made a dazzling background on sideboards and shelves against the walls. The table was laid for two with gold plates, knives, and chalices, with a high-backed chair of oak at each place. Smoke was rising from the hearth in the kitchen outbuilding beyond the window, and he caught a glimpse of two slave women hard at work there.

"I was hoping you'd come home to eat," Theodora said. "If you hadn't, I was going to send you a message."

He sank into the chair at the head of the table, too dazed to reply, and when she clapped her hands a slave woman appeared with a damp, hot cloth of linen.

Still unable to speak, he automatically wiped his hands and face.

"I found a bell rope," Theodora said, "and a majordomo came from the palace when I pulled it. These servants are just here temporarily, of course. We'll find others, if they don't please you."

"I'm overwhelmed," he muttered.

"You should do the overwhelming. Leaders of the Blues who have visited you have commented on the way you live, but I never knew until last night what they meant. The same is true of the nobles. The Lord Chamberlain, Cassius, isn't sure whether to support you or Vitalian for Emperor, and it's no secret that he's been courted by Vitalian at grand banquets."

Justinian tried to interrupt.

"I know what you're going to say—a man should be respected for his merit, not the outer trappings, but that isn't the way of the world. We're judged more by appearances than by our talents and accomplishments."

The arrival of a slave woman with a steaming bowl of food made it impossible for him to reply, and he waited until the servant deposited the bowl in front of Theodora. "My tastes are very simple," he said, looking askance at the dish. "My inner humors become unbalanced if I eat rich food."

"So I gathered last night, and I also took the precaution of questioning the majordomo this morning." She ladled a generous helping onto a plate. "But I also know that a man who works as hard as you do needs nourishment."

Justinian stared at the dish she placed before him, then sniffed cautiously. "This is a Macedonian stew!" he exclaimed, poking with his knife at millet dumplings, chunks of lamb, and onions. "I haven't tasted it since I was a boy! How did you know—"

"I didn't. I guessed." She tried not to sound smug as she poured water into his chalice, then added snow that had been brought to the palace from the mountains by relays of runners.

He waited with ill-concealed impatience until she served herself, then ate heartily.

Theodora speared a piece of meat and a small dumpling, and tried to sound enthusiastic as she tasted them. "This is good, far better than the Theban stew the Greeks eat."

"Of course. It's Macedonian."

Under no circumstances could she tell him she found the dish too hearty, and that it needed the leavening of a light, dry wine in place of water.

Justinian was studying her as he ate, and his eyes became veiled. "You spoke with great authority of the chieftains of the Blue party, and the Lord Chamberlain. How do you know so much about Imperial politics—and about me?"

"A woman in my position needs to know all she can find out—about many things—if she hopes to survive."

Her reply was blunt, which pleased him, but he wasn't yet satisfied and, still eating, worded his next question with care. "Why did you choose to single me out when there are many men of wealth and standing in Constantinople who have reputations for their liaisons with—ah—ladies in your profession?"

She decided it was best not to pretend their meeting had been accidental. "Perhaps," she replied lightly, "it was because you have neither a wife nor a mistress, and you have no attachments other than your occasional visits to the harlots at the Square of Venus." Her smile faded. "My principal reason is that I can help you, and you need help, far more than you know."

His manner changed, and, no longer the Macedonian peasant eating a favorite dish, he looked like a powerful and cunning nobleman playing for the highest stakes on earth. "I'm listening," he said, his voice rasping.

"General Rincius fawns on the Emperor and pretends to be your friend, but he's in league with Vitalian. They made a secret agreement at least a year ago, and Rincius never loses a chance to defame you when he visits the Empress Euphemia."

Justinian forgot his food for the moment. He knew his uncle's wife had always disliked him, perhaps because he reminded her of her own humble origins, and he had suspected that Rincius was working against him, but his espionage agents had been unable to obtain any real evidence against the senior troop commander. "I hear many rumors," he said, "but I never accept them without proof."

Theodora faced him, her gaze unflinching. "What I've

said is true. When a man and woman have been together, he often relaxes and tells her many things."

He found her candor so startling that to cover his confusion, he concentrated his surface attention on the meal, and began to sop up the gravy on his plate of gold with a chunk of bread.

"There are some who admire you for working harder than any slave," Theodora said, "and there are others who ridicule you. This much I know—a man who buries himself behind papers and relies on others to act as his eyes and ears misses much of what happens. In the palace as well as in the city. I'm not unselfish, Lord Justinian. A woman grows tired of going from one man to another and selling the baubles he gives her to the moneylenders."

"In all my life," he said, his voice suddenly hoarse, "I've never trusted anyone."

"If you wish, I'll leave at once." Theodora pushed back her chair and stood.

"Sit down!"

She obeyed silently.

"I know only that you can read and write, which is miraculous, that you've made over my house in a few hours, and that you have a mind as keen as any man's."

His failure to list her beauty among her assets amused rather than annoyed her. "I'll gladly tell you anything you may want to know. And I suggest you get a report on me through your spies."

"I've already ordered one." He smiled faintly.

She summoned a slave woman, who took away the dishes and put a pot of goats' milk cheese before them, then backed out of the chamber. "Let me tell you what it will say. My father is unknown, my mother was a bear-keeper at the Hippodrome circus, and I waited on my older sisters until I became old enough to wear scarlet, too. Anyone on the Mesé knows that much. I exchanged my red cloak for saffron when Hecebolus took me to Africa with him, and

I suppose I should be grateful to him for the improvement in my station." She heard the faint tremor in her voice and drank a little water. "After spending a few months with him, I left. Since then I've wandered through the Empire—"

"Becoming friendly with the patriarchs?"

"If it weren't for the kindness they and their priests showed me, I wouldn't have lived to return to Constantinople six months ago. But you'll find nothing of such matters in your spy's report. My friends in the Church never boast of their charity and compassion."

"Was it they who taught you letters?"

"No, they helped me to understand the writings of the Apostles in God's Book, but I taught myself to read when I was very young."

"How is that possible?"

"Why did you walk in the dust from Macedonia to Constantinople, Lord Justinian?" she countered.

He nodded, smeared a coating of cheese on a large piece of bread and ate it. "I can't be certain you aren't an agent for the Green party," he said at last.

"I could assure you that my relationship with men hasn't been political, but you'd be a fool to believe me. Your spies will find I've never plotted with anyone, or against anyone. The worst they can say about me is that I'm penniless."

Justinian was surprised. "I've always assumed—that is, I've taken it for granted—that one in your profession becomes wealthy."

"A few who will accept any protector may save a little. But I've been too busy preparing—for this." Having told him everything, she felt relieved. If her gamble succeeded, her long campaign would be crowned with triumph; if it failed, she would be forced to sell her saffron cloak for a scarlet one, and return to the Square of Venus.

Justinian rose and began to pace up and down the dining hall, clasping and unclasping his hands behind his back. "My mind is on my work, so it isn't easy to decide what to do. All I know is that this is the best meal I've eaten since I left the home of my parents, may they be enjoying eternal salvation, and my house looks so magnificent I scarcely recognize it." Suddenly he halted and turned to her. "I've won my place as Praefect. My uncle gave it to me grudgingly. I know my friends and my enemies, and I need no help from anyone."

She vowed she would never forget that he considered himself self-sufficient, and knew a placating smile, combined with a humble lowering of her head, would be a sop to his male vanity.

He paced again, more rapidly. "When I was a boy working in the fields," he said, "my mother often gave me a dish of sausages and barley for my supper."

"They're cooked together," Theodora replied, "with a few bay leaves and a clove of garlic to give them flavor. I sent to the market for the ingredients this morning, and the barley is already simmering."

"I find it uncanny that you should be able to read my mind. For years I've longed for the taste of that dish."

She had no intention of telling him she had spent a full week eating all her meals at a tavern frequented by Macedonians, tasting, observing, and then questioning the cooks. The dish he craved was the universal favorite of the broadshouldered workmen who had come to the city from their distant farms, so it had not been difficult to guess his preferences.

"Stay until I learn the truth about you," he said gruffly. "Take any sleeping chamber you want—except mine."

Obviously he had no intention of allowing a physical or emotional entanglement to cloud his judgment, and his caution made her smile admiringly. Never had she known such caution in any man.

"Here," he said, reaching into his purse and handing her a gold aureus, then another. "You've ruined your clothes moving furniture, and you'll need others." Embarrassed and uncertain of his own motives, he stomped out and started back toward the palace.

Theodora clutched the gold pieces, realizing that over a period of years he had forgotten the value of money; he had given her far more than she needed for a dress. In fact, she could buy a complete new wardrobe and live comfortably for many weeks. Her foothold in the house was precarious, but she certainly had no cause for complaint. All the same, it had not occurred to her that she could achieve even this much without giving in to sexual demands, and she knew she would have to revise her thinking and her approach to Justinian in order to strengthen her hold on him. To put it mildly, he was the most unpredictable man she had ever encountered.

❦ ❦ ❦

Not the least of Theodora's talents, Justinian thought, was her ability to handle servants, and in less than a week she had assembled a full staff that worked efficiently and harmoniously. Regardless of whether a slave was a Persian or a Vandal, a Goth, a Hun, or a crude Bulgar from the wilderness beyond Macedonia, she could speak the servant's language and had impressed on everyone she brought into the little palace that she would not tolerate slothfulness, dishonesty, or disloyalty. The cook, who went off to the markets each morning to buy the day's food, accounted for every copper he spent, knowing it would be both useless and dangerous to try cheating someone who knew the price of every item on sale at the stalls. Even the majordomo, a haughty Greek freeman, quickly learned it was best to ignore her saffron cloak and stockings, and to treat her with the respect she demanded.

It had become a pleasure to spend time at home, which was new in Justinian's experience. No matter how early in the morning he arose, Theodora was waiting for him when he came into the dining hall for breakfast. And no matter when he returned for his midday and evening meals, large quantities of hot, delicious food appeared within a few moments of his arrival. Obviously she had a remarkable organizational ability.

Even more extraordinary was the way she had created order out of the chaotic state of his books and scrolls. She had set aside a special room for him to use as a work sanctum, had lined it with shelves, and then arranged his reading matter according to subject. When he wanted books of philosophy or theology, studies of engineering, road-building, taxation, or military affairs, he could find them at once. She had even purchased a heavy strongbox of iron for him, insisting that he himself have a lock and single key made for it by the palace smith, so that he could bring secret documents home in the knowledge they would be safe.

Above all, he enjoyed relaxing with her at meals and for an hour after they ate their supper, before he went back to his interminable work. It bothered him, however, that he hadn't yet been able to arouse her interest in *The City of God*, but they seemed to have so much to discuss that there had been no opportunity to read to her at length from the work of Augustine.

What continued to surprise him was her apparently unlimited store of knowledge of people in high places. No matter what noble or high official he might mention to her, she was not only familiar with the name but knew something of his character traits. She swore she had met virtually none of the great, however, and when he tried to find out the sources of her information, she merely smiled and told him that her friends in the Square of Venus used methods as effective as those employed by the Crown's espionage agents. And she gave him every reason to believe her.

He appreciated her respect for his work habits, and neither she nor anyone else disturbed him when he retired to his sanctum for a long evening of reading. So he was doubly surprised one night when she appeared at the door.

Looking up from a report on the storage of grains in the outer reaches of the Empire, he was vaguely aware of the fact that she had changed her attire since supper and was wearing a new lilac-colored gown of silk that seemed to emphasize her violet eyes. A gold-colored metal chain made him realize how incredibly tiny her waist was, and the desire for her that had been increasingly difficult to control surged up within him.

"Forgive the interruption, Lord Justinian," she said, "but the principal secretary, Narses, and the centurion Belisarius are here to see you. I sent word through the major-domo that you're busy, and would see them only if you wished, so you needn't feel obligated."

"Oh, I must. Something out of the ordinary has happened, obviously. Come on."

If she thought it unusual that he was expecting her to accompany him, she kept her views to herself.

Belisarius, a broad-shouldered young officer with chiseled features, jumped to his feet and saluted, but Narses rose more slowly. The director of the Emperor's secretariat was a slender man who looked far younger than his years, and in no way resembled a clerk. His wavy, shoulder-length hair was oiled and perfumed, he wore several rings and a massive bracelet of gold, and his calf-length, girdled robe was of the purest silk from Cathay. He bowed to the Caesar Praefect, but covertly studied the girl.

She appeared more interested in Belisarius, but when Narses persisted, she returned his scrutiny.

Justinian either felt no need to present the men to the young woman or was too embarrassed. "What's wrong?" he demanded without preamble, waving them to their seats.

"A problem of great delicacy has arisen," Narses said, carefully arranging the folds of his robe as he sat. "I can't go to Caesar Augustus with it. You know how he demands only demonstrable facts and becomes annoyed when there's the least speculation. Besides, the matter is of direct concern to you, Caesar Praefect." He paused and glanced significantly at Theodora.

"I'm listening," Justinian said tartly.

The girl felt uncomfortable, although flattered because he wanted her to stay.

Narses made it plain that he would speak in her presence only with reluctance. "Just two days ago," he said, "the Caesar Augustus drew up a secret realignment of our frontier regiments."

"I know," Justinian cut in. "I helped him."

"And just yesterday he sent out the orders to the regional frontier commanders."

"I was with him," Justinian said, "when he placed the Imperial seal on each set of orders."

"I myself made the copies, as I always do when I'm dealing with highly secret material." Narses was becoming agitated. "I made two copies of each, putting one in the Emperor's personal file and the other in his military file. This evening the copies in his military file disappeared."

"Who has access to that file?"

"The Emperor, you and I. No one else."

"If my uncle wanted to refer to the matter," Justinian said, "he'd look in his personal file, which is in his own sanctum. He certainly wouldn't go searching through the strongboxes in your office at the other end of that long corridor. And since you and I were both familiar with the orders, neither of us would have any reason to take them."

"Tell him, Belisarius," Narses muttered.

"I'm in command of the palace guard tonight, Caesar Praefect," the young officer said. "Earlier tonight, as I was making my rounds, I saw the consul coming out of Narses' file room. He was in a great hurry, and when I went into the room after he'd gone, I found that the Emperor's military strongbox had been forced open, so I notified Narses immediately."

The atmosphere became tense, and Justinian frowned. "If I remember the law correctly, Vitalian has no right to see the Emperor's private military file, either in his capacity of consul or that of general in command of Constantinople's defenses."

"He has no right whatever," Narses said flatly, "and I want to bring this whole matter into the open, Caesar Praefect. At once."

"Can you prove Vitalian took the orders?"

"No, milord. We know only that the papers are gone, and that Belisarius saw Vitalian coming out of the file room. I'm sure it was he who forced open the strongbox, but I haven't proof that would satisfy the Emperor."

"I'm afraid," Justinian said, "that the word of even the most trusted of centurions would carry little weight if a man of Vitalian's standing denied he was guilty."

"That's why I've come to you," Narses declared. "The weight of your influence would balance that of Vitalian. This is our chance!"

Everyone present knew what he meant, that this was an opportunity to discredit the consul and remove him as Justinian's rival.

But Justinian shook his head. "It isn't that simple. Belisarius, what good would a copy of the orders do Vitalian?"

"If he were preparing a revolt, they'd be useful to him, but I'm reasonably sure he has no such scheme in mind. He's enormously popular in the army, but the troops still put the Emperor first. Every man who carries a Roman shield knows he rose through the ranks, and is loyal to him."

"But in a contest between Vitalian and me, they'd support Vitalian, of course."

Belisarius was too embarrassed to reply, and nodded. "What other reason could he have for taking the papers?"

"I don't know, Caesar Praefect."

"Narses?"

The secretary shrugged elegantly.

Theodora could not keep silent any longer. "It's very plain. It couldn't have been accidental that Vitalian came out of the file room at the precise moment that the centurion Belisarius was making his rounds there. You follow a regular schedule, don't you?"

"Well, yes," Belisarius said.

Narses was annoyed because the girl had dared to interrupt, but Justinian was regarding her intently.

"Then General Vitalian, of all people, knows that schedule. He wanted you to see him. He knew the secretary would come to Lord Justinian, and he hoped a charge would be brought against him. Don't you see? It would be his word against Justinian's, and the army would take the word of a successful general in a dispute with a civilian. Don't you see?" Theodora asked earnestly, almost pleading. "Except for the War That Never Ends, with the Persians, we're at peace with everyone, so Vitalian has no real need for secret military information. He's thinking far ahead, as he always does, and wants to discredit the one man who stands between him and the throne."

Grudgingly, but with a trace of admiration, Narses agreed.

Belisarius really looked at the girl for the first time, seeing her as something more than a courtesan.

Justinian was conscious of the young officer's interest and felt a stab of jealousy.

"I spent more than two years as Vitalian's aide-de-camp," Belisarius said, "and the lady is right. That's the way he thinks and works. I'm willing to wager my soul that she's right."

Justinian remained silent, and his expression indicated neither approval nor disapproval. He was stone-faced, and it was impossible to guess his reaction.

Belisarius' discomfort was obvious, and even the sophisticated Narses seemed ill at ease.

Theodora was equal to the situation. "I'm sure you'd like some mead," she said, and went herself to fetch several cups of the honey brew.

"That was a brilliant analysis," Belisarius said, filling an awkward pause. "I've seen Vitalian maneuver many people in just such a manner."

"She must know him well," Narses added, an edge of malice in his voice, "to understand his mind so thoroughly."

Justinian was still slumped in his chair, his chin almost touching his chest, and did not stir until Theodora returned with the bittersweet mead. "Narses," he said, "have the smith make a new strongbox for the Emperor's military files. Order a new lock, too, one that can't be broken by thieves. Let the smith and his helpers work all night, if necessary, but make certain the box and lock are finished by morning. Belisarius, hereafter I want two armed sentries posted outside the Crown file room. No one except the chief of the secretariat is to be admitted unless he carries a signed permit from the Caesar Augustus himself. *No* man may enter, not even the general in command of the Constantinople defenses or the Caesar Praefect. Tomorrow, when I see the Emperor, I'll find some excuse to change the alignment of the border regiments again, so the information stolen this evening will be useless. Have I made myself understood?"

"Yes, sir," Belisarius said.

Narses, whose attitude had been one of familiarity with his superior, stiffened and, half-rising from his chair, bowed.

"This evening's unfortunate incident will be forgotten.

Mention it to no one, and write nothing concerning it in your logs for the day. Does anyone else know of it?"

Narses and Belisarius both indicated that they alone had any knowledge of the affair.

"Good," Justinian said. "If Vitalian is the culprit, as we believe, he'll be disappointed when nothing further develops. If someone else was the thief, the information will be of no value to him, either." He hauled himself to his feet, indicating that the conference was at an end.

The other men rose at once, and Narses raised an eyebrow when he saw that Theodora had remained seated. "May I provide you with an escort?" he asked her, a hint of unpleasantness behind his seemingly thoughtful gesture.

"You're very kind," she replied sweetly, "but my escort arrangements are already made."

The cleverness of her rebuff, which did not indicate whether she was leaving or staying for the night, made Belisarius laugh aloud, and he quickly averted his face.

Anger flashed in Narses' dark eyes for an instant, then he controlled himself and, paying no more attention to her, dropped to one knee and kissed Justinian's hand, his lips pressing against it longer than protocol required.

The Caesar Praefect accompanied his visitors as far as the terrace before turning back to the great hall.

Theodora, waiting for him, was still unable to read his mood. She wished he had taken at least a token sip of the mead, but as he had not touched his, she thought it wiser not to drink her own.

"I think I should warn you not to match wits with Narses," he said. "He's easily offended, and he never forgets an injury, so he can be dangerous."

"The moment one meets him, one knows the stories told about him on the Mesé are true. No woman could be his friend, particularly a woman attached to your household."

"His preferences are no secret, certainly, but why would he dislike you?"

"Apparently you've never noticed the way he looks at you." Theodora realized she was taking a chance by speaking so candidly; for all she knew, the enigmatic Caesar Praefect and Narses already had a complicated relationship.

Justinian stood for a moment, stroking his chin. "You observe much, and have explained something that has puzzled me. I'm doubly in your debt." He drew her to her feet and, taking her by the hand, led her to the stairs.

She accompanied him in willing silence, having learned not to question his abrupt decisions.

He took her to his private quarters, which she had just finished refurnishing. The suite consisted of a sleeping chamber, a dressing room almost as large, and a balconied sitting room overlooking the Golden Horn, where he could read, meditate, or even enjoy a meal in solitude. It was the first time they had been there together.

Justinian left her in the sitting room, and she wandered out onto the balcony. Merchant seamen of a half-score nationalities and girls from the Square of Venus were walking in the street below, and their laughter drifted up to her, as did the cries of pastry and fruit vendors and the angry shouts of outriders clearing a path for their noble masters. The world of the street was her world, the world she knew, far removed from the luxury of the little palace in spite of its physical proximity, and she felt an uneasy shiver creep up her spine as she awaited the man whose moods and attitudes she found so difficult to judge.

He tarried for a time in his dressing chamber, and when he finally rejoined her he appeared to be holding something in his thick, peasant's hand. "Your dissection of Vitalian's strategy was superb," he said. "I've never heard a magister react so quickly or accurately at a Council of State meeting. If it weren't for you, I'd have bumbled tonight, which is precisely what Vitalian hoped I'd do. I can't repay you, but this will at least show you my gratitude." He thrust his hand toward her, opening it.

Theodora saw the ring in the light of a clear, three-quarter moon, and gasped. An emerald larger than a gull's egg was set in a bed of diamonds and rubies, but it was the luminous sheen of the stone even more than its enormous size that awed her. She had heard there were such gems on earth, but had found the allegation difficult to believe; even the emerald in the crown of the Patriarch of Antioch was a relatively insignificant bauble.

"This was the Emperor's gift to me when he made me Caesar Praefect. He gave me the rank, and tonight you saved it for me, so I want you to have this."

She continued to gape at the ring.

He forced it onto her finger, scraping the skin.

Theodora felt paralyzed, unable to move or to speak, but at last she tore her gaze from the fantastic stone and looked at the man who towered above her. "This ring," she said, "would pay the ransom of an Empress captured by the Vandals. It's a symbol of your place of high trust, and was a gift to you from the Emperor Justin. I—I can't accept it."

"It belongs to you now. Do what you please with it."

Again she stared at the ring, then suddenly began to weep.

The alarmed Justinian drew her into the sitting room, where she threw herself onto a divan. Uncertain what to say or do, he stood, shifting his weight from one foot to the other and fidgeting.

Exercising all her faculties of self-discipline, the girl managed to control her feelings. "No man—except the priests of the Church—has ever given me a free gift. Until now I've had to earn every crumb, in the one way expected of me. So forgive me for weeping."

"I refuse to buy you." Justinian's voice sounded high and thin. "If you should ever give yourself to me, you'll do it freely, of your own will."

She took a deep breath, then stood. "I've assumed that

you prefer to wait until your spies report that I'm not in league with your enemies."

"I know the report will be favorable. How could it be otherwise?"

She saw the desire in his eyes, the same expression she had read in the faces of so many men over so many years, and knew he wanted her, here and now. Once again she had to revise her plans drastically: although she had intended from the outset to win a place in his household by becoming his mistress, that place was already assured, at least for the present, and a terrible fear seized her.

She had been able to dissemble with others, to simulate passion when there had been only a void inside her, to pretend she was giving love when she made meaningless gestures. But she could not play the role of an actress with Justinian, whose sensitivity was greater than that of any man she had ever encountered. He was capable of being as ruthless as he had been generous, and a single false word or insincere move might enrage him and cause him to destroy her.

To deny him, however, would be an equally unbearable insult, and she wished desperately, but in vain, that she could return his yearning. Steadying herself, she said, "Whenever you want me, I'm here."

"You'll never have to earn your way in my bed. I've already told you the ring belongs to you, so there's no way you can repay me for it." His voice became even more shrill.

Theodora unpinned her gown at both shoulders, and when it fell away she stood before him, unclad.

Accustomed only to the coarse bodies of the peasant women who had become daughters of Venus, he stared at the slender girl in much the same way that she had gaped at the emerald ring. Her breasts were small but perfectly formed, and, unlike the harlots, she had not rouged her pointed nipples. Her waist was even tinier than it had appeared when she wore clothes, her hips and thighs were firmly rounded, and her legs were long, giving her an illusion of being taller than she was.

Justinian picked her up, carried her into the inner chamber, and deposited her on the bed, where he joined her. In spite of the intensity of his desire, he took his time, kissing and caressing her slowly, his hands gentle as they roamed and explored. Although clumsy in almost everything he did, he displayed surprising qualities as a lover, curbing his own eagerness in order to arouse his partner.

Theodora found herself responding to his ardor and discovered there was far less need for her to simulate than she had feared. She had imagined he would be boorish and inept, but his patience and consideration were unique in her experience, and it astonished her that she wanted him.

They reached a climax simultaneously, and then, their desire spent, remained close as they rested on the silken cushions. Justinian appeared to be asleep, his face slightly averted, and Theodora was relieved. If he saw the tears in her eyes, he would ask too many questions that she was incapable of answering. Until now she had believed herself unable to obtain complete satisfaction from any man, and it confused her that this gaunt, awkward Macedonian giant, this dedicated public servant who prized intellect above all other human qualities and who drove himself unmercifully, should be the one who had freed her from lifelong bondage.

His power, his exalted rank, his dazzling prospects for the future were irrelevant at moments such as this. A man wore neither his insignia of high office nor his medals when he went to bed with a woman. And it was ironic that Justinian, almost twice her age, from whom she had expected nothing in an intimate relationship, should have achieved what so many others had failed to give her.

Too bewildered to think clearly, Theodora nestled closer to him, and she, too, dropped off to sleep.

✿ ✿ ✿

The routines of daily living in the little palace were flexible but firm and were adjusted to meet Justinian's arduous, ever-changing work schedule. No matter what time of night or early morning he might return home from a conference with the Emperor Justin or a meeting with the Imperial ministers of state, a freshly prepared meal of his favorite dishes awaited him, hot water was poured into a silver tub for his bath, and clean clothes were laid out for him.

At least one day each week friends came to dine with him, and at his insistence Theodora always joined them at the table. Sometimes he became absorbed in discussions with Anthemius, the architect, or Timeus of Corinth, the philosopher, and when these talks lasted far into the night, Theodora discreetly vanished, but was always nearby to bring the guests refreshments or to listen to the talk for a time when there was something that Justinian particularly wanted her to hear.

His friends and associates sang her praises everywhere. She was as perfect a hostess as she was lovely, Anthemius declared, and the hard-bitten John of Cappadocia, the tax collector, who was the least sentimental of men, said that she had the mind of a man. Belisarius saw her in still another light. Theodora, knowing that Justinian's one weakness was a lack of understanding of military affairs, encouraged the development of a friendship with Belisarius, in whom she detected an incisiveness of intellect and strength of character that his own superiors had not seen. And the young officer returned the compliment, in a sense, when he told some of his army comrades, "Theodora is changing the Caesar Praefect into a human being. He doesn't just work for the sake of efficiency anymore, but is always asking whether this or that decree will help the people."

To be sure, the change in Justinian's way of life did not meet universal approval. Noble ladies complained to the Empress Euphemia, members of the Green party ridiculed the Caesar Praefect for taking a harlot into his household, and the consul, Vitalian, privately confided to his intimates that he thought Justinian was ruining his own future.

The Emperor, who could have ended the affair or stifled the gossip with a word, did not mention the subject to anyone, his nephew included. It had always been his opinion that a man's private life was strictly his own business, provided his dedication to his work and his efficiency were not impaired, and it was obvious to everyone in the higher ranks of the government that Justianian was more energetic and clear-headed than he had ever been.

Theodora, obviously, had become an influential woman, but the limits of her power were sharply defined. At no time did she ever accompany her lover into the palace of the Emperor, she received no invitations to dine at the homes of nobles, and even the wives of artists like Anthemius took care to avoid her. Her unsavory past made it impossible for any respectable woman to associate with her.

She seemed content, however, and it did not occur to Justinian that her life might be less than complete until one evening, after spending several hours at his work, he found her on the balcony of the private suite she now shared with him.

Theodora was leaning against a Doric column at one side of the balcony, and as she listened to the hubbub drifting up from the busy street below, he caught sight of a wistful expression on her face.

She heard his footsteps, her mood changed instantly, and she smiled at him.

Justinian was not fooled, however. "Why are you sad?" he demanded.

"I'm not."

"Don't lie to me."

"I swear it."

He preferred to see her more clearly when they talked, and led her to the sitting room, where he lighted both of the oil lamps and several tapers.

Theodora waited patiently, thinking that he was sometimes out of sorts when the pressures of his responsibilities became too great. She would suggest that they entertain a poet and perhaps a composer of music in the next day or two. Light conversation that was nevertheless stimulating would provide him with a welcome change.

"Now, then," he said, sitting and motioning her to a place opposite him. "What's wrong?"

"I've already told you, my dear, nothing whatever. I have everything I need or want."

He stared at her for a time, his blue eyes lidded as he carefully and logically discarded one possibility after another. "You have everything—except human companionship," he said at last.

"My sisters visited me again just this week."

"I know," he replied with a grin, momentarily distracted because her efforts to find powerful protectors for both of her older sisters amused him. Then, suddenly, a thought struck him. "You haven't once left the grounds of this house since the night you first came here with me. And that was five months ago."

"Six. I have no need to go anywhere," she said defensively.

"You send the cook to the markets for food, which is fair enough, I suppose, but it's my understanding that ladies go to the bazaars when they want cloth for new gowns. You've had the sellers of silk and linen bring their wares to you."

"I find it more convenient to make my selections in private, where I won't be disturbed." Uncomfortable under his scrutiny, Theodora stood and wandered toward the shadows at the far end of the chamber.

"That isn't your real reason," Justinian said quietly.

She hesitated for a long time, then forced herself to face him. "You're quite right, it isn't."

He gripped the arms of his chair and braced himself. Until this moment it had not occurred to him that she might be bored by her life with him, and he wasn't prepared for the possibility that she might want to leave him.

"I can't tolerate the thought," she said, moistening her dry lips with her tongue, "of going out into the city wearing the yellow cloak and stockings of a courtesan. I've grown accustomed to something very different here, and the—the shame of it would be too much for me."

He was simultaneously relieved and indignant. "You're no longer a courtesan, and I forbid you to wear saffron."

"Then I must stay here. You spoke just now of ladies going to the bazaars. I'm no lady, and I can't hide my past when everyone in Constantinople knows it." Now that she was no longer trying to conceal anything from him, she felt freer than she had in many days.

Justinian's heavy fist pounded the arm of his chair. "You'll go where you please in Constantinople—or anywhere else in the Empire you may want to go. You'll wear one of your new gowns, and you'll ride in a carriage with the fasces of the Caesar Praefect in gold on its doors!"

It was just like a man, she thought, to brush aside insurmountable obstacles as though they did not exist. "You forget there's a law," she told him, "that forbids any courtesan to appear in public without the saffron that identifies her standing."

He became very angry for the first time since she had known him, and his eyes glittered. "Who will place you under arrest? The officers of the watch, whose centurions are responsible to me? Someone in the army? Not even Vitalian would dare!"

"I'm sure no one would harm me. I could wear whatever I please, and the worst that would happen—to me—would be a few whispers behind my back."

"Then that settles it!"

"But I'd still be breaking the law, and you'd suffer. Vitalian and the Greens would say that Justinian places himself and his mistress above the law—and they'd be right, unfortunately. Your reputation would be hurt, and you'd find it much more difficult to enforce your authority."

Still clenching his fists, he frowned.

"You know I'm right," Theodora said. "Even if you could persuade the Emperor to make an exception for me—"

"I'm sure I could!"

"—it still wouldn't be enough. We'd be guilty of evading the law. How often you've told me the laws of the Empire apply to everyone, from the Emperor himself to a slave. You'd be denying the very principles on which you base your concept of justice!" Theodora raised her own voice. "I shall stay here, within these walls!"

"You can't be caged here forever—like an animal!" Justinian bolted from his chair and hurried out of the chamber.

She could hear his footsteps as he descended the stairs and wanted to call him back, afraid he might do something impulsive. But she did not dare and returned to the balcony, knowing she would see him if he went off to the Imperial palace.

Instead he stayed in his own garden, pacing its length interminably, his head bowed and his hands clasped behind his back, and fear numbed Theodora when she thought she had set forces in motion that might destroy the only happiness she had ever known.

THREE

❦ ❦ ❦

A bright sun was rising in a cloudless, pale blue sky when
Justinian came into the house after his night-long vigil in
the garden. The servants, who had never known him to
eat breakfast and go off to the Imperial palace later than
dawn, looked at one another uncertainly as the gaunt man
wearily trudged up the stairs. The same thought was in
every slave's mind: Was he dismissing his mistress? And if
that happened, would they be sold to another master in the
great market near the Arsenal, overlooking the Bosphorus?

Theodora, still dressed in the gown of deep blue she had
worn the previous evening, thought it unlikely that her
lover would terminate their affair, but otherwise did not
know what to expect. She had not rested, either, and had
remained on the balcony all night, watching Justinian until
his restless pacing had made her dizzy, and she was hollow-
eyed and exhausted, too.

But she made an attempt to greet him cheerfully as he
dragged himself into their sitting room. "Good morning,"
she said, forcing a bright smile. "Shall I order breakfast?"

"I'm not hungry." Justinian dropped into the nearest
chair.

Wishing she could soften his adamant opposition to the drinking or serving of alcoholic beverages, even mild wines, by everyone in the house except dinner guests, she filled two chalices with honey-sweetened barley water and handed him one.

He took it, scarcely aware of what he was doing, and drained it. "Have your serving maids bathe you and anoint you with your most potent scents," he said. "Dress in a gown that will make a man know you're the most feminine of women in the Empire. Wear your emerald ring and the necklace of rubies I bought from the Ethiopian trader. Oh, yes—and the earrings of diamonds and onyx from Damascus. Be ready to leave no later than the eleventh hour, and if I can't come for you myself, I'll send Belisarius and a guard of honor as your escort."

"Where are you planning to take me?" she asked warily, unable to imagine a situation requiring her to wear her finest jewels so early in the day.

"I'm asking my uncle to receive you privately as soon as he's finished with his public morning audience. We'll need his approval."

"What is it you want him to approve?"

"We can't marry without his permission," Justinian said testily.

Theodora was stunned. It hadn't occurred to her that he might want to marry her, and she would have been happy to remain his mistress.

"Don't you like the idea?" His red-rimmed eyes were sharp.

"I—I'm overwhelmed."

"So am I." He softened, and rising swiftly, went to her. "I realized, out there in the garden, that I can't do without you. I want a permanent, formal relationship with you, one that can't be broken. I hope it's what you want, too."

She realized what she should have known the night they

had first gone to bed together, that she loved him. "I do, more than I can tell you."

"Then it's settled." He searched for the pitcher of barley water, found it, and refilled his chalice.

"There's a very strict law prohibiting the marriage of nobles to courtesans or harlots."

"Believe me, I'm aware of the law. I also know that laws can be changed. I'm directing Tribonian to draw up a new one this morning, and all it will need will be the Emperor's seal. Charm him, as I'm sure you will, and we'll be married tomorrow. In the Sancta Sophia, if you wish, by the Patriarch of Constantinople himself."

He reduced the problem to its simplest terms, but she could not believe it would be that easy. "Vitalian will stand in our way," she said. "He'll know at once that a marriage to someone of humble birth will make you more popular with the ordinary citizens, and he'll do everything in his power to prevent our marriage."

"Let him try," Justinian said with a hoarse laugh. "I have the Emperor's confidence, and if I know my uncle, he'll be delighted to welcome you into the family. So what can Vitalian do?"

🏵 🏵 🏵

White would have been virginal, and therefore a travesty, so Theodora wore a demure, cream-colored gown of heavy silk with long sleeves, a high neckline, and a skirt that touched the floor. Her hair, unfettered by gems or pins, fell in loose waves down her back, and the absence of cosmetics, except for a light touch of kohl around her eyes, made her look very young and vulnerable. She had chosen to ignore Justinian's instructions, too, and after forbidding her serving maids to daub her with scent, had donned none of her jewelry.

Nobles and high-ranking army officers, magisters and ministers and other government officials, stared at the slender girl as she walked quietly at the side of Belisarius along the marble-arched colonnade of the Imperial palace, and her seeming unawareness of them and their interest in her was only a slight exaggeration of the way she actually felt.

The excitement she created made it obvious that Imperial officialdom had learned of Justinian's intentions, but there would be ample time, if he succeeded, to study her future associates with care. In the meantime the palace itself absorbed her full attention.

Augustus Caesar, nephew of the great Caius Julius and first of the Emperors, would have been dazed by such splendor, and so would those of his successors who had lived in the old capital, Rome. Proud courtiers were fond of boasting that never in all human history had such magnificence been created in one place, and they were probably right. It was improbable that Solomon of the Israelites, the kings of Cathay, or Ramses II of Egypt had known such luxury.

The wealth of Europe, Asia, and Africa, the talents of every known civilization, had been combined to make the compound within the walls of the Imperial palace, a city within a city, the wonder of all the world. Peacocks strutted down tailored garden paths, observed by brilliant effigies of themselves fashioned of rare jewels, and even the benches and seats in the gardens were made of solid silver or gold, set beneath trees of sculptured brown marble with unfading leaves fashioned of jade.

Justinian had told Theodora that more than 3,000 people lived and worked in the palace, which was a complex consisting of more than 150 buildings, all connected by covered walks with floors, walls, and ceilings of mosaic tile, most of them inlaid with precious and semiprecious gems. Marble and alabaster statues of past Emperors, their wives, children, and favorites, their heroic subordinates and sycophants, were everywhere. Superbly wrought tapestries covered the interior walls of building after building, and guards in the gorgeous uniforms of more than a score of private armies zealously patrolled their own preserves.

The Imperial sanctum was the largest and most impressive of the structures in the compound. Surrounded by its own garden, in which rare fruits, herbs, and flowers were cultivated, it was set off from the surrounding buildings by an ornamental fence of pure gold. The mosaics inside the entrance were inlaid with gold, as were those on the steps leading to the throne room and the private chambers beyond it.

Gold-helmeted guards stood at rigid attention as Theodora walked past them with Belisarius, and the silent girl gasped involuntarily when she caught a glimpse of the empty throne room. Its ceiling had been made to resemble a night sky, and set in the face of blue silver were huge diamonds and sapphires, any one of which would have enabled an ordinary citizen to live in the greatest of comfort until the end of his days.

"Everyone is awed by this place," Belisarius murmured. "Some of the foreign ambassadors who come here actually lose their voices."

"I can't help thinking," Theodora replied, "of how few beggars would go into the streets if just a fraction of these riches were sold and the money given to the poor."

Her thoughts were so similar to those entertained by the younger generation of army officers that Belisarius grinned, but he quickly caught himself. "It's said that the walls here have ears."

Theodora smiled, but fell silent again. Given the opportunity, Belisarius would go far, and it would be wise to win his permanent loyalty.

Justinian was pacing up and down an anteroom of marble

and gold, but he stopped short when Theodora appeared, and his anxiety faded. "I was afraid you'd be late. He's waiting."

She took his arm, and Belisarius opened the door of an inner chamber, then stood aside and mounted guard outside.

Heavy cloth-of-gold drapes lined the room, which overlooked the garden, but the table and chairs were of plain cedar, and the grizzled old man who was cutting his signature in documents with a curious little instrument made of steel looked so unpretentious in a faded wool dressing gown and scuffed slippers that it took Theodora a moment to realize she was in the presence of the Emperor Justin.

She dropped to her knees, intending to prostrate herself in the prescribed manner and kiss his left foot, but he reached out, stopped her, and pulled her upright again. "I'm required to tolerate such nonsense in public," he said, his rough voice remarkably like his nephew's, "but it makes me feel foolish in private. So you're Theodora." A hardened soldier's eyes looked her up and down.

The girl had no idea whether he approved, so she stood still, a faint smile on her unpainted lips.

"Justinian," the Emperor said abruptly, "your fidgeting drives me mad. Pour us some of that white grape wine from Jerusalem and leave us so we can enjoy our chat."

The younger man went to a cedar cabinet in the corner and splashed some wine into a battered pewter cup.

The Emperor seemed to have eyes in the back of his head. "Fill it," he said, "and give one just like it to Theodora."

"She doesn't care for wine," Justinian said.

The old man made a strangled sound of exasperation. "You mean you don't drink the stuff, so you've assumed she doesn't. Have you ever asked her? Do as I say!"

It was impossible for Theodora to keep a straight face, but she tried to look solemn when Justinian reluctantly placed two full cups on the table.

"Tell Belisarius to instruct you in the cavalry tactics the Hittites used against the Egyptians in the Battle of Kadush," Justin said. "That'll keep you occupied."

His nephew went to the door, hesitated a moment, and finally left the room.

The Emperor's laugh sounded like a wheeze. "This is distilled wine. It's very potent." Suddenly he pointed to a chair near his. "It makes me nervous when people hover over me."

Theodora sat and uncertain of protocol waited until the Emperor drank from his cup before tasting her own wine. It was delicious, but she warned herself to be careful after so many months of abstinence.

"If I were twenty years younger and thought my virago of a wife wouldn't learn of it, I'd bed you myself."

She was startled but recovered quickly. "If Caesar Augustus demanded my life for the good of the Empire, I'd be willing to die for him, but I'll go to bed with no man except Justinian." She met his piercing gaze without flinching.

"By God, you mean it!" the old man said after a long silence. "The things I've heard about you are true."

Theodora said nothing.

"You must be curious." He sounded annoyed, but there was a glint of amusement in his eyes. "Aren't you going to ask what I've heard?"

"Caesar Augustus will tell me what he wishes me to know," she replied. "Besides, I know the truth about myself."

"So do I. Never have I had so many reports on one person."

She wondered which members of her household staff were in the Imperial employ, but knew it would be useless to inquire.

"Anthimus of Antioch is very fond of you."

"He's a wonderful and devout man." The Emperor was far more thorough than she had imagined.

"Only one report was less than candid. I had to learn elsewhere of your relationship with Hecebolus."

Theodora felt her face burning. "I despise him."

"I don't blame you. Have you told Justinian about him?"

"No, Caesar Augustus. What good would it accomplish?"

"You really aren't vengeful," he said, sipping his drink.

She took another small swallow of her own. "When it serves a purpose, I can be ruthless."

He held up the steel instrument. "This," he said, seemingly changing the subject, "is a little knife with my signature carved in it. Here. Press it on this parchment. That's it. You've now signed a decree affecting the people of Apollonia. Does that please you?"

"It depends on the decree, Caesar Augustus."

The Emperor handed her the document. "Any citizen of Apollonia who stones a harlot will himself be put to death by stoning."

Tears welled up in her eyes and she quickly blinked them away. "Thank you," she said. "It pleases me very much."

His touch was surprisingly gentle as he took the scroll and knife from her. "When I was young," he said, "I couldn't get the smell of cow dung out of my clothes. But I'm not ashamed of it. The smell was honest. My wife was a peasant, too, and to this day she doesn't recognize her own name when she sees it written. You wouldn't know it, though, from the airs she puts on." He fell silent for a moment, biting his lower lip, then spoke crisply. "It doesn't matter to me that you were a whore. I damned near married one myself when I was a leader-of-fifty on the Persian front."

Theodora realized that a reply would be an insult to the Empress, no matter what she said, so she merely nodded.

"An Emperor isn't necessarily free to do what he wants, though, as Justinian might discover someday. Would you marry him if I sent both of you into exile?"

"No," she said without hesitation, "but I'd do it if you sent me into exile alone."

He grinned broadly and drained his cup. "Justinian," he said, "needs a woman like you. He loses himself in his books and reports, and he loses touch with the real world. As you know."

"I admit no such thing, Caesar Augustus. There are men who act hastily, and there are others, wiser men, who study a subject thoroughly before committing themselves."

"Well said. All the same, you'll give him the backbone he needs."

Theodora realized she had won his approval and felt like shouting.

"What's more, you can hold distilled wine better than most men. I hope you'll visit me again, soon. I grow tired of the flatterers who agree with anything I say to them even when I call them fools to their faces." Again the sound of his wheezing laugh filled the little room. "Send Justinian to me, and don't wait for him. Go home. I'm sure the whole place is already buzzing like a sealed hive of hornets."

She was surprised when he stood, an honor few of his subjects had ever been accorded, and bent down to kiss her on the cheek.

"I still say that if I were younger, I'd take you away from Justinian," he said.

The anteroom door remained open when she went out, so she could not speak freely for fear the old man might overhear her. Nodding almost imperceptibly to convey the good news, she told Justinian, "Caesar Augustus wants you to join him."

Belisarius fell in beside her, a junior officer taking his place on sentry duty, and the escort of household troops surrounded the pair when they emerged into the corridor.

It would be strange, Theodora thought, to be accompanied everywhere by soldiers, to live a life almost totally devoid of privacy. The hampering of her freedom would be a constant source of annoyance after she and Justinian were married, but perhaps she could change the custom that prohibited female members of the royal family from going alone from their private apartments.

Lost in her own thoughts, the girl was scarcely aware of the expensively gowned woman of middle years who passed her on the staircase and who looked at her with eyes narrowed to slits. In any event she would not have recognized the Countess Sylvia, the wife of the consul, Vitalian, nor could she have known that the noblewoman was making her way to the suite of the Empress on an urgent errand.

🏵 🏵 🏵

Euphemia, Empress of Rome, was grossly overweight and spent most of her days in a huge bed with a coverlet of purple silk spread over her. Visitors saw only her bloated, tired face and pudgy hands, on which she wore an Imperial fortune in rings. Unable to learn Latin, the official language of the court, she insisted on conducting all conversations in Greek, which the nobility considered fashionable, even though her Macedonian accent was so strong it constantly reminded visitors of her humble origin. Her eyes, dark, brooding, and stubborn, were those of a peasant, too, and when she was angry she had a habit of staring into space over the head of the person who had annoyed her.

Her husband had found it almost impossible to converse with her when she was in a disturbed frame of mind, but Justinian had no choice, and pulled his chair closer to her bedside in the hope she would not be able to avoid meeting his gaze. "Aunt Lupicina," he said, addressing her by the name she had used all her life prior to her coronation, "I wish you'd be sensible."

"The subject is closed. Hand me that bowl of stuffed dates."

He rose, crossed the room for the confection, and returned to his seat. He couldn't help wishing that gluttony would kill her, and the thought did not make him feel guilty. "But you can't just tell me you forbid me to marry Theodora—without explaining your reasons."

"But that's just what I've done, and I've told your uncle I won't stand for such a marriage, so that's the end of the matter." She tried to decide which of two nut-filled dates she wanted, and solved the problem by shoving both into her mouth at the same time.

"But just this morning Uncle Justin told me he approved!"

"He has often been fooled by the lascivious face and body of a cheap woman. That's been one of his weaknesses." Her mouth was so full that she spewed bits of chopped nuts onto the coverlet.

"Theodora isn't that sort!"

"I thought you knew better, but you're as shortsighted as your uncle."

"You've been listening to women like Vitalian's wife!"

The old woman's eyes hardened. "Do I need your permission to entertain my friends?"

"Hardly." Justinian knew it was useless, even dangerous, to argue with the Empress, but was too upset to care. "The least you can do if you're going to be fair is receive Theodora in an audience and make your own judgment."

Euphemia became so furious she lapsed into her native Macedonian. "Never, as long as I live, will I allow a trollop to enter my presence."

"Some of the high-born ladies who fawn on you," he replied in the same tongue, "are adulteresses of the worst sort, and go to bed with more men in a year than any daughter of Venus! Shall I tell you their names?"

She popped another date into her mouth, then clamped her hands over her ears. "I refuse to hear lies about my good friends!"

Justinian was in despair, but tried another approach.

"You've always told me you hope I'll succeed Uncle Justin on the throne."

"Provided you behave with the dignity of an Emperor, I might be persuaded to support your cause." Her manner became sly, like that of a peasant bartering eggs for vegetables in the market.

Justinian was willing to descend to her level, if necessary, but thought he could use a far stronger approach. "Why do you suppose Vitalian's wife came to you today? Because my marriage to Theodora would be popular with the people—and would weaken Vitalian's chances of being accepted as Emperor!"

Euphemia shook her head. "The slut you took into your house has corrupted your mind as well as your body. Do you think Sylvia is completely lacking in patriotism? Or in gentility? It distresses her because the Caesar Praefect of the Roman Empire consorts with a loose woman. It's you who are destroying the respect of the people for their masters, and if you refuse to get rid of her, I'll do everything in my power to persuade Justin to make Vitalian his heir!"

Not satisfied with ruining his marriage plans, she was now demanding that he rid himself of Theodora, and the challenge was too great for Justinian to ignore it. "Do what you must," he said.

"You refuse to dismiss her from your house—even if I command it?" She propped her sagging body higher on the pillows of royal purple.

"If you alone command it," he replied slowly, "I'll defy you. If you persuade Uncle Justin to command it, I'll leave Constantinople, taking Theodora with me!"

"Where could you go?"

"At the moment, I have no idea. But I'll find a haven somewhere. Preferably a place," he added with quiet emphasis, "where the leaders of the Blue party won't be able to follow me and try to persuade me to return. The Emperor has my loyalty to the end of his days, no matter how much you may try to interfere with my personal life. I'll never do anything to undermine his position."

The old woman understood the threat behind his words. He was the champion of the Blues, the stronger of the political parties, and if he appeared as a martyr by going into exile, the repercussions could conceivably shake the throne. Less than a quarter of a century had passed since the people of Constantinople had revolted against an Emperor, and Euphemia well remembered the frightening three days of rioting, looting, and burning that had been a nightmare.

Justin had been a general then, and rather than lose popular support by playing a role in the crushing of the rebellion, had feigned illness, remaining at home behind barred doors and heavily shuttered windows. The citizens of Constantinople had remembered, and his own popularity had stemmed in part from the tacit support he had given the commoners.

Now, if there should be riots and demonstrations in Justinian's favor, the old man on the throne might not be able to cope with them. He had given so much power to his nephew that he might not be able to rule without Justinian's help, and he wouldn't be the first Emperor who had been murdered by the mobs.

Euphemia raised a jeweled hand to her thick throat, almost as though warding off the daggers of assassins. "I suppose," she said, "it will do no real harm to keep the woman in your house, if you insist, provided she continues to remember her place and doesn't seek the company of her superiors. But," she added, rallying, "under no circumstances will I permit you to marry her. That subject is closed, now and for all time!"

❦ ❦ ❦

Theodora listened intently to Justinian's account of his meeting with his aunt. Her hands folded in her lap, she looked down at the colored tiles of the terrace floor and neither spoke nor moved.

"I promised her an insurrection when she told me to send you away," he said, cold anger forcing his voice to rise. "And now I'll suggest to the Blues that they demonstrate in our favor at the chariot races on Saturday. She knows nothing about racing and doesn't really care about the sport, but she always goes with Justin, and when she hears an aroused crowd of 25,000 shouting your name, I have an idea she'll take the hint and stand aside so we can be married."

"We can do nothing worse," Theodora said.

"It's the only language she understands. She retreats when she's afraid."

"But the Emperor doesn't."

"Of course not." It was Justinian's private opinion that his soldier-uncle was too callous and unimaginative to fear anything, but he could not speak disparagingly of his relative and mentor, even in private.

"You'd be challenging him, too—"

"He'd know why the Blues were demonstrating!"

"I dare say, but a deliberate defiance of his wife's authority would leave him no alternative. He'd be forced to discipline the Blues, and you know what would happen if he called out troops to chastise them."

"That's what I mean. Rather than let a civil war develop, he'd tell his sow of a wife not to interfere in matters that don't concern her."

Theodora's long hair swished from side to side as she shook her head. "You don't understand him."

"But you do, I suppose, after spending a quarter of an hour with him. I lived under his roof from the time I was seventeen—"

"If he's maneuvered into a corner and forced to make a

choice between his wife and his nephew, he'll agree with her, no matter what his private feelings. We like to think of ourselves as Christians, remember, and not even an Emperor can disavow his wife with impunity!"

"You may be right," he admitted grudgingly.

"I know I am. If you push this dispute into the open, you and I are certain to lose."

"But if we let her bully us into accepting her ultimatum without a struggle, she wins the war without even sending her legions into battle."

"The Emperor," Theodora said, "wants to leave you the throne, and will abandon you only if you deny his prerogative—either directly or through his wife—to rule as he thinks right."

"You're like everyone else on the outside," Justinian said irritably. "The throne isn't as monolithic as we lead the commoners to believe. Even at his best Justin was unable to grasp any principles of kingship beyond that of using the military to enforce his will. He's never heard of Plato's ideal state, he's done nothing to prevent corrupt officials from enriching themselves at public expense, and I don't think he's capable of realizing that the Empire is decaying. Surely you know I make almost all of his administrative decisions for him!"

"Nevertheless," Theodora said stubbornly, "he's the Emperor, and we'd flout him at our peril."

"Euphemia committed herself today," he said, his annoyance increasing. "I wouldn't bow to her exorbitant demands, so she's going to support Vitalian, no matter how lightly you and I might tread. If you've ever known any Macedonian peasant women, you'd realize her pride is even more important to her than all the food she swills. She'll never forgive me for what I did to her today. I'm positive she's already started telling Justin I'm untrustworthy and that Vitalian is the only man who can hold the Empire together."

"All the more reason not to make her hate us even more," Theodora said.

"Then what do you suggest we do?" he demanded, his exasperation complete.

"There's nothing you could or should do. But there's one thing I can do, and must." She averted her eyes. "I'll quietly disappear."

Justinian was too shocked to speak.

"It's the only solution. Let her think you've sent me away, and she'll forgive you immediately."

"Either you've been inhaling the poppy incense of the Medes," he said hoarsely, "or you've completely lost your mind."

"I can't deny you the throne," Theodora said, "and once I've gone, you're sure to inherit it."

Justinian's sallow face became flushed.

She ignored the danger sign. "The necklace you gave me will buy a house and a little garden in Antioch or Edessa, with enough income to make certain I'm never cold or hungry—"

"Enough, woman!" He jumped to his feet, trembling. "I'll strangle you with my own hands before I'll permit you to leave me! I won't hear of such idiocy!"

She felt certain his shouts could be heard in the street at the foot of the hill.

"I won't be separated from you." He started toward her, breathing hard, his face distorted.

He loomed over her, and for an instant Theodora thought he intended to strike her. Then, suddenly, he collapsed, dropping to his knees and burying his face in her lap.

The servants could see that he was making a spectacle of himself, but he required her full attention, so the problem of how to prevent untoward, maliciously harmful gossip would have to wait. She cradled his head in her arms, stifling his sobs.

The Emperor had been right: Justinian's need for her was so great that if she left, he would be incapable of ruling alone, and probably would be denied the throne for that very reason, thereby negating her sacrifice. "I'll stay," she whispered, "no matter what may happen."

☙☙☙

In a ceremony held without advance notice to anyone, the Emperor made Vitalian Consul-for-Life, a newly created position that broke the old Roman tradition preventing any man from holding the post for more than three years. Since the title was honorary, conferring only prestige, Justin also appointed Vitalian his permanent deputy in command of the army, which meant that every military man, from general to conscript, needed the consul's help and goodwill if he wanted advancement and security.

"Unless Justinian acts swiftly," the shrewd John of Cappadocia said, "Vitalian will be so strong that no one will be able to stand in his path when he makes a bid for the Crown."

The Green party celebrated in the taverns, staged parades through the streets, and gave their champion a wild ovation when he appeared for the chariot races at the Hippodrome. The Blues were spoiling for a fight, but Justinian passed the word that discipline had to be maintained. His supporters felt cheated, so he alleviated their disappointment by giving them a purse so large that he refused to tell even Theodora the amount.

But he took no other steps, open or covert, to protect himself or advance his own cause. He extended his warm congratulations to Vitalian at a meeting of magisters, thus indicating his seeming approval of the appointment, and, following Theodora's advice, made no mention of the subject to his uncle. The rumor spread through the Empire that he was reconciled to the loss of the throne, but he continued to be unstinting in his direction of the government's business, and even his friends were unable to understand him.

"You can't persuade the Emperor to retract the appointment," Theodora said in the privacy of their bedchamber, "so anything you might say or do will only harm you. Let people think what they please, and the gossip will soon die away. Vitalian is a vain man, and may do something that will displease the Emperor, so we'll keep watch, and sooner or later our chance will come."

As the months passed, however, the consul lost no opportunity to strengthen his position. One by one the commanders of garrisons and frontier outposts were summoned to Constantinople for private conferences with him, and returned to their duties satisfied. The Countess Sylvia became the Empress' constant companion, attending her daily, and it appeared that no impediment ᴐd between her husband and the throne of Caesar Augustᴜᴐ.

On the surface Justinian appeared untroubled, and only Theodora knew he lived in quiet despair. "Wait," she counseled him repeatedly. "Wait."

"If I wait much longer," he said as they ate their usual early breakfast one morning, "Vitalian will be able to destroy me whenever he wishes. He meets alone with the Emperor every afternoon, and no one knows what they discuss. Narses can't find out and has no record of their talks."

"Or so he says."

"Perhaps. But I can hardly blame Narses—or anyone else—from trying to protect himself. If Vitalian were to ascend the throne tomorrow, and then send me off into exile, not a single voice would be raised in protest. The Blues wouldn't like it, but they're no match for the army."

"You still have friends."

Justinian shrugged. "Belisarius and Mundus are jeopardizing their army careers by making it plain they prefer me, and so are a few other young officers who believe Vitalian is accepting bribes from the Persians. But they can prove nothing, and probably will pay for their disloyalty to him with their lives when he's in a position to do what he pleases."

She sought in vain for some logical, reasonable consolation that would ease his orderly mind.

A serving maid tapped at the door to announce the arrival of a messenger from the Imperial palace. Theodora wrapped herself in a cloak of thin wool that concealed her flimsy night-robe.

An agitated young leader-of-fifty came into the room, and almost forgot to salute. "Caesar Praefect," he said, "I bring sad tidings. The Empress Euphemia died in her sleep no more than a quarter of an hour ago."

Justinian jumped to his feet and donned his heavy sandals. "Tell the Emperor I'll come to him immediately."

Theodora made no move, and not until she was alone did she smile and stretch sinuously. The time of interminable delay had come to an end, but she alone knew it.

❧ ❧ ❧

Two patriarchs and a Western bishop conducted the funeral service, which was held with full Imperial pomp in the presence of foreign ambassadors, every nobleman and army commander from outlying districts able to reach Constantinople in time, and the entire court. Euphemia was buried in a sarcophagus of royal purple marble, topped by a statue in her likeness carved from stone of the same color, and a team of twenty-four horses dragged the huge coffin to the burial ground of the Caesars at the far end of the palace gardens, beyond the stables.

The Emperor Justin retired to his private quarters, instructing Belisarius to admit no one.

For the next two weeks Justinian acted as Regent in all

but name, making final decisions and signing decrees without referring even the most vexing questions to his uncle. He carefully avoided Vitalian's sphere of influence, however, and took no action that might offend the consul. Then, fifteen days after Euphemia's funeral, he requested and was granted an Imperial audience.

Theodora waited anxiously for her lover, but when he came home she curbed her desire to greet him in the courtyard and remained in their private suite, where their conversation could not be overheard. "How is he?"

Justinian looked a trifle bewildered. "I've never seen him in a happier mood, and I'm afraid he might drink himself to death. He finished a half-jug of his Jerusalem white wine in the short time I was with him."

She smiled, certain that the Emperor was relieved because he had been freed of a burden. "Did you ask him?"

"It wasn't necessary. As I came into the room he said that there was no one to stand in the way of our marriage now." Justinian went to Theodora, kissed her, and then held her at arm's length. "We'll have a wedding worthy of an Emperor's niece. The patriarch will marry us in the Sancta Sophia—"

"He will not." She did not explain that she wanted to be more than an Emperor's niece by marriage, but felt some sop was necessary. "After we've lived together all this time, a royal wedding would be rather foolish—as well as in bad taste, so soon after your aunt's death."

Justinian was forced to agree with her judgment.

"I don't suppose he mentioned the succession?"

"No. As I was leaving, he remarked that Vitalian would be pounding on his door as soon as he learned I'd been there, but that was all."

"It was enough," Theodora said, becoming thoughtfully silent.

❦ ❦ ❦

At the instigation of Justinian, they were married in the tiny church of Saints Sergius and Bacchus, built at the end of the Imperial palace garden by Anthemius. An elderly priest who had no special standing in the Church hierarchy performed the ceremony, with a magister and two ministers of state as official witnesses. Theodora's sisters were present, as were a few friends of both the bride and groom, among them a blond actress, Antonina, whom Theodora had known most of her life, and Belisarius. The young officer and the courtesan from the theater were attracted to each other, and the bride celebrated her new status by inviting them to dine at the little palace on the hill the following day.

Immediately after the ceremony Justinian went off to a Council of State meeting at which he would preside, and Theodora returned home. She did not remain any longer than necessary to change into a gown of pale lavender that suggested the purple of royalty, and to don the thin, multicolored headband worn by every matron in the Empire, regardless of her rank, station, or wealth. The new carriage Justinian had just purchased for her was waiting at the seldom-used main entrance of the little palace, pulled by a team of four matched horses. Then, flanked by eight outriders in the silver and black tunics, breastplates, and leg shields of the Caesar Praefect's household staff, she drove out into Constantinople for the first time since the evening she and Justinian had met.

He had supposed she would be content with an airing, perhaps stopping briefly at the bazaars and markets to buy some trinkets, but she was anxious to make up for the time lost in the months of delay, and directed the coachman to take her to the section of the city bounded by the old Wall of Constantine, where many of the wealthier and more powerful nobles lived. On another occasion, when she wasn't preoccupied, she would enjoy the stares of the people as she and her entourage swept through the busy streets.

The largest of the private palaces was that of the Consul-for-Life, and Theodora's manner was that of one who had spent all her life in such places. When the majordomo hurried into the courtyard to greet her and help her alight from her carriage, she used her new title for the first time, saying, "Inform the consul that the Lady Theodora wants to confer with him in private."

She was kept waiting for only a short time before being ushered onto an inner terrace, its graceful roof supported by Corinthian columns, its open sides looking out on massed beds of flowers. If Sylvia, who had so successfully blocked her marriage, was aware of the younger woman's presence, she was watching from the concealment of the drapes that covered so many of the palace's windows.

Vitalian, a ruggedly handsome man in his early fifties, glowed with the vibrant good health of one who had spent much of his life in the field. He was noted for his charm as well as his dashing uniforms, and if he was surprised by the visit, he gave no sign of it when he came to the terrace entrance to greet his unexpected guest.

Noting Theodora's headband with a swift glance, he bowed as he would to any high-born lady. "Permit me to offer my felicitations on your marriage, Madame."

She gave him her sweetest smile. "Thank you, Lord Consul."

Ushering her to a chair of carved ebony, he sent a servant for a snow-chilled jug of Greek wine, and then began to chat about the recent arrival of the largest merchant fleet from Beirut ever to reach Constantinople. "There must be something in the blood of the old Phoenicians that makes them superb traders," he said. "I've been told they have bolts of silver and cloths of precious metals on board that are superior to anything ever sold here."

Theodora had not come to discuss cloth and women's fashions. "Lord Consul," she said, ignoring his idle remarks, "I'm deeply distressed."

His expression changed, and his dark eyes became calculating. "I'm sorry to hear it, Madame."

The servant returned with the wine, and Theodora did not forget that her husband was noted for his abstinence. "None for me, thank you, but I appreciate your hospitality." She waited until the slave disappeared. "I've been distressed to hear you and Justinian mentioned as rivals."

"I haven't been happy about it, either." Vitalian was politely noncommittal.

"The Empire needs both of you, each in your own sphere."

He inclined his head. "It's generous of you to say so."

"You know as well as I, Lord Consul, perhaps better, that when two great men, each of them supported by one of Constantinople's political parties, are opposed to each other, the result is always the same. The people riot, heads are cracked, and the churches are filled with women in mourning."

Vitalian nodded.

"So I've been wondering whether it might not be possible—for the good of everyone—to reach an agreement."

His light tone belied the expression in his eyes. "You say you've been wondering about this, Madame. So I'd like a clarification, if you don't mind."

"Of course." Theodora matched his graciousness.

"Have you come to me as the emissary of the Caesar Praefect—or on your own initiative?"

She realized he knew that Justinian would not utilize her services as an intermediary, but would deal through a government official or one of the few army officers close to him, but she refused to give Vitalian the satisfaction of thinking he had scored. "My husband and I are always in concert, Lord Consul, in all things."

He had learned nothing from her reply, but his shrug indicated that the issue he had raised was of no consequence. "What sort of agreement did you have in mind?"

"In all probability," Theodora said, speaking with an air of confidence she did not feel, "my husband will succeed our uncle on the throne." The assertion was sheer speculation, of course, and her reference to the Emperor as "our uncle" was preposterous effrontery, but she presented her case with self-confident calm.

Vitalian was not fooled, however. "There are some," he said, "who might not accept that premise."

"I imagine there are, unfortunately." She was determined to carry her bluff through to the end, having realized from the outset that it was unlikely the Emperor had told Vitalian he would be named the heir to the throne, but that the old man might have been more free in a confidential talk with his blood relative.

The consul, however, refused to consider anything she told him authoritative. "To the best of my knowledge the issue of the succession is far from settled."

It was her turn to shrug, prettily, with a faint but distinct hint of condescension indicating that he was entitled to believe what he wished but would suffer the consequences if he failed to accept her word.

"What did you have in mind for me?" Even his voice became grave now.

"A man of your military standing and reputation could control insurrections everywhere and protect our borders. I'm certain my husband would be pleased to make you Imperial viceroy for the provinces." She was blandly innocent, although it was obvious she was suggesting that—if and when Justinian became Emperor—his rival would be banished from the capital with a glittering new title and authority that might seem great to outsiders but could be countermanded at any time by the supreme ruler above him.

A glint of hard humor appeared in Vitalian's eyes for a moment, then vanished again. "In the unlikely event that the Caesar Praefect should succeed the Emperor Justin," he said, "I suppose a post as Imperial viceroy would be as good as any to put me safely out of the way. But I fear no man, you see, and should I win the throne, I'd certainly keep Justinian in his present post. He's an excellent administrator, even though he may lack the—ah—broader vision required of one who sits on the throne of Caesar Augustus."

There would be no compromise, and the battle would be fought to the end, regardless of the consequences. Theodora had not expected a capitulation, but she had at least hoped to be spared a direct insult. But now she knew where matters stood, and so would Justinian when she repeated the conversation to him.

Not bothering with social proprieties, she gathered the full skirts of her gown, then stood. "Thank you for taking time from your busy affairs of state to see me," she said.

His response was equally constrained, and he did not see her to the courtyard, letting the majordomo accompany her.

Although Theodora had seen nothing of Constantinople for many months, she was indifferent to the city's bustle as she drove home. She sat low in a corner of the coach, twisting her emerald ring, her eyes unseeing. She was Justinian's wife now, so it was her right as well as her duty to protect his interests, and it was plain that he and Vitalian could not compete amicably. Therefore the consul would have to be eliminated by any means she found necessary.

FOUR

❦❦❦

Belisarius and the actress Antonina were married by the Patriarch of Constantinople in the Sancta Sophia. The younger army officers and their wives were present, as were a number of minor nobles and their spouses, who attended because they knew Justinian and Theodora would be there. But Vitalian and Sylvia were conspicuous by their absence, as were the magisters, ministers of state, nobles of consequence, and higher-ranking officers. It was whispered in the Mesé that Sylvia had said, "I refuse to recognize that harlot, and would absent myself from Imperial audiences if she were there." Everyone in Constantinople accepted the comment as authentic.

Unfortunately, it was impossible to test the challenge, the Emperor having abandoned all audiences and gone into the seclusion of a virtual recluse. He remained in his private apartments, where he saw no one except Justinian, Vitalian, and occasionally a magister or minister. According to a popular account that his secret police tried to keep alive, he had vowed to stay in mourning for his late wife until the end of his days. Anyone who had known the real nature of his relations with Euphemia smirked in private but was careful to accept the absurd tale in public. Those who doubted the officially inspired word of the Emperor had been known to suffer heavy taxation, confiscation of their property, and in some severe cases had permanently vanished from their homes. The few who were familiar with the royal dungeons beneath the palace were particularly zealous in sympathizing with the Emperor in his time of sorrow.

Constantinople was split into opposing camps, each supporting the candidacy of its favorite to succeed Justin, and as both freely used spies to learn what its opponents were thinking, saying, and plotting, the social life of the Imperial capital withered away. It became impossible for nobles to entertain guests when their servants and even their friends might be reporting their confidential comments to their foes. Theaters closed, ladies who had been close to one another for years barely nodded when they met in the bazaars, and only the races at the Hippodrome were still held regularly, the Caesar Praefect and the Consul-for-Life having informally agreed that there might be fewer violent outbreaks if the people had normal outlets for their feelings.

Life was changed at the little palace on the hill, too. Although Theodora was free to go where she pleased, she visited only her sisters and Antonina, or made occasional, prudent purchases in the markets and bazaars. "If I buy a single bolt of cheap linen," she told her husband, "Sylvia claims I've bought fifty, all cloth-of-gold, and calls me a spendthrift. It's best that I not call myself too much to the attention of the people these days."

Virtually no one was invited to dine at the little palace, and Theodora insisted that she and Justinian take their meals in the privacy of their bedchamber. There, with the sitting room between them and servants in the secret pay of Vitalian who might be eavesdropping, they could speak their minds to each other. But their opportunities for exchanging views at length were few; Justinian was working longer hours as the pressures increased, keeping himself informed of everything that went on in the Empire, and usually gulped his meals.

Theodora was not surprised when he did not come home until almost midnight one night in the early autumn of 526, and she quickly brought him one of the towels she had kept hot and damp for him.

He groaned, stretched out on the divan opposite their bed, and wiped his face, then left the cloth over his eyes.

"You'll kill yourself unless you rest," she said. "Would you like antelope steak or Macedonian stew for dinner? Both are ready."

"I'm not hungry," Justinian said in a muffled voice.

"But you'll become ill if you don't eat!"

He threw the towel aside and sat up, his feet thumping on the floor. "Don't nag at me, woman."

Theodora looked at him sharply. "What's wrong?"

Habit caused him to peer into the adjoining room to assure himself it was empty before he replied. "Justin can't last much longer. He was so drunk again today that I had to bar everyone from his chamber, even Vitalian, and I can tell you *his* nose was out of joint!"

"Tell me about Justin."

"He couldn't see clearly enough to sign the day's decrees and orders, so I simply borrowed his signature knife again. Then, tonight, he began raving and shouting like a lunatic, and I had to call a physician."

"Which one?"

"Servetius. My most reliable agents swear he's completely loyal to me, and I've got to trust *some* medical men. I can't cope with Justin alone, much less keep watch over him day and night so Vitalian doesn't persuade him to sign a paper naming him Regent or co-Emperor."

"You were telling me about Servetius," she said patiently. Their principal topics of conversation were Justinian's inability to cajole the Emperor into granting him full authority, and his fear that Vitalian might succeed in a similar attempt.

"After Justin fell unconscious, Servetius examined him. I brought in Belisarius and Mundus as witnesses, much as I hate letting anyone find out that the Emperor's problem is drink."

"Surely the officers of the household guard know!"

Justinian shrugged wearily. "They do now. If the Emperor had died, Vitalian might have accused Servetius and me of murdering him. Be that as it may, the physician swears he can't live more than a few months. Liquor has decayed his core and spleen, and his heart is filling with poisonous fumes. So, one way or another, the end will come soon, and then the civil war will begin. This morning, when Justin seemed relatively sober, I begged him to name a successor, no matter who it might be. But I don't believe he recognized me, and I very much doubt that he heard a single word I was saying."

"One way or another," Theodora repeated, "the end will come soon." Rising, she left the suite.

When she returned a short time later, Justinian was still sitting on the edge of the divan, an ink-stained hand drumming on a cushion.

Theodora handed him a silver ladle and knife, placing the food on a table beside him. Experience had taught her not to urge him to eat, and she felt relieved when he absently tasted the stew, then began to eat it in earnest.

"What did you mean?" he asked at last.

They had covered the same ground so often that she could not curb her impatience. "If Justin dies with the issue unresolved, there's certain to be a civil war." She ticked off the principal points on her slender fingers, the emerald gleaming on one hand and on the other a new sapphire picking up the light of a scented oil lamp. "Since Vitalian controls the better part of the army, you're certain to lose. Vitalian will crown himself, and his first act as Emperor will be to take you prisoner, torture you, and put you to death. If Sylvia has her way, the same will happen to me." She paused. "You know all that."

"I also know it mustn't happen." The ladle remained poised between the bowl and his mouth. "There's something I've never told you, and I don't want you to laugh at me."

"I couldn't!"

"A secret dream I've had ever since I first came to Constantinople has given me strength. Eight hundred and fifty years ago another Macedonian united the entire civilized world. Yes, Alexander made a contribution as great as Plato's and Aristotle's. He brought the world peace and gave people justice. His government was the most efficient in all history. I've learned almost all there is to know about administration and the principles of justice. I'm convinced that if I'm given the chance, I can repeat Alexander's triumph and can even succeed where he failed." He lost interest in his meal.

Theodora was silent. Whenever she thought she truly understood him, he revealed another facet of his character, and it had not occurred to her that he was such an ambitious dreamer.

"Alexander's mistake," he said, "was that of allowing all the people he conquered to keep their old gods. I intend to reunite the entire Roman Empire and expand its borders through Persia to India, even to Cathay. And the whole world will become Christian!"

If he tried to force his faith on others, he would create more problems than he solved, Theodora thought. Her own travels had convinced her that men were willing to die for their religious convictions more readily than for any other cause. But this was not the time to dispute the matter.

"If I'm given the chance," he said again.

"You won't be given anything. You'll have to make your own opportunities."

He looked at her, uncertain of her meaning.

"You say your dream has given you strength, and I believe it. I've never known any man who works as hard or who tries so hard to increase his knowledge. But there are different kinds of strength. How much do you believe in your dream?"

A trace of a smile appeared on her lips and she picked up his untouched food-cutting knife, holding it by the blade and extending the hilt as she offered it to him.

When her meaning became clear, he shrank from her.

Theodora continued to offer him the knife.

Too stunned to thrust it away, he took it.

Justinian stared at the blade, turning it over in his hands. "Belisarius?" He was muttering to himself. "He can be ruthless, but he's a gentleman. Mundus, perhaps. He was born a barbarian—"

"This is a task that only one man can perform," Theodora said quietly. "Justinian."

The knife clattered to the floor, and he stared at it.

She picked it up and handed it to him again. "He'd do the same to you, and will if he can."

Gingerly, his distaste evident, he felt the cutting edge of the blade. "He's a professional swordsman, of course, and I was hopeless when I tried to learn self-defense. That's one reason my uncle decided I was better suited for a civilian career."

"You'd be stupid to cross swords with him." Theodora had thought of every approach to the problem, and going to a locked chest, opened it and removed a small dagger with a double edge. "This is what you'll need."

Justinian examined it, his revulsion equaled by his surprise. "The insignia of the Consul-for-Life is engraved on the hilt."

"Precisely."

"Was it stolen from his palace?"

"Surely you don't think I'd give him advance warning. I had it made by a swordsmith I can trust. Someone I befriended long ago, and who was in my debt. He lives far from Constantinople, and he's very discreet."

"You've been planning this for a long time."

"I, too, have my dreams," Theodora said. "Well?"

"I need time to think."

"You're more than ten years younger than he, and your native strength is greater. My idea—"

"Never mind. I understand."

"Then you agree?" She was unrelenting. "You'll do it?"

"I'm—not certain. The Ten Commandments—"

"There's an eleventh, unwritten," she said. "When you know your enemies intend you harm, strike first."

☙ ☙ ☙

The old man's sleep was heavy. Stretched out on the coverlet of royal purple, unshaven but fully dressed, he made no move. But his breathing was labored, and there were splotches of color in his pale face.

His two principal subordinates stared down at him. "You've seldom seen him in this condition," Justinian said. "We've been locking the doors when he's this bad to make certain no one comes into the room by mistake."

"I knew, of course," Vitalian replied, "but seeing him like this is still a shock."

"I had to show him to you before discussing what I have in mind." Justinian ignored the throbbing of his temples, and spoke with a remarkable calm that was only simulated in part. Now that the hour for action had come, it was surprising how calm he felt, how clear-headed and in control of all his faculties.

Vitalian continued to look down at the Emperor, which enabled him to appear only remotely interested.

"He can't be deposed, of course," Justinian said, speaking his well-rehearsed lines with seeming spontaneity. "But if you and I issue a joint proclamation, we can declare him incompetent and name ourselves as co-Regents to rule in his stead."

For a few moments Vitalian appeared lost in thought, but at last he turned to his rival. "We could manage well enough while he continues to live."

Justinian nodded while his right hand, already beneath the folds of his robe, closed over the hilt of the dagger.

"But it would be only a temporary solution."

"True." Justinian balanced himself.

"What the Empire needs is a clear decision to end the sense of uncertainty that has been straining the tempers and patience of the people. One of us," Vitalian said firmly, "just one should become Regent."

"I quite agree," Justinian replied, and struck.

The consul caught a glimpse of the dagger and tried to ward off the blow, but it was too late. The blade penetrated deep into his stomach, causing him to double over in agony as blood spewed onto the carpet from Cathay and the tiled mosaic floor beyond it.

Justinian, trying not to let himself think of his rival's suffering, took two steps backward, precisely as he and Theodora had planned, and picked up a cushion from the Emperor's bed.

When Vitalian toppled to the floor, still trying to remove the blade, Justinian was ready. Moving forward again swiftly, he clamped the cushion over his victim's face.

Vitalian tried to free himself, but the severity of his wound weakened him, and he was no match for his foe.

Long after the consul stopped struggling, Justinian continued to hold the cushion over his face. Finally, after what felt like an eternity, he removed it and saw that his enemy was dead. Vitalian's hands gripped the hilt of the knife.

Shoving the cushion under the head of the unconscious Emperor, Justinian retreated to the far side of the room. He discovered his legs were trembling, his robe was soaked with sweat, and now that he had accomplished the deed, he felt ill. But he couldn't relax as yet; only the first part of his task was completed, and his future depended on his ability to remain composed.

He slipped into his uncle's dressing chamber, which adjoined the bedroom, and closed the door softly behind him. No one was in the garden outside, and the sentries stationed about twenty feet away stood with their backs to the window. When he succeeded Justin, he told himself, he would see to it that a tighter security guard was maintained.

Climbing out of the window he had opened earlier for the purpose, he dropped to the gravel path, and then, sauntering as though completely relaxed, accepted the salutes of the sentries with a pleasant nod.

He made a half-circle to the front of the building, re-entered it, and climbed the main stairs to the Emperor's anteroom, where Brutus of Alena, the magister in charge of Imperial roads and transportation, was waiting in the hope of being granted an audience.

The burly Mundus was standing duty outside the door of the bedchamber, and his eyes widened when he saw the Caesar Praefect, but he gave no other indication that he had believed Justinian to be inside the bedroom.

"Good morning, milord." Brutus, a member of Vitalian's faction, was reserved. "I was told you were in conference with the Emperor."

Justinian exchanged token wrist-clasps with him, and suddenly remembered he hadn't checked to see if there was blood on his hands. Now he would have to wait before risking a surreptitious glance. "No, I had business elsewhere. The consul has been received in audience, I think. Isn't that right, Centurion?"

"Yes, sir," Mundus said, looking straight ahead.

"It's urgent that I see the Caesar Augustus. Will you tell him I'm here, Centurion, and that Magister Brutus is also waiting?" Justinian saw a smear of dried blood on his right hand, but checked the impulse to wipe it off on his robe.

The young officer dutifully tapped at the door.

Feigning irritation when there was no response, Justinian said, "My business can't wait. Tell the Caesar Augustus it's imperative that I see him." The presence of an important supporter of Vitalian was an unexpected stroke of good fortune, and he intended to exploit it to the full.

Mundus hesitated, opened the door, and then stiffened. "Caesar Praefect!"

Justinian peered over his shoulder. "My God!" he muttered, and motioned Brutus forward. Not until he was certain that the magister had seen his fill did he command, "Alert the guard and send at once for the physician Servetius!"

The centurion raced out through the anteroom, and Justinian carefully refrained from entering the bedchamber, as did Brutus.

Belisarius arrived on the run, accompanied by a platoon of household guards, who formed a tight cordon around the suite, and a few moments later the breathless physician appeared.

"Examine the Emperor!" Justinian ordered, and followed Servetius, with Belisarius, Mundus, and Brutus at his heels.

The physician wasted no time. "Caesar Augustus is sleeping peacefully," he said. "He's unharmed."

"You're sure he hasn't been wounded?"

"Quite sure, Caesar Praefect."

"Then examine the consul."

Servetius took even less time. "He appears to have died of a wound in his stomach."

"Self-inflicted?" Justinian asked.

"So it would seem, Caesar Praefect." Servetius removed the blade, then pried it from the dead man's stiff fingers.

Justinian edged slightly to one side so the magister would be forced to take the blade from the still-kneeling physician.

Brutus accepted the dagger reluctantly, holding it as though fearful it would spring to life.

"The Ministry of Safety must take custody of it, of course," Justinian said. "What's wrong, Lord magister?"

"It bears Vitalian's own seal!" Brutus stared at the crest on the hilt.

Servetius stood, and there was a long, tense silence, no one knowing what to say or do next.

Justinian waited deliberately, then cleared his throat. "There is no mystery here," he said.

The others looked at him, aware that whatever the now unopposed heir to the throne might say would become the sole official version of what had taken place.

"The Caesar Augustus is ill. He finds it difficult to remain awake for more than short periods." Justinian glanced at the physician.

Servetius nodded hastily in confirmation.

"The Consul Vitalian came to the Emperor with the request that he be placed first in the succession. The Caesar Augustus refused to grant his wish, and because he was exhausted, fell asleep. Vitalian was in despair, and killed himself."

Even Brutus of Alena agreed with him.

After all, as Justinian realized, he had suddenly become so powerful that it would be dangerous for any man to oppose him. Other government officials and nobles would accept his version of what had transpired, and no one would openly question the story.

"Belisarius, attend to the removal of the body. Supervise the task yourself, and be discreet. Vitalian served the Empire well, and we want no scandal that will reflect on the integrity of a Roman hero who gave in to a moment of weakness. Mundus, take charge of the dagger, and deliver it yourself to the Minister of Security."

Both officers saluted.

"You must handle this matter with delicacy and care," Justinian told them. "You'll need additional authority, so I promote both of you to the rank of colonel, effective immediately." No one would question his right to promote army officers, and the rise to a higher rank would insure that Mundus, already his partisan, would not mention his belief that Justinian had been inside the bedchamber with the Emperor and Vitalian.

"Lord magister," Justinian continued, turning to Brutus of Alena, "I shall be grateful if you'll take the sad news to the Countess Sylvia. Shield her if you can, and spare her the details. And be sure to express my sympathies to her."

"It will be done, Caesar Praefect." Brutus spoke earnestly, anxious to win the favor of the future Emperor who knew he had supported the wrong candidate.

"Tell the Countess Sylvia, too, that the funeral must be private. Although I'd personally prefer a public ceremony in recognition of Vitalian's services to the Empire, that cannot be. The spirit of the troops might suffer, since everyone is certain to learn that he took his life with his own hand. I'll prepare an official order later in the day, but I'm sure the Countess Sylvia will understand."

Brutus swore there would be no problem.

Belisarius had gone into the anteroom to confer with several junior officers, and when he returned with two soldiers who placed a cloth over Vitalian's body, Justinian turned away.

The Emperor, all but forgotten, began to snore softly.

"Colonel Belisarius," Justinian said, "see that Narses is told I'll return in an hour. I'll want to see every magister and minister of state before the day ends. And I want all senior army officers informed that I'll meet with them at my house this evening. Right now I need a short time to compose myself. This has been a frightful morning."

A squad of tall household guards, each man armed with a sword, javelin, and shield, formed a cordon around Justinian as he left the Imperial suite, under the command of a leader-of-fifty. No one commented on the sudden change in routine, but it was obvious Belisarius was making certain no harm would come to the man who was certain to become the next Caesar Augustus. Never again would Justinian be free to wander alone wherever he pleased; until the end of his days he would know no real privacy.

He accepted the change with aplomb, but concealed his right hand in the folds of his robe, hoping the gesture looked casual.

🏵🏵🏵

The reaction set in while Theodora was bathing her husband's hand with scented water. He had been sitting quietly for a time, saying little, but suddenly became annoyed. "Scrub it!" he demanded. "We must have a brush of boar's bristles somewhere!"

She calmly examined his palm, then the back of his hand. "You're clean now." She dried the hand with a linen towel.

"I'll never be clean," he replied morosely.

"Nonsense! You had no choice. When Vitalian refused to act as your co-Regent, you knew that one of you would have to die. Had he put you out of the way, he'd be suffering no qualms of conscience!"

"He was a soldier, so he was accustomed to killing. I've always thought of myself as civilized."

Theodora stood, her mouth a hard line. "The Emperor of Rome," she said, "can't afford the luxury of remorse. There will be plots against you and those who stand close to you in the years ahead. Men you trust will try to betray you. Insurrections will break out when you least expect them. Your position will force you to sign many death decrees, and if you brood, you'll hurt no one but yourself."

"There's a difference between signing a death order and killing with my own hands."

"Now you're being a sophist. When you're responsible, you can't pretend your hands are cleaner than those of your hired executioners."

Justinian hastily wiped the palm of his right hand on his robe.

Theodora became contemptuous. "I've heard it said that Justin killed two of his rivals. Did you ever know him to feel remorse?"

"No, but he wasn't the sort who—"

"Neither are you, if you intend to be a real Emperor! You'll have your chance to bring your dream to life, but you'll accomplish nothing if you're squeamish. You conducted yourself well this morning, and only one thing bothers me. Mundus must know you were with Vitalian in the Emperor's bedchamber, so he undoubtedly has guessed what happened."

"Mundus behaved superbly."

"Yet he knows. Transfer him to a remote border garrison, and there won't be as much as a ripple when he's killed there."

Justinian was horrified. "He's loyal to me, and what's more, I've just promoted him in order to guarantee—"

"The loyalty of no man to anyone but himself and his own interests can be 'guaranteed.' One who has worked as many years as you have in the Imperial palace must know that! The intrigues, the shifting alliances—"

"The Emperor of Rome," Justinian said, "cannot rule

alone. He needs men he can trust, men who'll serve *his* interests. I'll be forced to depend on others."

"But not on an officer who knows too much about a very delicate incident that outsiders might not understand."

"I can't and won't send Mundus off to his death. There are few enough officers in the army who supported me and jeopardized their military careers. He and Belisarius are reliable, and I refuse to get rid of either!"

Aware she could not argue with him when his mind was set, Theodora bowed her head slightly to indicate that she accepted his verdict. She was far from satisfied, however, and instantly made up her mind that if he refused to take adequate measures of self-protection, she would have to intervene in her own way. Now that the road ahead was clear, she would form her own espionage service, reporting to her alone. She would keep watch not only on Mundus, but on every other man Justinian trusted, and sooner or later her caution would be of help to him at a time when he would need her assistance.

There had been Empresses who had devoted themselves to wallowing in luxury, but she refused to follow their example. Power rotted away when it was not used, and she could not and would not permit her husband's position to be undermined. If he was naïve, she was not, and would become his watchdog.

❦ ❦ ❦

The crowd waiting on the terrace and in the great hall of Justinian's house grew larger, but no one seemed to resent the delay. One by one the magisters and ministers of state, the heads of government departments and bureaus, were ushered into the Caesar Praefect's inner sanctum for a private talk, and Justinian took his time with each. It appeared that no one was being discharged, and the civilians, most of them men with whom he had worked for years, did not feel that their positions or influence would be jeopardized in the months and years ahead. The future Emperor was conservative in his approaches, and those who had been closely associated with him were pleased that the issue of the succession to the throne had been settled.

The military men who arrived singly and in pairs for their joint conference with the future Emperor were less sure of themselves, however. In spite of their burnished, plumed helmets, breastplates, and leg guards of gleaming gold, they glanced at one other apprehensively and refrained from any but the most subdued conversation. Almost without exception they had been Vitalian's supporters and felt they had good cause to be afraid they would be retired, sent to far distant posts where they would be out of the way, or even discharged.

Theodora, resplendent in a new gown of pale lavender, but unseen behind an Indian screen of heavy silk, looked into the great hall and then returned to the small room outside her husband's sanctum. There, Narses had established himself at a small table and was keeping a meticulous record of those who went in and out of the inner room, how long each conferred with the Caesar Praefect, and, most important, whether he was in a good mood or bad after being told his future duties and responsibilities.

Narses glanced up from his work long enough to incline his head in a half-respectful, half-insolent gesture of recognition. "Justinian is at least an hour behind his schedule," he said, "but it will do the generals no harm to cool their heels."

His calm assumption that he was sharing in Justinian's strategy was as irritating as his failure to stand when Theodora came into the room. "The generals are all here and shouldn't be kept waiting," she said.

The secretary raised an eyebrow. "Justinian doesn't need

to cater to men who were Vitalian's most ardent supporters. Let him show them that he's their master now."

"He'll need their help," she replied acidly, "far more than he will that of men who do nothing but sit at tables all day, reading reports."

"That's a matter of opinion, Lady Theodora."

She was outraged, but before she could put him in his place, Justinian emerged with his most recent visitor.

Narses studied the man, and, while Theodora told her husband she believed he should see the army commanders at once, the secretary jotted down his impressions of the departing official. Finally, when the woman had finished speaking, he repeated what he had said to her.

Justinian smiled. "Narses is right," he said. "I'll see my friends first. The generals will be more malleable, more inclined to do anything I ask of them, if they're put on edge and are afraid they'll be stripped of their rank. Who is next?"

"John of Cappadocia, the tax collector, Caesar Praefect." Narses had won a clear-cut victory and, despising all women, made no attempt to conceal his triumph.

John, a burly man in a fur-trimmed cloak that most nobles would have hesitated to wear for fear of being thought ostentatious, swaggered through the outer room, his bow to Theodora perfunctory.

Again she felt slighted, but her anger was not directed at the tax collector. Her enemy was Narses, who had dared to defy her wishes and persuade Justinian to follow a course she opposed. She would have known how to deal with another woman who threatened her standing, or how to cope with a man who failed to pay homage to her, but Narses was neither. It was humiliating to realize that her rival was a homosexual, but she tried not to think in terms of personal vengeance or the possibility that Narses might entice an unwary Justinian into an affair.

What mattered was that her husband would become Emperor, and needed her help if he hoped to stem the tide of Imperial deterioration, much less realize his dream of restoring the grandeur of Rome. She alone, Theodora told herself, wanted nothing other than Justinian's success, so she alone could serve him selflessly, completely. She had not imagined it possible that she would rise this high, and thought it miraculous that she, too, would wear royal purple, but she was discovering she wanted nothing for herself other than the utilization of power for the ends Justinian sought.

Having already acquired riches far beyond her expectations, she found that wealth and luxury meant little to her. It was enough that she would never go hungry again, dress in rags, or give her body to men in order to survive. At the risk of losing the throne, Justinian had given her his love, so she would devote herself to protecting him from the greedy and the unscrupulous, even when she was forced to act without his knowledge or consent.

As Narses—and anyone else who stood in her path— would learn when she became Empress, she intended to be more than a mere consort.

Shutting the smirking secretary out of her mind, she stood, lost in thought, then went straight to the great hall, where the army commanders were assembled. The generals stood, although she saw some of them frowning while others were obviously reluctant to honor her as they rose to their feet.

But she ignored their pettiness, aware—as Justinian and Narses were not—that Emperors could be deposed if they failed to win the support of the army chiefs. "Milords," she said, "the Caesar Praefect has asked me, on his behalf, to beg your indulgence while he listens to the fearful whines of the clerks and scribes who cower and hide whenever there's an emergency."

She was rewarded by a smattering of chuckles and several broad smiles.

"He hopes you'll accept some refreshments while you wait," she continued, and summoning the majordomo, ordered him to bring several casks of the expensive, distilled white wine from Jerusalem that was the Emperor Justin's favorite.

Even the commanders who had unfailingly damned the harlot who had risen to such heights brightened at the prospect of drinking the potent wine.

Theodora quickly took advantage of the momentary goodwill she had created. "Milords, I hope you'll feel free to call on me whenever you want a sympathetic ear. The Caesar Praefect's background having been exclusively civilian, he doesn't understand some of your problems until they've been carefully explained to him. But we've had our experiences in bivouac tents, you in your way and I in mine, so we speak the same language. At least I know how to listen, and if need be I hope I can act as your interpreter."

The thaw was complete. The commanders whose wives had told them that Justinian's slut was putting on airs now had evidence of their own to the contrary, and without exception the blunt soldiers admired Theodora's frankness. She was offering them her friendship, and the realization that she would act as their intermediary made them more amenable to the future they had been regarding with distaste.

Servants appeared with the wine, and Theodora broke her self-imposed rule, accepting a cup so she could share a drink with the generals.

Hippolytes, principal inspector of the army and Vitalian's lifelong comrade, raised his cup. "Brothers," he said, "I give you the Lady Theodora!"

She smiled at each of the generals in turn, then suddenly realized that Belisarius and Mundus, who were present in their capacities as co-commanders of the royal household guard, although junior to the others in rank, were watching her from the far end of the great hall. Both were conscious of what she was doing, and both approved.

But she warned herself not to let Mundus' attitude weaken her resolve to keep him under close observation. Any man who knew the secret he had gleaned was dangerous, and she would be of use to Justinian only if she remained alert, and when necessary, always struck the first blow.

❋ ❋ ❋

The Emperor Justin's health deteriorated steadily, and his mind became so muddled that he was no longer capable of making even simple decisions. He failed to recognize most of the subordinates who came to his bedchamber and took pleasure only in the daily visits of his nephew's wife, whom he often confused with a girl he had known almost a half-century earlier.

For all practical purposes Justinian was already the ruler of the Empire, issuing decrees and proclamations, acting as the arbitrator of disputes between ministers of state, and, with the help of Tribonian, reviewing judicial sentences that had been appealed to the Emperor. He took care not to hold Imperial audiences, however, and as he told Theodora, "The power of the Crown still isn't really mine. No matter what I do or decide, I'm still acting in my uncle's name. So as long as he continues to live, I'm nothing but a caretaker. I can't institute any of the reforms I'm planning, or make any appointments of my own."

For her part, Theodora was content to bide her time. She worked assiduously to cultivate the friendship of the generals and paid informal calls on their wives. She dressed modestly on these occasions, wearing no cosmetics or jewelry, and her manners were impeccable. If the proud ladies continued to dislike her, they had little active reason to complain about her, and aware of the power she would exercise when she became Empress, they accepted the inevitable.

Even more important to Theodora was the creation of her own network of espionage agents. Justinian had settled an income on her, and she was spending the better part of the sum in wages, but she had no need to match the fees paid by Justinian's official police or the spymaster of Chosroes, King of the Persians. Her service was unique, and many of her volunteers refused to accept money.

All of her spies were women.

Theodora held a personal interview with each recruit in Constantinople, and her philosophy made women of every class eager to join her band. "In many ways," she told them, "we are little better than slaves. I am free to do as I please because my husband is kind, generous—and trusts me. But there are many, including the wives and daughters of some of our most powerful nobles, who spend their entire lives behind the walls and locked doors of the women's quarters in their palaces. A husband may obtain a divorce when he pleases, but a wife may not bring suit against him, no matter how he treats her. A wife may inherit property other than the jewels she has been given only if the Emperor signs a decree granting her a dispensation from the general law. An illegitimate child has no rights whatever, and the children of harlots and courtesans must follow their mothers' profession, be they girls or boys.

"When I sit on the throne of Augusta, I intend to begin an intensive campaign to assure women of the rights they deserve. But I need help. I need weapons, every scrap of information about the men who have suppressed and humiliated us for centuries. My assistants and I want to know everything that takes place, anywhere within the Empire and beyond its boundaries, no matter how insignificant. When we understand a man and his weaknesses, we know how to handle him."

The prostitutes and courtesans of Constantinople and the smaller cities of the Empire were the first to enroll, which was what Theodora had expected, and many chaste women of the lower orders, among them housekeepers and slaves, were anxious to take part in the campaign, too. What surprised her was the reaction of the high-born. Wives of Imperial viceroys throughout the realm sent her letters inscribed for them by priests whom they swore to secrecy. Great ladies came to the little palace on the hill for earnest, private conversations, as did the wives and daughters of merchants and sea captains, traders and farmers. Antonina recruited the wives of several generals, and soon it seemed as though every woman married to a soldier, no matter what his rank, wanted to join the secret army of the future Empress.

No one was turned away. "Some will talk out of turn to their husbands," Theodora told Antonina, "but it doesn't matter, because they won't know anything worth repeating. Only a few will receive the information and analyze it, and they'll be women I know I can trust."

It was inevitable that the men learned of the enterprise. Justinian shrugged, saying he thought no harm would be done, and most of the magisters, generals, and lords were equally indifferent. Some indignant husbands ordered their wives to take no part in the group's activities, so these women were quietly replaced by other female members of their households.

John of Cappadocia was one of the few who recognized the potential power of the organization Theodora was forming. "There will be almost no secret in the Empire these women won't know," he said, "but I don't see how they can use what they find out. They hold no offices and wield no real power."

Theodora smiled quietly when his words were reported to her. "John forgets," she murmured, "that I shall be sitting on a throne draped in purple."

One of the few who ridiculed the endeavor was Narses. "They'll make nuisances of themselves, as women always do," he said, "but I doubt if they can do any real harm. Let Theodora amuse herself, and she'll be too busy to meddle in affairs of state."

Theodora curbed her anger when she heard Narses' comment, but immediately sent an order to her operatives in the Imperial palace. "Keep me informed of everything Narses does," she said.

❦ ❦ ❦

Constantinople seemed to be marking time in the winter of 526-27. The Emperor's condition remained unchanged, and the government took no initiatives. King Chosroes of the Persians thought the temper of the period appropriate to increase the price he charged for maintaining peace, and sent Justinian a demand for fifty boxes of gold, threatening to send an army across the border if his request was not met.

"The Emperor," Justinian wrote in reply, "has been informed of your desire, and a decision will be made as soon as his health permits."

The same day that a special ambassador left Constantinople to carry the message to Chosroes, ten regiments of troops were dispatched to the Persian border, and the Roman generals, already influenced by Theodora, decided that their Emperor-to-be had blood rather than ink running in his veins.

Suddenly, early in the spring of 527, the Emperor Justin took a sharp turn for the worse. "He can't live more than a day or two," the physician, Servetius, told Justinian, and a deathwatch was established in the Imperial bedchamber.

The old man fell into a coma, but refused to die, and lingered for three long weeks, trying the patience of every official concerned with an orderly transition from one regime to another. But finally, after what seemed like interminable waiting, a messenger came to the little palace outside the Imperial grounds to inform Justinian the end was at hand.

Theodora accompanied her husband as he hurried to his uncle's bedside. The early morning air was damp and cold, no hint of dawn had as yet appeared in the dark sky, and except for the inevitable sentries pacing their rounds, the palace and gardens appeared deserted. This was the day she had long anticipated, the day when the harlot daughter of a circus performer would become the Empress of Rome, but she felt no elation, no sense of pleasurable anticipation. Her life would change, she suspected that her relationship with her husband would be altered in ways she could not predict, and a faint but persisting sense of dread nagged at her.

Perhaps, Theodora told herself angrily, she was depressed because she had become fond of the old soldier who had put up such a gallant battle for life.

Physicians and priests filled the Emperor's bedchamber, and all of them except Servetius and the Patriarch of Constantinople stepped aside as Justinian and his wife came in. The last rites had already been administered, and everyone awaited the end in silence. Justinian stood for a moment, looking down at his uncle, then dropped to his knees and prayed. Theodora did the same on the opposite side of the bed, and her voice, like his, was barely audible.

Then the silence closed in again, until Servetius said in a clear voice, "The Emperor has gone to his Maker."

A candle was lighted at the head of the bed and another at the foot.

Household guards pushed into the room, and Mundus helped Justinian to his feet. "Long live the Emperor," he said, "and long may he prosper."

A small cordon of soldiers surrounded Theodora, too, and her husband, who saw that she was weeping, performed his first act as Emperor by giving her a large square of linen to wipe her eyes.

"Tomorrow," Justinian said, trying in vain to get rid of a huskiness in his voice, "Caesar Augustus will be given a state funeral worthy of his memory. I'll want a full report on the plans and arrangements no later than noon. The Empress and I," he continued, flicking a glance in the direction of Theodora as he referred to her for the first time by her new, exalted title, "will move into the Imperial palace after the ceremony. She will decide what quarters we will occupy, and the master of the Imperial household may go to her later this morning for a conference. The coronation will be held two days after the funeral, and because of my grief, I don't want an elaborate celebration." He offered his arm to his wife, and they retired to a chamber on the far side of the corridor, opposite the anteroom.

When they were alone, Theodora turned on him furiously. "We should have waited at least a week for the coronation."

Justinian shook his head. "Impossible. The longer we delay, the greater the opportunity we give the demented to assassinate me. And if I should be killed before I'm crowned, at least a score of candidates would claim the throne. The army would split into factions, and there would be a civil war that might last for years."

Theodora, who was proud of her ability to think and act like a man, was completely illogical. "I'll have to spend all of today preparing for the funeral and arranging for our move here. That will leave me only two days to make ready for the coronation. How can I possibly have a gown made in that short a time?"

He was unimpressed. "If you don't have enough clothes already—"

"I own nothing in Imperial purple, naturally," she snapped. "I'll be on display before the whole city, and my portrait will be painted in my coronation robes, so I can't possibly wear something I already own."

There were other matters on Justinian's mind, and he could not sympathize with her. "Your sewing women will have to do their best."

"I suppose you realize," she continued, still upset, "that there won't be time to have new crowns made for either of us."

"There's no need for new crowns when I have so many other uses for money. We'll wear Justin's and Euphemia's."

She had long envisioned the crown she wanted, a dazzling object set with precious gems that would be remembered for all time, and her disappointment was crushing.

"They're very handsome," Justinian said, beginning to write notes to himself.

Theodora hated the sound of a stylus squeaking on a clay tablet. "Must you?" she demanded. "You have hundreds of clerks to write down everything for you now."

He paid no attention.

"My gown will be makeshift, and I'll be wearing that old iron crown of Euphemia's," she said, "but I won't complain. However, I do insist on one thing."

Justinian gave no sign that he heard her.

"I demand that the people of Constantinople be admitted to Sancta Sophia for the ceremony."

Justinian raised his head slowly and, the stylus poised above the tablet, blinked at her. "According to tradition, only the nobles, government officials, military commanders, and members of the Senate attend coronations. And their wives, of course."

"You've told me again and again how you want to revitalize and expand the Empire. You'll need money, volunteers for the army, sacrifices, and self-discipline from every one of your subjects. Do you think they'll follow you simply because you're the Emperor? If you do, you're so lost in your world of books and reports that you've forgotten what little you may have known about human nature."

A hint of amusement appeared in his somber eyes. "Belisarius and Mundus will be very reluctant to allow ordinary citizens to approach that close to us. The Sancta Sophia is so dark that a knife could cut one of us down from a distance of fifteen or twenty feet, and no one would ever know who committed the murder."

"Let Belisarius worry about protecting us. You'll need public support!"

Justinian began to smile. "Well," he said, "your advice is usually good—"

"In this instance I know I'm right. Set aside as many seats as you need for the really important nobles and officials. We can hold a reception of some sort after the coronation—in the garden, perhaps—for the others, who'd be feeling hurt. But throw open the doors of the Sancta Sophia to the people, and they'll cheer you, work for you—yes, and die for you!"

FIVE

✿ ✿ ✿

The coronation was unique in the five-hundred-year history of the Roman Empire. The nobles, generals, senators. and government officials crowded into the front of the Sancta Sophia were stunned as they watched commoners by the hundreds file past the troops of the Imperial household guard into the great church, filling every pew, lining the interior walls, and choking the aisles. Thousands more gathered in the square outside the building, and in a holiday mood sang and cheered lustily.

But the throng of cargo handlers and sailors, street venders and petty shopkeepers, bricklayers and stonecutters and butchers, showed remarkable self-control, and when the religious procession began, fell silent. They, like the aristocrats, watched as the priests of Sancta Sophia marched through the square and into the church, the patriarch and deacons behind them, followed by the couple who would mount the twin thrones.

Both were bareheaded, and Justinian, at his wife's insistence, was attired in a short tunic of royal purple, with a breastplate and leg shields of pure gold. "You can't afford to look like an instructor from the university," she had told him, "and no one will respect you if you appear in those impossible, flapping robes. You aren't a teacher, you know, or a monk. You're the Emperor!"

She herself required no guidance, and everyone who saw her knew her role. She wore a heavy cloth-of-gold gown, dyed purple on the outside, with the inner facing showing here and there in a skirt slit almost to her knees and an eight-foot train, the ends of which were carried by two ladies-in-waiting, one of them the younger daughter of Vitalian. A circle of pure white fur was draped around her shoulders and cascaded down her back, her cosmetics had been boldly but carefully applied, and, after experimenting at length, she wore no jewelry, having discovered that even a modest ring or necklace made the ugly iron crown of Euphemia look dowdy.

The crowd in the square, although quiet, pressed forward against the javelin barrier of the household troops to see the woman they regarded as one of their own, and inside the Sancta Sophia the noble ladies were only a trifle more polite, standing, craning their necks, and openly ogling the former harlot, who, in spite of her disreputable background, had promised them a freedom never attained by women.

Justinian and Theodora took seats on low stools of raw wood directly below the main altar, but were required by tradition to use these symbolic reminders of their mortality for no more than a few minutes. They alone were administered the rites of Holy Communion by the patriarch, who then took a battered crown of tarnished laurel leaves, supposedly that of the first Caesar Augustus, and handed it to the Emperor.

Justinian placed it on his own head, taking care not to press the metal against his forehead and temples. It was far too small for him, as it had been for all of his predecessors who had worn it, and he well remembered that his uncle had suffered from a blinding headache after his own coronation. It was something of a consolation to realize that only once each year, on the day of his annual reception for foreign ambassadors, would custom require him to don this crown again.

The patriarch reverently took a second crown from a box of purple-lined gold and handed it to Justinian. A plain band of iron with a small icon rising from the front, it was an object totally lacking in aesthetic or historical significance. All the same, every woman present wished she had the right to wear it.

Theodora approached her husband, fell slowly to her knees before him, and waited for him to place the crown on her head, an act they had rehearsed earlier in the day to make certain he did not inadvertently spoil the arrangement of her hair.

The new Emperor took great care to place the heavy object squarely on her head, but was so intent on the task that he used more force than was necessary. Theodora winced and then, aware that only Justinian could see her face, giggled.

He resisted the impulse to return her laugh and, helping her to her feet, walked with her up the steps of a dais on which the twin thrones of the Roman Empire had been mounted. These seats, regarded as the ultimate symbols of Imperial authority, were carved from matching blocks of rare, purple marble, and officials tried to foster the impression that they were the traditional thrones of the Roman Emperors and their consorts. Virtually the entire court, however, knew they had been made for the weakling Theodosius II at the instigation of his sister Pulcheria, whose desire to occupy one of them herself had at first been thwarted by outraged bishops and patriarchs, who had forgotten their differences long enough to close ranks and prevent a scandalous marriage. It was small wonder that the loyalty to the Crown of magisters and nobles was limited.

The marble was cold, hard, and slippery, and the seat had been made for a much larger woman, so Theodora had to grasp the arms in order to stop herself from sliding to the floor. Since this was the throne she would use daily for the rest of her life, she made up her mind to have some cushions made for it at once, and was sorry she had not been permitted to try the chair before using it in the presence of such a multitude.

But the roar of approval that seemed to shake the walls of the old church made her forget her discomfort. She held her head high and sat unmoving, accepting the applause.

The priests began to form for the procession that would take the Imperial couple back into the square and from there to the palace compound, but Justinian suddenly broke with tradition, surprising everyone in the assemblage, his wife included.

He raised his right hand, demanding quiet, and the cheers instantly subsided, the throngs outside the open doors at the rear of the church pressing forward to hear him, too.

"We have inaugurated a new era," he said. "We promise all our subjects justice and equity, honor and glory. In return we demand obedience, and should it prove necessary, sacrifice. The decrees we shall issue, beginning on the first day of next week, will make clear our intent."

Theodora found it difficult to stare straight ahead, looking as though she knew what he was planning. He had said nothing to her, which was his prerogative, of course, but she couldn't help feeling annoyed, wishing he had been less secretive. It wouldn't be easy to help him unless he took her into his confidence.

Most of the nobles and officials who sat in the front pews, facing her, seemed startled and bewildered, too. Tribonian was calm, which wasn't necessarily significant, as he rarely became ruffled. John of Cappadocia, resplendent in a fur-trimmed cloak and matching hat, was smiling quietly, which meant he had some idea of Justinian's plans, and Theodora decided to keep him under close watch. In her experience men of his birth who dressed ostentatiously were greedy.

Her glance met that of Narses for an instant, and the secretary stared at her haughtily, revealing not only that he knew Justinian's secrets, but also that she had been excluded. A feeling of jealous rage welled up in her, and she fought to control it so she could concentrate on what Justinian was saying.

"Until next week, when we shall start to work together, side by side, for the benefit of Rome and of all mankind, let us rejoice together. All churches in Constantinople will remain open day and night so that our subjects may give thanks to Almighty God for the opportunities He is giving us to make this a better world.

"Each afternoon chariot races will be held in the Hippodrome, the expenses to be paid out of our personal treasury. We regret that our mourning for our beloved uncle, the Caesar Augustus Justin, will prevent us from attending these festivities. In his memory we have directed that alms be distributed to the poor every morning at all four of the main palace gates."

Theodora's irritation increased. A wise man would have given alms to the poor in his own name in order to insure their goodwill, and she thought it absurd that Justinian's generous gesture would be wasted. He had so much to learn.

"Next week, too, we will receive in audience any who wish to see us, no matter what the reason. We are reviving the ancient custom of the first Caesar Augustus, who himself dispensed justice to any Roman who sought to meet him, face to face. So be it, our reign has begun."

He rose so quickly that Theodora, jumping to her feet, too, became tangled in her long train and needed the help of her attendants. She quickly recovered her poise, however, and her smile was graciously amiable as she walked beside Justinian into the square.

"Why haven't I been told your plans?" she demanded, scarcely able to make him hear her above the sustained roar of the crowd.

Justinian, bowing to the throng and waving, did not break his stride. "You were busy with your sewing women," he said, "but I was working."

Theodora privately vowed not to be caught napping again.

❦ ❦ ❦

No magisters or ministers of state were dismissed from office, contrary to the custom of new Emperors, but Justinian had developed a new method of delegating authority to men he trusted. Two of his appointments were of paramount importance, as his initial decrees attested.

Tribonian became president of a twelve-member Council of Law that was ordered to undertake a gigantic, unprecedented task. The commission was directed to codify, modernize, and unify the entire body of Roman law that had grown ever bulkier and more unwieldy since the early days of the ancient Republic in old Rome, on the banks of the Tiber. In effect, the Empire would be governed under a complete new set of laws, applicable to all men of all ranks and stations, with citizens, foreigners, and slaves guaranteed justice.

Tribonian, who would also act as Supreme Judge of the Empire, with authority to make binding rulings in the name of the Caesar Augustus, was ordered to complete the task in no more than three years, with the promise that thereafter he would revise the courts themselves. Lawyers, judges, and virtually everyone else who knew anything about the complex legal system said that the new president of the Council of Law had been given an impossible assignment, but two men—Justinian and Tribonian—were supremely confident that the work would be completed on schedule.

John of Cappadocia became equally powerful, leaping over men who had been his superiors to become the Caesar Praefect of Finance, a newly created post. He was directed to impose new, equitable taxes on the citizenry that would require the wealthy as well as the poor to pay their fair share. He was given the power to fine and imprison those who evaded or cheated, and all fund-raising was placed in his hands, including the imposition and collection of customs duties. He was granted control of the Imperial mints, and of the storage of gold, silver, and copper.

The Emperor made no changes in the high command of the army, which surprised even the generals, but a curt Imperial decree prohibited nobles, military leaders, and others from maintaining their own private armed forces. Anyone who violated the order would be sentenced to death, and all troops were required to swear allegiance only to the Crown.

"People everywhere are saying your plans are too ambitious," Theodora told her husband when, one evening, he joined her for an inspection of the private quarters she had established for them on the third floor of the Imperial palace. "Some say you're a dreamer, but most think you're a fool."

"My security police reports are more discreet." Justinian, still unaccustomed to his short tunic, tugged absently at its hem.

"My agents," she retorted, "are honest!"

He made himself comfortable on a divan, pleased that a pitcher of barley water was close at hand. "They'll discover they're wrong," he said calmly.

Theodora took a seat opposite him. She was afraid the acquisition of supreme power had unbalanced him, and was determined to make him face the future in realistic terms. "No one," she said, "can perform the task you've given Tribonian!"

"Is that your agents' opinion, or your own?"

"Both!"

"To the best of my knowledge you've never studied law. Have they?"

"Well, no. But—"

"Then leave the problem to experts," he said, his voice suddenly firm. "Tribonian and I have been making our plans for more than ten years. Every member of his council was appointed for a specific purpose, and most have been at work, quietly, for years. Tribonian will use a guide, an outline, that we developed together, a document of more than six thousand pages, and I've authorized him to hire as many legal assistants as he needs. We believe he'll use a staff of between seven and eight thousand trained men."

Theodora was stunned, and told herself she should have known her husband would be thorough in his preparations beyond the capacity or even the imagination of ordinary mortals. "Perhaps Tribonian will succeed," she said slowly. "It would be wonderful, almost miraculous. And I'm willing to grant the possibility."

"Thank you," he said dryly.

For his sake, not her own, she ignored the sarcasm. "But your other plans are too ambitious. No one can change the system of taxation that has been used for hundreds of years!"

Again Justinian became gentle. "Is that your agents' opinion, or your own?"

"Both." Theodora was beginning to feel uncomfortable, and became more aggressive. "You've given far too much power to one man, and your trust in John of Cappadocia is misplaced."

The Emperor's eyes narrowed. "Do you have any evidence to that effect?"

"Nothing specific—"

"Until you do, I'll trust my own judgment—and John. He was my colleague for twenty years, and my friend when nearly everyone else turned against me. I have absolute faith in his talents as an administrator, and if anyone can reorganize our system of taxation and bring in revenues without huge sums seeping into the purses of corrupt officials, John of Cappadocia will do what I've ordered. You seem to forget my own years of training as a member of the Imperial staff. I may be a dreamer, but my dreams are based on what I know can be achieved."

She saw he was becoming aroused and realized it was dangerous to continue the argument, but could not stop herself. "I never forget your experience, my dear, and I know you'll become a great Emperor, provided your own loyalties don't mislead you. I know nothing of finances and taxes, but I do understand something about people, and my instinct tells me not to trust John!"

"When you can prove to me that he's disloyal to me or has stolen from the Imperial treasury, I'll act accordingly. Until then, he stays."

She knew that for the present it would be unwise to press.

"John is the only man in the Empire who can fill the palace vaults with gold."

Theodora realized she had to tread delicately. In all the time she had known Justinian he had never been greedy, and his sudden desire to accumulate great wealth made no sense to her. "Gold that's locked in the Imperial vaults," she said lightly, "is as useless as the coppers a miser buries near a fig tree."

Although they were alone, their suite guarded by sentries who would allow no one to approach, the Emperor lowered his voice. "The gold," he said, "will be used."

She waited, hoping he would elaborate, but not daring to ask questions after being so free in her criticism.

"Do you remember my telling you that I want to restore the old boundaries of the Empire—and expand them?"

"Of course."

"When I'm ready, I'll move, although I know it will take a few years to build a war chest. That's my greatest secret, and not even John knows why I want him to fill the vaults."

"He won't learn your reason from me," Theodora said tartly, "nor will anyone else."

"I'm quite sure of that."

The compliment gave her renewed courage to speak her mind. "I hope you aren't intending to send your uncle's generals to conquer the world. Not only were they Vitalian's friends, but years of inactivity have made them soft."

Justinian's long sigh was lugubrious. "I sometimes wonder whether you credit me with any sense. By the time I'm ready, they'll be older than they are now—and ready for retirement. Until then, you see, they'll be loyal. Well, loyal enough. They're relieved because I haven't dismissed them from their posts, and since there's no logical candidate to succeed me, they won't conspire behind my back."

"You're farsighted, my dear, as always." Her mind working rapidly, she thought her own position would be strengthened if she could establish cordial relations with the future leaders of the army and if possible put them in her debt. She saw virtually no officers except those assigned to the household guard, however, and knew little about the brigade and regimental commanders in the field. "It was last year, I think, that you told me Alexander the Great gave his lieutenants special training that made it possible for them to win so many victories."

"Yes. Alexander's system was remarkable." His expression indicated his awareness of her attempt to glean information from him, but he wasn't certain he wanted to share all his secrets with her. She was displaying a desire to exercise power in her own right rather than live as a charming and graceful consort, and he had no intention of sharing his own authority with her. "Must you always wear purple?" he demanded, suddenly.

"It's been the custom of empresses for the past five hundred years, I believe."

"Even when we're alone?"

Theodora recognized the hint, and knew, too, that her hold over him depended at least in part on her physical appeal. "When we're alone," she said, "I'll dress only to please you."

He smiled, his tension draining away.

She had just learned another lesson she would not allow herself to forget: The Caesar Augustus might be the most powerful potentate on earth, but, like any other man, had to be soothed and pampered, and became infinitely more malleable when flattered.

❧ ❧ ❧

The quarters traditionally occupied by the Empress, the tiny throne room in which she granted courtesy audiences to foreign ambassadors and the chambers in which she received the great ladies of the realm, proved far too cramped for Theodora's purposes. With her husband's freely granted consent she established her own court in a building adjacent to the main palace. Until the present Imperial headquarters had been constructed one hundred years earlier, it had served as the Emperor's own, and Theodora found it perfect.

She refurnished the old throne room, paying no attention to the pleas of John of Cappadocia that she spend less money, and she quickly created her own court, inviting the daughters and widows of nobles and other prominent citizens to make their home there. It was rumored that she also gave refuge to a number of notorious women, including the former mistress of a high-ranking general, several shrewd harlots, and a Greek actress-courtesan who had been intimate with magisters and ministers.

It was impossible to verify these tales, however. No man could let himself forget the Empress' own background, and care was taken to avoid offending her by referring to her old friends of dubious virtue. Even more important, it had become almost impossible to learn what took place in the women's palace, or seraglio, as it was sometimes called. The building was closely guarded by its own detail of sentries, and although Theodora automatically granted audiences to any woman, men were admitted only at her express invitation. She received these visitors either in her magnificent throne room or in a pleasantly furnished sitting chamber, but men were excluded from the rest of the building.

A young nobleman who had been found sleeping with one of the Empress' ladies was put to death in the Imperial dungeons, and a leader-of-fifty in the household guard who had been unable to resist temptation had been whipped and dismissed from the military. Both sentences had been passed by Theodora, and Justinian had not countermanded her orders.

She won his approval for anything she wanted, and the court developed several theories to explain his amenability. "She has bewitched him," John of Cappadocia said, expressing a point of view shared by the more sophisticated nobles and officials. "I have no idea whether she feeds him love potions or uses other magical charms, but that doesn't matter. What's obvious is that he's infatuated, just as he was when she first went to live with him. She smiles at him, she kisses him—and he grants her every wish."

Narses had a far different idea. "The Emperor," he said, "is the busiest man in the history of Rome. From the papers

I've seen, and I know only a fraction of what goes on in his mind, his plans are staggering. He simply doesn't want that woman and her female spies underfoot, distracting him. He prefers to let her amuse herself in her seraglio, where she's not only out of the way but harmless."

Only Theodora, to whom both concepts were duly reported by her agents, knew that both were reasonably accurate. She used no magic, of course, to keep Justinian entranced; that claim was absurd. It was enough that she was a woman, and that, loving him, she knew how to please him. As for Narses' statement that she was harmless, he and many others would learn, in due course, that they were mistaken.

Some of the men invited to audiences at the seraglio were openly curious about the place, and the others made amusingly surreptitious attempts to pry into its alleged secrets. Only Tribonian, coming there for the first time, at the Empress' request, seemed completely indifferent to his surroundings.

A lean, spare man, the Caesar Praefect for Justice, his new title, was immersed in his codification and revision of Imperial laws, and also was forced to spend several hours each day passing judgment in cases referred to him by lower-ranking magistrates. No one had ever seen him flustered or angry, however, and even now, accepting Theodora's invitation to sit on a divan overlooking the inner courtyard gardens, he was calm, polite, and remote.

At first glance he looked, as Justinian had for so many years, like an instructor from the university. But there were subtle differences. His long gray robe was made of expensive silk, the cord that encircled his waist was of gold, the gems of its tasseled ends hidden in the folds of his garment, and the Empress knew instantly that his shoes of fine kidskin had been made in Antioch, where the best and most expensive tanners in the Empire lived and worked.

She tried to chat with him, but Tribonian remained

aloof, and Theodora soon discovered that rather than put him at ease, she was becoming upset, while he remained tranquil. So she decided to waste no more of his time or her own.

"You may have heard, Caesar Praefect," she said, "of my interest in the plight of unmarried mothers."

Tribonian's expression remained unchanged. "To be sure. No matter how busy a man may be, he's told of all the Augusta's whims and hobbies."

The suffering of the young women was no whim, but she curbed her temper. "Let me tell you something that isn't yet known. The little palace beyond the wall—our former home, which the Emperor presented to me as a gift—is going to be converted into a home for unmarried mothers and daughters of Venus who no longer want to ply their degrading trade."

"You're very generous." He nodded, obviously bored, and wondering why she was choosing to confide in him.

"You may remember some conversations in that house, on occasions when you visited us. I swore that should it ever be in my power, I intended to change the status of those women."

Tribonian vaguely recalled something of the sort.

"It's a disgrace that the father of a bastard isn't required to support his child or pay the mother compensation of any kind."

The Caesar Praefect for Justice shrugged. "The attitudes of men and of women in these matters are different."

"Very different. I also believe it's a disgrace that the children of a prostitute are themselves condemned to spend their lives in the same profession."

Tribonian gave her his full attention now. Neither he nor anyone else in the Empire forgot Theodora's own background, and although he couldn't agree with her views, he could understand why she was upset. "Tradition," he said, "always favors the moralist's point of view."

"Is it moral to force innocent children to sell their bodies? Is it moral to give them no choice?"

"I'm only a lawyer," Tribonian said uncomfortably. "It would be more appropriate to ask the bishops these questions."

"I have, and they agree with me, even though they think the problem is insoluble. I happen to believe that any condition created by humans can be cured by humans."

"The Augusta is an optimist." He was becoming increasingly uneasy.

"No, I think it takes generations of gentle persuasion, teaching—and obedience—to change the nature of people." She poured some wine into a goblet for him, then took a little for herself, pleased that in the seraglio it wasn't necessary to abide by Justinian's injunctions against the use of alcoholic beverages.

"By obedience," Tribonian said, weary of fencing, "I assume you mean observance of the law."

"Precisely."

He raised his glass. "The laws are very clear in the matters you've mentioned."

Theodora returned the salute. "Laws," she said succinctly, "can be changed. And should."

Now he knew why she had summoned him, and was annoyed. Her approach was ridiculously simple and unrealistic. "The council," he said, "considers recommendations made to us by the staff—"

"The president of the council could dispense with the usual routines, if he chose."

"Well, yes," he was forced to admit. "I suppose I could, provided the Emperor and I agreed that a law should be changed."

"In this instance, do you believe the situations I've mentioned are unjust?"

"Taking a purely legal approach—"

"Justinian's views are the same as mine," Theodora said.

"He has other matters on his mind, and is leaving the solution of these problems to me."

The Caesar Praefect for Justice felt he could not grant her wish without referring the questions to subordinates for study and recommendations. His manner that of a university lecturer, he tried to explain.

The Empress cut him short. "I want to correct a rank injustice to women and their children that has existed for centuries, Tribonian. Don't prattle about legal methods!"

She might be Justinian's wife, but no one knew more than he about the law. "If I accepted all the advice I've been given, the new body of Imperial law would be an unholy maze."

"I've made a few suggestions, that's all, and I can't see how the body of law would be either complicated or corrupted by them."

"I'll tell the council what you want, and we'll put the questions on our agenda," he said, privately cursing her for interfering with his work.

Perhaps Justinian was right when he said Tribonian would become immortal after finishing his great task, but Theodora refused to admit defeat to any man. "You'll do better than that," she said evenly.

He was too startled to reply.

"I want a new law made that will compel fathers of illegitimate children to recognize their financial responsibilities. And I want another that will grant the children of prostitutes freedom from bondage." Her violet eyes blazed, but she did not raise her voice. "You'll prepare these laws yourself, and the Emperor will sign them."

"Are you threatening me?"

"Certainly not! But I do have something of a personal problem that only you can solve. I dare say you know that your wife has become my good friend. I'm very fond of the Lady Minerva."

Tribonian, watching her, didn't know quite why her smile made him shudder.

"I've discovered some things that might hurt her, but I can't help wondering whether it's my duty to tell her what I've learned, and I'd like your opinion. It's been brought to my attention that every Tuesday night, when Minerva's husband is working late at the new council building, a red-haired courtesan from Egypt pays a private visit to his quarters."

Tribonian became pale.

"What I find particularly interesting are the practices in which the couple engage. Some of them are unusual, don't you agree? What bothers me is that Minerva has told me that her husband lacks imagination as a lover. Now, I could refer the problem to a committee of my ladies, or I could ignore the routines and go straight to Minerva. Which do you suggest?"

"You have no right to spy on me," Tribonian said in a strangled voice.

Theodora's smile broadened. "That's only one of the matters I think I should discuss with her. The other is more delicate because—as you know better than anyone—she values the high place in society that she and her children have achieved. She'd be crushed if she learned her husband had sired a child by a daughter of Venus—"

"That's not true!"

"—and that the child herself became a harlot."

He found it difficult to breathe and gulped his wine.

Theodora, the considerate hostess, refilled his goblet. "Surely you don't deny your relationship with a woman named Mera, about two years after you and Minerva were married."

"I'm not on trial!" Tribonian gasped.

"Mera not only swears that her child is your daughter, but she has a small ring that bears your seal, the only gift you could be persuaded to give her when you learned she was pregnant. But your daughter herself is the best evidence. She bears a remarkable resemblance to you."

Tribonian slumped in his seat and covered his face with his hands.

Theodora waited, but there was no sympathy in her silence; her eyes were cold and her face wooden.

"I'm prepared to make amends," he muttered. "I'll give them whatever money they need to make new lives elsewhere—"

"As harlots? And when your daughter gives birth to a child, must she become a harlot, too?"

"Do you want to destroy me because of a mistake I made almost twenty years ago, Theodora?"

"I want justice, Tribonian, justice which you've been commanded by the Emperor to provide for all Romans. Mera and her daughter have been taken under my protection, so there's nothing you can do for them. I'm prepared to provide them with a new home and new identities, far from Constantinople, where they won't embarrass you. In return, and as a gesture that may persuade me not to tell the Lady Minerva what I've learned, I want those new laws ready for the Emperor's signature no later than tomorrow."

The Caesar Praefect for Justice made an attempt to recover his shattered dignity. "Once I've prepared them, it will take two days to copy them and incorporate them into the new codification."

"On the day after tomorrow, then, I'll expect you here at this same time of day. I want to read them myself before you present them to Justinian." She relaxed, then added politely, "Since you're very busy, and so am I, you'll be prompt, I know."

"Very prompt," he said in wry surrender.

The Empress stood. "Your work for Justinian is overwhelming, so I don't want to be selfish. In fact, I'm prepared to wait—until next month, perhaps—to discuss some revisions in the divorce laws that I have in mind. I believe that wives as well as husbands should have the right to obtain divorces, and on the same grounds."

Tribonian laughed hollowly.

Theodora escorted him to the main staircase, as a gesture of respect to one of her husband's principal lieutenants, and not until she returned to the privacy of the sitting room did she allow herself the luxury of a brilliantly triumphant smile. In a single, brief interview she had done more to improve the lot of her own sex than others had accomplished in centuries, and she knew now that her extraordinary espionage service was worth all the time, effort, and money she lavished on it.

SIX

❧ ❧ ❧

New forces of unprecedented strength were stirring in the long-dormant Roman Empire. The Justinian Code, completed by Tribonian and his council after four years of hard labor, granted equal rights under the law to every man and woman. The Emperor immediately appointed a new commission, with Tribonian as its head, to prepare a precise digest of all Imperial laws so they could be made available to every judge, governor, and praefect in the realm.

John of Cappadocia demonstrated extraordinary efficiency in finding new methods of taxation, then applying them to men on every social and financial level. Huge sums poured into the Imperial treasury, but contrary to the dire expectations of the magisters and ministers who held seats in the Council of State, the Emperor remained popular. The poor no longer resented taxation because the rich were paying more, and the wealthy were discovering, to their astonishment, that new sources of moneymaking were opening.

The Emperor's vigorous construction program was partly responsible. In Constantinople, Antioch, and all the smaller cities and towns of the Empire new public buildings were erected and new roads were built. Privately, sometimes secretly, Justinian personally invested in new inns, iron forges, and the enterprises of those who spun cloth. The nobles and merchants, seeing their opportunity to become wealthier, gave their financial support to the makers of other items, thousands in all, demanded by a prosperous, civilized people.

The government erected its own yards for the construction of ships at Constantinople, and both naval architects and builders were brought to the capital from Beirut, where the ancient Phoenician arts of seamanship still flourished. Lebanese cedars were used in the vessels, too, as was hard oak from the highlands of Asia Minor. The Emperor took care to emphasize that he was building a merchant fleet for the purpose of expanding Imperial trade, but men familiar with naval affairs looked at the ships gradually taking shape on the new Constantinople waterfront ways and realized that at least half were intended for the making of war. The largest, which would carry crews of 150 to 200 men, were armed with huge catapults, high-sided deck shields to protect archers, and a strange new device, somewhat similar to a catapult but much smaller.

The army conducted a quiet but vigorous recruiting campaign. Groups headed by leaders-of-fifty and sergeants traveled through the Empire, awarding cash purses to healthy young men who joined the service, and warriors of tribes living in the outer portions of the realm were granted special privileges when they entered as units. Even young slaves were guaranteed purchase from their masters and promised their freedom if they volunteered for duty in the foot brigades.

The nation's farmers were not neglected in Justinian's distribution of largess, which took a form that seemed to confirm the suspicions of those who believed he was preparing for the most extensive military adventures in generations. The minister of grains bought large quantities of wheat, barley, and millet from growers, paying prices that encouraged the production of still more, and storing the crops in special warehouses that were built for the purpose and placed under heavy army guard.

Rumors of an impending, major war were carried by Persian spies to their king, Chosroes, who became alarmed, and Justinian found it necessary to sign a new peace treaty with Rome's ancient foes. He doubled the size of the annual payments made to the Persians as a bribe to induce them to keep the peace, but refused to explain his reasons to the unhappy John of Cappadocia or the angry generals. In time, he said, they would understand and would accept his long-range strategy.

While the Emperor worked indefatigably, the Empress was expanding her own spheres of influence. Her network of female espionage agents and informers grew larger and more efficient, and the power of her seraglio court increased. With Justinian engaged in vast enterprises of significance to future generations, Theodora concerned herself with day-to-day affairs. A merchant who had been cheated, a citizen whose home had been ransacked by a mob, a shipowner whose cargo had been stolen from the docks, could attend her regularly scheduled audiences, plead for her intervention, and obtain swift, effective help.

Women of every class were particularly fortunate, and under no circumstances were turned away from the seraglio. Those who came to the Empress with legitimate complaints were granted justice never before accorded members of their sex. Men who tried to take advantage of their weakness frequently disappeared, and it was whispered they were held as prisoners in the ancient dungeons beneath the seraglio, where they were subjected to strange and humiliating tortures. Husbands who had failed to support their families or had beaten their wives, vanished for a time, and from then on, after their return to society, were subdued and lived up to their responsibilities. Without exception they refused to reveal what had happened to them, and their stubborn, frightened silence made other men apprehensive.

There were many who felt that Justinian had granted Theodora too much authority and should put her in her place, but few dared to express their views, even to their closest friends and associates. The Empress' spies were said to be everywhere, and even a minister of state was called before her, then ordered to make adequate financial payments to the wife he deserted for a younger, more attractive woman.

High-ranking government officials and members of the palace household staff wondered whether the Emperor either knew or cared what his wife was doing, but it was impossible for anyone to ascertain the truth about the relationship of the Imperial couple. It was known that they dined together nightly, alone, in their private apartment, where their food was served by the most trusted of Theodora's followers, and it was believed that on most nights they slept in the same chamber. But no one was able to glean even a hint of what transpired between them, although wealthy nobles and magisters discreetly offered large sums of money for any useful information.

Not even Justinian and Theodora quite realized that their marital ties had become so complicated they defied ordinary definition, or that the Empress herself sometimes wondered where she stood. One evening, as they dined together on a simple dish of broiled lamb that had been rolled in a batter of wheat and minced plums, Theodora carefully told her husband the highlights of her day's audiences, omitting anything that might annoy or upset him.

In order to save time, it had become his custom to bring with him to the table new laws, decrees, and orders requiring his signature, and he glanced through them as he ate, sometimes signing his name, sometimes affixing the Imperial seal with a blob of wax he scooped from a warmed dish. As usual, he nodded occasionally, but rarely replied.

And, as usual, Theodora was uncertain what he heard and what he failed to note. She had been fooled too often by his seeming inattention to hurry her recital or cut it short, however, even though it was unnerving to be speaking into what appeared to be a vacuum.

Justinian sighed, frowned, and scrawled his name at the bottom of a communication to his immediate subordinates.

"The wives of sailors are complaining that their husbands are deserting them to join the crews of your new ships. There were eleven who came to me today." Theodora saw Justinian stir and knew the remark had made an impression.

"Under no circumstances," he told her, scanning still another scroll, "are you allowed to threaten seamen or take them into custody. I forbid it."

"Why should they have the right to abandon their wives?" Theodora was indignant.

"I care nothing about their domestic lives. We've never been a nation of sailors, and I need every experienced seaman I can get."

"If they go unpunished," she said, "you'll be encouraging them to become irresponsible."

Again Justinian signed his name, then looked at her, faintly amused. "If they're unmolested by your people, they may be all the more anxious to join the Imperial service."

"Then you won't be keeping your pledge to deal with all injustice in the same way!"

"Correct. I need seamen."

"But—"

"Sometimes your enthusiasm for justice, especially

justice for women, clouds your judgment. If one sailor is brought before you for as much as a little speech on his domestic obligations, I'll order the security police to disband your army of private guards and seal off your dungeons for all time with blocks of stone."

Never had Theodora seen him so firm, and found it difficult to believe he would subject her to a semipublic disgrace. "You'd be hurting yourself as well as me."

Justinian remained surprisingly tolerant. "There are two things your espionage agents haven't been able to learn. One is my military master plan, and the other is the secret of the citadel I've built at the university. Narses tells me your people tried on eight different occasions in the past week to get into the citadel."

"Narses." She made the name sound like a curse.

"You've won great popularity and you're performing a valuable service, but keep your ambitions within bounds," the Emperor said, turning away from the papers to face her, while continuing to eat methodically. "I have too much on my mind to tolerate interference with my major projects—even from you."

"I hope you realize that the people are becoming more and more disgruntled," Theodora said, counterattacking. "Your recruiting sergeants are trying too hard to force men to join your legions, and everyone is complaining because taxes go higher every month."

"Is that what your spies tell you?"

"Yes, and I'm hearing the same thing in every class. The wealthy are annoyed and the poor are becoming angry."

"Apparently we don't hear the same reports. The security police haven't told me of a single complaint."

"Of course not. Everyone knows your agents, and in their presence people say only what they think you want to hear."

"My dear," he said, reaching out and covering her hand

with his, "you begin to take yourself too seriously, and you're enjoying power too much—because it's new to you. I've seen the same thing happen to others—"

"Like Narses and John of Cappadocia?"

"They've been efficient administrators for years!" For the first time he showed irritation. "I appreciate your help, but don't try to take my place. I enjoy seeing you in that new gown, and I'm always pleased when you wear something other than purple for me. That's more important than trying to rule independently. Just try to remember there can be only one Emperor."

"I think of nothing but your good, Justinian." She thought it pointless to tell him that he had seen her gown of pink silk on a number of occasions, and that it was at least six months old.

He was forced to admit she had rendered him assistance greater than the work performed by any magister, and that the enthusiastic support given her by the women of the Empire had made his own task easier. "Come with me to the citadel tomorrow morning, and I'll show you the greatest of surprises in all human history."

She was uncertain whether he meant it or was merely trying to make amends for his unaccustomed severity toward her, but was grateful for the gesture.

"Wear an old cloak and sandals, and leave your jewelry here."

Theodora's curiosity became greater.

Justinian patted her affectionately on the shoulder, stood, and went off to his work sanctum, twice dropping documents that he clumsily stooped to retrieve.

Theodora remained at the table, nettled and disturbed. On the surface, she told herself, she had every reason to be satisfied with her lot. She was the first woman of the wealthiest and most civilized of nations, a power in her own right. Her clothes and gems were worthy of her title, the plates and serving dishes on the table were made of pure gold, and not only the members of her staff and her servants, but countless thousands of Roman subjects, would be eager to gratify every desire that occurred to her. Why, then, was she out of sorts?

Ringing a small jade bell with an emerald-inlaid handle, she ordered the lady-in-waiting who responded to her summons to bring her a cup of distilled Jerusalem wine from the late Emperor Justin's cellars. When she was alone and knew Justinian would be absorbed in his work for many hours she allowed herself the luxury of drinking the alcoholic beverages he despised.

Common sense told her she was far removed from the time of nightmare she could not let herself forget. Never again would she be forced to sell herself in the marketplaces of strange, alien towns to ward off starvation. Never again would she cater to the brutal, perverted demands of the lust-filled and greedy in order to buy rags that would cover her naked body, give her a temporary roof over her head, and enable her to survive. She was envied, respected, and feared by a world that catered to her whims and anticipated every request, so she had no logical right to feel so thoroughly dissatisfied.

Justinian, she supposed, was responsible. Even his awkwardness annoyed her. A corps of servants could have carried his documents and papers for him, and she wished he would start behaving with the dignity of an Emperor. But that, apparently, was asking too much. Ignoring the customs of centuries, he insisted on shaving, bathing, and dressing himself, and actually refused to let magisters and ministers of state prostrate themselves before him when they came into his presence. If he wasn't careful, people would begin thinking of the Caesar Augustus as an ordinary man, and he might lose his throne—and his head. She could not change his habits, but at the least would have to order some new tunics for him in the immediate future. Food stains frequently soiled his clothing, and it was difficult to remove spots from purple-dyed silk, linen, and wool without causing a garment to fade.

Perhaps, Theodora reflected, her frustration was caused by the realization that in some ways she and Justinian were drifting apart. Sipping her wine as soon as the chalice was placed beside her, she knew it was inevitable that the demands of the throne gave him less time to spend with her, less time to make love to her. He was driving himself mercilessly, of course, and consequently was too exhausted to express physical passion when he stumbled into their bedchamber late at night, but she couldn't help fearing that his basic desire for her had lessened, even though he continued to admire her appearance and seemed sincere in his compliments.

In all justice to her husband, her own interest in lovemaking had waned, too. Once, she had known of no other way to hold a man's attention and insure his continuing affection, but her life had become almost as full as Justinian's; she was subjected to incessant demands that occupied her time, absorbed her mind, and sapped her strength.

Drinking her wine too rapidly, she became angry with herself, aware she was rationalizing and unwilling to face facts. It was true that she was busy, but she was twenty years younger than Justinian, in good health, and was capable of arousing his desire for her whenever she wished.

What really disturbed her was his unusual order forbidding her to punish sailors who deserted their wives and children. Because of his own desire to create a navy—and she suspected he was more interested in building a war fleet than in enlarging the merchant marine—her campaign to win for women the rights they deserved would be thwarted. It was outrageous that Justinian should think only of himself and thereby nullify everything she had worked so hard to achieve.

She could not openly defy his command, to be sure. If she did, she would compel him to make good his threat to disband the carefully recruited regiments of her own household troops that enforced her will. Most of the complaints made to her by women and the reports of her agents would be meaningless unless she had the force that compelled men to observe the laws promulgated at her insistence. If she had no soldiers, no dungeons, no gifted female torturers who had developed extraordinary techniques of chastening men, her laws would be ignored and women would sink again to the state of bondage in which they had been held since the beginning of time.

Resisting the impulse to drink another cup of the potent wine, Theodora continued to sit at the dinner table, pondering. Only one course was open to her: although she could not disobey Justinian, she could circumvent his intent by taking advantage of the reputation she had acquired. She would pass the word to the daughters of Venus, the wives of waterfront tavern owners and other women who knew sailors that she planned to take swift, retaliatory action against any seaman who failed to make adequate financial provision for his wife and children when joining the Emperor's navy.

The threat alone might intimidate the men and cause them to accept their responsibilities. Within a few short years of unremitting effort she had given the men of the Roman Empire good reason to be afraid of arousing her ire. So she would organize this new campaign cleverly, and if Justinian heard of her threats, she could claim they were unsubstantiated rumors, that she had no idea how they had started.

Her sense of depression lifting, Theodora went off to the seraglio to initiate the most subtle of her attempts to secure the rights of the Roman women. Every move she made actually strengthened Justinian, she told herself, so she felt no qualms of conscience.

❁ ❁ ❁

The Emperor and Empress drove off to the university in a closed carriage, and the squadron of cavalrymen who escorted them through the streets of Constantinople rode in a tight formation around the coach, virtually blocking the occupants from the view of the city's people. Narses accompanied the Imperial couple, devoting his full attention to Justinian, and Theodora was sorry she had accepted her husband's invitation.

The presence of the secretary was enough to put her in a bad frame of mind, and she was already disappointed because she could neither see the citizens of Constantinople nor be seen by them. Probably the precaution was wise, since she did not look particularly regal in her oldest purple cloak and was wearing no jewelry, but she seldom ventured beyond the palace walls, and would have enjoyed the sight of familiar crowds and sights. But Justinian had insisted that she be kept from the public gaze, and Narses hadn't helped matters by explaining—unnecessarily, at length, and to Justinian alone—that the subjects of the Emperor and Empress enjoyed being overwhelmed when they saw their rulers.

The lecture halls, libraries, and laboratories of the university were handsome edifices, some of them built according to designs sketched by the Emperor Constantine. Students in their robes of dark gray were sitting on the lawns of the well-tended grounds, reading and chatting, seminarians were marching to their chapel to hear one of their number deliver a practice sermon, and several lecturers stood outside the faculty headquarters, engaging in quiet, earnest discussions. The atmosphere was serene, and virtually no one paid more than token heed to the Imperial cavalcade.

But a far different aura pervaded the citadel, a miniature fortress surrounded by an exceptionally high wall of thick stone. Troops of Belisarius' household regiment, wearing sashes of purple and white, stood sentry duty at the entrances, and men of Mundus' regiment, purple plumes rising from their helmets, patrolled the top of the wall.

The main gate was too small to admit the carriage, so the Emperor and Empress left the coach and, followed by Narses, walked inside. Only the commander of the cavalry escort accompanied them, and he was barred at the entrance to the building itself, where other household troops were stationed.

Theodora was paying her first visit to the place, and was reminded of a castle under siege. The soldiers wore battle armor and helmets, with swords at their sides and spears and shields in their mailed hands. There was no grass in the yard between the wall and the building, and in this open space the Empress saw several catapults, each loaded with a heavy boulder, each manned by a full crew ready for action. Apparently something of extraordinary value was being guarded here.

"The Augusta," Narses said, a hint of malice in his voice as he saw Theodora note the presence of the catapults, "begins to understand why her agents have learned nothing about this place. Anyone stationed here who speaks a single word about the secrets of the citadel would be drawn and quartered. It's a standing order."

Theodora glared at him. "It's good to know that a place can be made so secure," she said, hating him because he was gloating.

Two generals in battle dress awaited the Imperial couple inside the main entrance of the gloomy fortress and, like the sentries, saluted without ceremony. They were crisp, obviously unimpressed, and, the Empress thought, barely civil.

With the generals in the lead the party walked down a corridor that opened onto an inner courtyard, and the Empress was reminded of a prison she had known in the town of Ancyra, high in the Bithynian hills of Asia Minor. The entire floor was paved with huge blocks of stone, and the solid walls of the building were windowless on all sides. The area, thirty feet long and perhaps half again as wide, was like a large cell, with a patch of sky showing above the towering walls of the citadel.

Gradually Theodora became aware of something strange: the stone floor was streaked with huge patches of black, and so were the walls. If it had been possible for stone to burn, she would have sworn the courtyard was scorched.

A slender, exceptionally handsome young man, his hair a mass of golden ringlets, appeared out of the shadows and moved forward. He, too, was wearing battle dress without insignia, but his appearance combined with his mincing gait made Theodora suspect he was Narses' sort.

"Augusta," Justinian said, "we present to you the most important of all our subjects, Orestes of Athens."

The name meant nothing to Theodora, which increased her annoyance, but Justinian did not appear to be joking, and no one smiled.

Orestes bowed slightly, in the manner of a civilian, and then pulled a thick helmet onto his head.

The Empress felt snubbed. Subjects presented to her for the first time were expected to prostrate themselves before her, or, at the least, kneel and kiss the hem of her gown. But the Greek half-man was unimpressed by her high station and did not bother to address her.

"I received your message earlier this morning, Augustus," he said, using the familiar form of Justinian's title, "and I'm prepared for the demonstration."

"Splendid. Shall we take our places?" Justinian, far from resenting the informality, appeared to enjoy it.

Orestes nodded before turning away, and the generals led the Imperial couple and Narses to a wall, almost six feet thick and about eight feet high, that stood a short distance from the blank wall of the citadel itself.

"This is the shield," Narses explained.

Justinian, enjoying his wife's irritated mystification, grinned and said nothing.

A number of strange garments were heaped on the floor behind the "shield," and one of the generals helped Theodora don a floor-length gown of thick cloth, with heavy, overlapping metal plates sewn on one side. The sheer weight of the peculiar garment made Theodora weary, and she thought, angrily, that even though her cloak and gown were far from new, they would be ruined.

The others were climbing into similar robes, and then Narses handed her a cloth-lined helmet similar to that of Orestes.

Theodora's indignation came to a boil. "That thing would mash my hair and give me a headache!"

Justinian's smile faded. "Wear it," he said. "You'll need it."

Including him in her sense of general annoyance, she pulled on the cumbersome headgear.

One of the generals spoke to her.

Theodora suddenly realized that her ears were covered, making it difficult to hear.

Rather than repeat his words, the officer guided her to a place behind the wall and pointed to a small hole approximately eight inches wide and three inches high. Feeling foolish as well as angry, she peered through it and saw the center of the courtyard.

A door opened at the opposite side, and a burly figure, robed and helmeted, carried a thick metal bucket into the middle of the yard. He handled it with great care, moving a single step at a time, as though afraid it might burst.

Then a second man, also in protective gear, came out with two pails of water while a third, directly behind him, carried several short lengths of iron and brass.

All three retreated through the door, and Orestes reappeared, still wearing no armor except his brass helmet.

Justinian said something that Theodora could not hear, but she gleaned from her husband's expression that he was satisfied when Orestes pulled on a very heavy robe.

The Greek came to the end of the wall, where he deposited the lengths of metal and the pails of water, and then beckoned to the Empress.

She regarded the gesture as insolent, but Justinian made no objection, so she swallowed her pride and went to the Greek.

"The Augusta," he said, his lips close to her headgear, "shall have the honor of making the demonstration."

Justinian became alarmed and started to protest.

Orestes laughed. "I give the Augustus my solemn oath that she shall come to no harm." He handed her a metal-covered cloth, and when she only looked at it blankly, he snatched it and placed it over her face, just below her eyes, attaching it at either side of the helmet. Then he donned a similar contraption.

Blinking at him, Theodora realized that she herself probably looked like one of the veiled nomad women of the African desert.

"In one of these pails is seawater and in the other is fresh," Orestes told her. "Either will suffice, so take your choice, Augusta."

His informality was intolerable, Theodora thought, but saw that her husband was waiting and pointed at one of the pails, neither knowing nor caring which kind of water it contained.

Orestes carried it around to the front of the "shield," taking care not to spill even a drop, and again beckoned.

Theodora had not been treated with such curt disdain in years and was seething by the time she joined him.

"Standing right here, no closer, throw the water into the bucket," Orestes told her, "and then move, as quickly as you can, behind the protective wall."

--⚜ 130 ⚜--

Tired of being given orders by this rude stranger, she picked up the pail and deliberately started forward with it.

Orestes reached out for her, and surprisingly strong hands pulled her back to the spot he had designated. "I cannot be responsible for the Augusta's safety unless she does as she's told." His voice was surprisingly firm, and his eyes, the only part of his face that showed, were coldly angry.

Anxious to end the farce, Theodora grasped the pail and heaved the contents at the bucket in the center of the courtyard.

There was a hissing sound, followed almost immediately by a loud roar, and a column of searing flame shot high into the air.

Theodora was terrified, more frightened than she had ever been. The heat was so intense that she felt certain it was blistering her, but she felt rooted to the spot, unable to move.

Orestes swept her off her feet and carried her to safety behind the thick observation wall.

Awed, grateful to him, and confused, she watched as the fire continued to rage fiercely. Her eyes smarted, so she closed them for a few moments, but was so fascinated by the spectacle that she opened them again.

"Would you care to test the strength of the fire?" Orestes handed her a length of iron and another of brass. "Come."

She was docile now as she accompanied him to the front of the wall.

"Throw the pieces of metal into the bucket," he commanded.

She did as she was bidden, and the iron disappeared into the bucket, but the length of brass struck the edge and fell onto the stone floor.

"No matter," Orestes said, motioning her to safety. He

waited until she retreated behind the wall, then threw the contents of the second pail onto the fire.

The flame, orange-blue in its intensity, soared again, and the heat was so great that Theodora stood back from her observation post for a few moments.

The blaze rose still higher, and Theodora was almost blinded by it. She continued to feel its heat, her protective garments and the thick wall notwithstanding, and although she knew almost nothing of military matters, could understand why such efforts were being made to keep this devastating weapon a closely guarded secret.

At last the fire began to subside, diminishing slowly, until with unexpected abruptness it burned out and died.

Orestes removed his headgear and robe, then helped the Empress take off her outer garments and led her to the center of the courtyard. There, to her astonishment, she saw that the metal bucket had melted down into a glowing mass, and as the length of iron was no longer visible, she assumed it had melted, too. The length of brass that had bounced off the bucket had not been subjected to the fiercest heat of the fire, but it, too, was reduced to a semiliquid puddle.

"Although you can see none of the material used in making the flames," Orestes told her as Justinian and the others approached them, "enough of the composition remains, if more water is added, to create another brief spurt of flame." For the first time his manner became congenial. "If the Augusta would like a memento of this occasion, I will design and make her a necklace or bracelet of the metal she has melted."

"I would be very pleased," she replied, so impressed by all she had seen that she forgot to use the Imperial "we" when speaking of herself.

Orestes turned to the Emperor. "If nothing further is required of me, I have work to do." Not waiting for a reply, he stalked off, his walk as incongruously feminine as his treatment of the Caesar Augustus was unprecedentedly rude.

Justinian took no offense, however, and was smiling slightly as he guided her out of the courtyard. "When I first saw a demonstration, I felt much as you do," he told her.

She recovered her voice when they reached the corridor. "Orestes spoke of a composition in the bucket. What was it?"

The men roared with laughter, Narses' high-pitched giggle louder than the others.

"Only Orestes and a few members of his staff know the secret, which they brought with them from Greece, and they work constantly to improve the substance." Justinian was solemn again. "In the past six months alone, they've found some way to make a small amount burn longer."

Theodora accepted the farewell salutes of the generals and was silent as she and the Emperor returned to the carriage, Narses following a pace behind them. She did not speak until they had started the drive back to the palace. "What is the substance called?"

"For lack of a better name," Justinian said, "we've been calling it Greek fire. A crude form of it was first used by the Greeks more than one hundred years ago, and the secret has been passed down within a very small family group, with each generation refining and improving. I heard rumors that such a substance existed—"

"Through the Imperial espionage service, which is second to none in the world," Narses cut in.

"—and I was finally able to locate Orestes and his associates. Eventually I persuaded them to work for me," the Emperor continued.

"Was it difficult?" Theodora wanted to know.

"Very." Her husband did not elaborate.

"What I don't understand," she said, flicking a brief

glance in the direction of Narses, "is how someone afflicted with the ancient curse of the Greeks could devote himself to such a destructive, masculine activity."

Justinian was embarrassed for his secretary's sake, but knew an evasion would increase the tensions. "Orestes," he said, "isn't what he seems. He has no greater a liking for men than he has for women. His great tragedy is that he was captured by barbarians four or five years ago, and they emasculated him in an attempt to force him to reveal the contents of Greek fire. He feigned madness, so they finally released him."

"I see."

"No, I'm afraid you don't. When I first urged him to work for me, I couldn't tempt him with riches or even a high place in the nobility. Only when I promised that he'd be succeeded by his two young nephews, who came to Constantinople with him, and that I'd use Greek fire to destroy the barbarians who had crippled him—only then would he consent to enter my employ and make Greek fire for me."

Theodora sat quietly, absorbing what he had told her.

"Repeat nothing you've seen or heard today," Justinian said. "Greek fire is the weapon that will enable me to reunite the Roman Empire of old and create a world that hasn't existed since the time of Alexander the Great."

Theodora saw that Narses was not surprised, and resented the fact that her husband had shared his dream with the secretary.

Apparently aware of what she was thinking, Narses looked at her for a moment, a triumphant gleam in his eyes.

For the moment he was unassailable, but she told herself that the time would come when she would strip him of his influence and power. "What race of barbarians crippled Orestes?" she asked her husband.

"Since you already know I've promised Orestes I'll exterminate them," he said, "you wouldn't need much more to learn the whole strategy of the War Council."

"Members of the council," Narses explained gratuitously, "have sworn an oath never to reveal our plans to anyone. Our success, which is almost assured by Greek fire, will be guaranteed if our overall strategy is kept a permanent secret."

Theodora had been hurt because Justinian had waited so long before revealing the existence of the astonishing new weapon to her, and it was a double blow to be told she was not eligible to learn any details of the military plans he and his strategists were making. She had thought of herself as Justinian's partner and co-ruler, as one who shared everything with him. But, instead, she was being held at a distance by a wall as thick and high as that which surrounded the citadel at the university.

It was impossible for her to imagine that Justinian no longer trusted her, and she turned to him, the unspoken question in her eyes.

"If the choice were mine alone," he said, "I would keep no secrets from you."

His excuse was feeble nonsense. The powers of the Emperor were supreme, and he could do what he thought best under any circumstances, no matter what his War Council, the magisters, or the Senate might decide. The incredulity in Theodora's eyes was eloquent.

The Emperor shifted in his seat. "The members of the War Council," he said uncomfortably, "aren't yet accustomed to the idea of a woman—even an Empress—becoming an unofficial colleague. You would be a member, more or less, if I told you the details of our deliberations."

Her exclusion on the grounds that she was a woman and therefore incapable of understanding military strategy was intolerable, a negation of her struggle for equality. But Justinian's mind seemed to be closed, and she could neither argue the point nor plead with him, particularly in the presence of Narses.

A sudden thought struck Theodora, and she looked quickly at the secretary. Before he could avert his face she saw him gloating, enjoying her defeat.

"Is he a member of the War Council?" she asked.

"Of course," Justinian said. "He's one of our best strategists."

She folded her hands tightly in her lap and did not speak again on the ride to the Imperial palace.

SEVEN

⚜ ⚜ ⚜

To persons outside the Imperial court, Theodora's influence, like the size of her seraglio, had grown larger. Her campaign for an improvement in the rights of women had been waged and won, and it was universally recognized that her agents kept her informed of everything that happened in the Empire. Even magisters sent gifts to her and attended her audiences.

By January 532, however, those members of the Imperial court who daily saw the Emperor or Empress wondered whether the couple was drifting apart, and Theodora privately shared their bewilderment. She knew she was being totally excluded from the making of vital decisions that would, for better or worse, drastically change the future of the Empire.

Belisarius and Mundus, who had been promoted and sent off to frontier commands, had been recalled to Constantinople, and now, immediately following their return, Justinian issued a proclamation in which he announced the general outline of his grand design. He had spent years building a new army, a navy, and a treasury reserve of gold.

He had filled the government's granaries and warehouses with food and modern weapons.

At last everything was in readiness, and he would strike the first blow in a great campaign to recover the ancient glory of the Roman Empire. His victorious banner would fly from St. Peter's in ancient Rome, and from the ramparts of the Italian towns to the north that had been the provincial heart of the original Empire. His troops would conquer Spain and Gaul, and would drive the barbarians from the banks of the Danube River. His legions would capture Carthage from the Vandals and would return to the Empire Augustine's city of Hippo, Tripoli, and Regius, as well as the Roman hinterlands of Africa. Never had an Imperial declaration been more rousing, never had an Emperor's words burned with greater patriotic zeal.

And not once in the ten years they had lived together had Theodora been more deeply disturbed.

For ten days she listened to his optimistic forecasts. None of his potential enemies knew where he would strike. In fact, their spies in Constantinople undoubtedly believed he had no intention of conducting an overseas campaign; after all, no fleet was gathered at Constantinople and no troops were being mustered there. But he intended to fool them by employing tactics too clever for them.

The bulk of his invasion force was in bivouac a day's journey to the west, and supplies were being sent there. The fleet, which was maneuvering at sea, would pick up the corps, unnoticed, and would sail for a secret destination. Meanwhile a second corps, almost as strong, was already on the march toward the Persian frontier, where it would stand guard in the event that Chosroes, thinking his foes occupied elsewhere, sent an invasion force across the border.

With his plans completed, Justinian revealed the last of his secrets to his wife. Belisarius would command the offensive corps and would attack the Vandals at Carthage.

Mundus, whom he knew she disliked, would command the defensive corps on the Persian border. Both young generals were brilliant, both were loyal to him beyond question, both were devoted to the cause they served. They would not and could not fail, and Justinian would become immortal, the Emperor who had restored Rome.

Eleven days after the Imperial proclamation had been issued, Theodora's worst fears were confirmed. It was a Saturday, usually quiet in the Imperial compound because most members of the court stayed at home prior to attending the weekly races at the Hippodrome. But there was great activity at the seraglio. Women of all classes were admitted after showing the sentries at the outer gate the jade discs that identified them as agents in the employ of the Empress. One by one they were interviewed by Theodora, who listened, asked searching questions, and challenged every assertion.

The ladies-in-waiting knew something out of the ordinary was happening, and were shocked when the Empress took the extraordinary step of canceling her late-morning audience. Then, accompanied only by a young centurion and a few soldiers, she hurried to the main palace and went straight to the suite in which Justinian worked.

Narses, ensconced in a large chamber that adjoined Justinian's, concealed his surprise when she entered.

"Tell the Emperor I must see him at once," she said.

The secretary could not disobey her direct order, but hesitated. "The Augustus is holding a conference of paramount importance with several bishops of the West."

She knew nothing of the meeting, but had too much on her mind to feel resentful. "Tell him," she said, "or I'll go to him unannounced."

Startled by her willingness to ignore rigid protocol, Narses hesitated no longer; an Emperor's privacy was considered inviolable, and no one, not even an Empress, dared to disturb him when he was busy. But it was plain she had no intention of waiting, and rather than give the bishops something to whisper about for months, Narses disappeared into the Emperor's sanctum.

He returned immediately and conducted her to the small chamber on the other side of the Imperial workroom. There Justinian ate an occasional meal when his schedule was crowded and, even less frequently, rested for short periods on a divan.

Theodora impatiently waved Narses out of the room as her husband entered.

Never before had she interrupted him, and Justinian was surprised, but his mood was jovial. "Well, my dear, I have good news for you," he said. "I've been sounding out some of the bishops on the idea of holding an ecumenical council, and if the patriarchs are in an equally receptive frame of mind, I believe the differences between the two branches of the Church can be resolved."

"The business of the Church will have to wait!" Theodora was strident, but lowered her voice before continuing. "A revolt is brewing in the city, and will break out at any time—today, tonight, tomorrow, no one knows when."

"You've been listening to your women again."

"I have, for ten days, and this morning all the reports are the same. The people are furious. They've always resented paying higher taxes, and they've hated your enlargement of the army and establishment of the navy. Now that they know you're planning to conduct a series of foreign adventures—in which the casualties will be high—they're wild. All of my agents—responsible, sober women I trust—say that Constantinople is simmering, and that the pot will start to boil at any moment. You'll have to make a gesture to pacify the people. I suggest you distribute free grain to them, which will quiet them temporarily and give you time to think of long-range steps that will prevent a revolution that might spread through the Empire."

"Even if your reports were true, I'd be stripped of my

dignity if I tried to buy peace from my own subjects," Justinian said calmly.

Theodora's frenzy increased. "You wouldn't be the first Emperor of Rome to bribe the mobs with bread. And my reports are accurate!"

"Like all women, your agents exaggerate when they become hysterical. The security police have been keeping me informed of the city's temper, and it's true there's been grumbling since I issued my proclamation—worse grumbling than usual, actually—but it will soon pass. There's no need for concern, and I certainly don't have to demean myself by bribing my subjects!"

"The security police are wrong," Theodora insisted, her sense of foreboding increasing. "They've misled you, not deliberately, but they've failed to read the mood of the people accurately."

"Your women have been useful on occasion," Justinian said, sighing, "but you can't expect me to believe they're more efficient than an organization that has been in existence since the days of the old Roman Republic. I'm grateful to you, my dear, but I beg you not to worry. You've been working too hard recently, and I hope you intend to relax with me at the Hippodrome this afternoon. You'll want to hear what I have to tell you about the bishops. Which reminds me that I've kept them waiting long enough."

"Wait!" Theodora became desperate as he started back toward his sanctum. "The security police may be right. I pray they are. But on the very remote chance that they've misread the mood of Constantinople and that the reports from my women are correct, won't you at least transfer some of your regiments from their camp down the coast to the city?"

"Impossible."

"They could be here by tonight if you gave the order now, and—"

"You make it sound so simple, Theodora, but it isn't. Belisarius and Mundus will be finishing their conferences here in the next few days, and the expedition to Carthage will sail in no more than a week's time. Regiments transferred to the city would be required to bring their supplies with them, not to mention their bedding and tents, and the transfer back to the embarkation area would necessitate issuing still more supplies. The sailing schedule would have to be delayed."

"Better a delay," she said stubbornly, "than a risk of open rebellion!"

"Think how the people of Constantinople would feel if thousands of armed troops were stationed in the city. The regiments would be everywhere. In the Mesé gardens, on the grounds of the university, even in the Hippodrome itself."

"So much the better. When people are in a nasty mood, they know only one language, that of force."

"I must disagree with you," Justinian said, trying not to sound patronizing. "The resentment would grow worse, and as soon as the troops leave on the expedition, we'd be certain to suffer a revolt."

She wanted to beg him to abandon his grandiose scheme, but knew he would not listen to her, any more than he would believe the reports of her agents. There would be trouble in the immediate future, but he was not prepared to cope with it.

❦ ❦ ❦

The Hippodrome was a mammoth, roofless amphitheater of stone, rising on all sides from a field larger than the Imperial gardens and tended as carefully. Although it had been based, roughly, on the Colosseum in old Rome, the citizens of Constantinople, virtually none of whom had ever seen the older structure, proudly claimed that their auditorium was infinitely superior in every way to that of the original. Fifty thousand people could sit in comfort on the stone benches, and entertainment to please everyone was available, not only in the arena itself, but in the open areas beneath the stands.

Purveyors of food sold hot minced-meat pastries, roasted chestnuts, and such delicacies as figs stuffed with chopped fruits and nuts. There was wine, mead, and a cheap, potent drink called *loka* for the thirsty. Daughters of Venus circulated freely, and if a man wasn't too fussy about his surroundings, a wench would be happy to accommodate him in the sections beneath the stands that were unoccupied when the races or a circus was in progress.

Members of the Blue and Green, the rival political parties, usually sat in solid blocs opposite each other, jeering in rivalry that was sometimes less than good-natured, and placed their wagers on the races with the uniformed attendants who circulated through the crowds. Until recent years the wager-takers had been private citizens, but John of Cappadocia had given them government posts—and kept a large share of their earnings. The wager-takers had been given no voice in the matter, and there were some who thought it unfair that they had become symbols of the city's anger. Frequently they were hissed and cursed, and on several occasions minor riots had erupted when the badgered wager-takers had replied in kind.

The front rows, separated from the rest of the seats by stone partitions, were used as permanent boxes by the nobles, senators, heads of government departments, and high-ranking military officers. So great was the demand for these boxes that most men left them to their heirs, but under the terms of a new law sponsored by John of Cappadocia, these holdings could not be sold. When a family line died out, a man went bankrupt or was required to forfeit his property because he was in official disgrace, his box at the Hippodrome reverted to the Crown, which then made a handsome profit by selling it to the highest qualified bidder at a private auction.

The largest and most comfortable of the boxes, of course, was the Emperor's. Thick cushions covered the hard benches for parties of as many as twenty guests, and small, cushioned thrones were used by the Emperor and Empress. A covered passageway provided a direct connection with the Imperial palace, and heavy double doors, one of teak-wood and one of iron, were under permanent guard. Some monarchs had ordered the erection of curtains and drapes at the sides and rear of the box in order to give them privacy, but the wiser rulers made certain that no obstruction concealed them from the view of their subjects. It was as important, Justinian had said soon after mounting the throne, that the people see their Emperor as it was that they be entertained by the races and circuses.

Theodora, accompanying her husband down the passage-way between rows of saluting household troops, always found it necessary to steel herself before entering the Hip-podrome. It invariably brought back some of the most pain-ful memories of her early life, the childhood years she had spent helping her mother care for the trained bears, the em-barrassment of attending her sisters when they had become daughters of Venus, and the mortification she herself had suffered when she had been forced by law, custom, and financial need to take up the life of a harlot.

The deep-throated roar of the crowd made her flesh crawl, and she suffered agonies of fear and shame in the mo-ment before she stepped through the opened double doors and took her place on her throne. Only the knowledge that it was her duty to attend the chariot races and other events kept her from absenting herself from the Hippodrome; she needed all of her courage and her talents as an actress to smile blandly and appear calm as she presented herself to the gaze of her subjects.

Acutely sensitive to the Hippodrome's moods, she knew, as she and Justinian reached the end of the passageway, that the warnings of her agents had not been exaggerated. The preliminary races were already in progress, and ordinarily men would be cheering, the Blue and Green would be exchanging barbed insults, and the wager-takers would be offering odds in penetrating singsong voices. Today, however, she heard only a low-pitched rumble that neither rose nor fell in either intensity or volume.

Steadying herself, she took a deep breath, glanced for a moment at the oblivious and unconcerned Justinian, and then moved into the open.

Every seat in the huge amphitheater was taken, people were standing or squatting in the aisles, and most of the entrances were blocked, choked by the overflow throng of spectators. The experienced Theodora estimated that nearly sixty thousand of Constantinople's citizens were present.

As the Emperor and Empress took their seats, the crowd reacted in an extraordinary manner. The rumble of conversation died away, and it was so quiet in the auditorium that the creaking of chariot wheels and pounding of horses' hoofs could be heard by everyone in the place.

Men with Blue armbands and Green were not sitting in facing blocs, but mingled freely. Never before had Theodora known the members of the rival political parties to forget their differences.

"I don't like this," she murmured to Justinian as they smiled and raised their hands in greeting.

"I must admit it's odd." He was bewildered by the failure of the crowd to respond.

Suddenly his subjects came to life. Spontaneously, with one accord, men jumped up and stamped their feet, clapping their hands together over their heads in a time-honored gesture of disapproval.

The stunned Justinian continued to smile and wave.

Theodora tried to follow his example, but fear paralyzed her.

Belisarius, resplendent in the gold and bright blue tunic and armor of a general, left the box where he had been sitting with his wife and young son, and hurried to the Emperor. "Augustus," he said, leaning close to make himself heard above the rhythmic clapping and stamping, "this crowd is looking for trouble, and anything might start a riot. You ought to leave before your dignity is compromised."

Theodora saw that Mundus had left his own seat and had gone to the rear of the Imperial box, where he was giving orders to junior officers. The household guard was being reinforced, and she revised her opinion of Mundus somewhat.

Justinian, ignoring the tumult, pondered Belisarius' advice, and finally shook his head. "I must speak to them," he said, and hauled himself to his feet, an ungainly figure in the short, purple tunic that revealed his bony knees and thin, flabby calves.

Theodora saw that the occupants of the other boxes were streaming toward the passageway that led to the sanctuary of the palace. One of the first, pushing and using his elbows to clear a path for himself, was Narses, and she forgot her own danger long enough to smile contemptuously.

Justinian raised both hands for silence.

Only a few in the huge crowd obeyed him. The rest continued to clap and stamp, the echoes reverberating across the amphitheater.

The Emperor tried to speak, but even his wife, less than an arm's length from him, could not hear a word.

The charioteers discreetly vanished from the arena.

Justinian doggedly continued to shout, but remained inaudible.

Somewhere on the far side of the Hippodrome a stone was thrown, and all at once a hail of rocks descended, some bouncing against the front of the Imperial box.

Belisarius and Mundus waited no longer. An escort of household guards formed around the terrified Theodora and the frustrated, protesting Justinian, and forming a wall of shields around and over them, swept them to the passageway and safety.

There the Emperor insisted on halting and watched with dazed eyes as the nobles, officials, and their families followed. The orderly withdrawal had become a panic-stricken retreat.

The crowd in the amphitheater had become a mob and began to press forward.

At Mundus' command the double doors were closed and barred, and a strong detachment of troops was left on guard, under the command of a colonel renowned for his ruthless treatment of rebellious barbarians in the provinces.

The thunder of stamping feet was so loud overhead that conversation in the passageway was impossible.

Justinian and Theodora, still escorted by a strong detachment, were the last civilians to leave. They crossed the Imperial compound and made their way to the roof of the main palace, from which they could obtain the best view of what was happening outside. Others had the same idea, and the roof was crowded, but both of the young generals were elsewhere, organizing the defenses of the compound.

Several officials, among them Tribonian and John of Cappadocia, tried to join the Emperor and Empress, and Narses was particularly insistent, but the colonel to whom the safety of the Imperial couple had been entrusted kept everyone at a distance. "I've had my orders from Mundus," he said, "so you might as well save your breath. Anyone who tries to go near the Augustus and Augusta will be cut down."

Scarcely aware of what was happening around them,

Justinian and Theodora stared at sights they could scarcely believe. Mobs had spilled out of the Hippodrome, although thousands had remained there, still clapping and stamping. And the whole city appeared to have joined the rebels.

Huge crowds had gathered near every palace gate, but were held at a distance by the alerted troops of the household guard, who had taken battle stations, in full strength, on the high walls. A merchant ship of wood, not yet completed on the ways at the harbor, had been set on fire, and a column of smoke was rising from the far end of the Mesé. Another, even more ominous, curled up from the hills where many of the nobles lived, indicating that the residences of the wealthy were being looted.

Justinian broke the heavy silence. "I was wrong and you were right," he said. "I've never been more mistaken in all my life."

Theodora was too sick at heart to reply.

Still more fires were lighted, and the conflagration spread rapidly through the district overlooking the Golden Horn, where so many of Constantinople's poor lived. Huge swarms could be seen on the Mesé and other principal thoroughfares, and it was evident that the people were uncontrolled and uncontrollable.

Belisarius appeared on the roof, and the guards opened their ranks to let him pass, then formed a solid phalanx again to keep the officials at a distance.

"We're under siege," the young general said crisply. "Every gate, every entrance is thronged by mobs. We've even put guards at the passage that leads to your former house outside the walls."

"Judging from what we can see, the whole city is in danger," Justinian replied. "What can be done?"

"We have about three thousand household troops in the Imperial compound, and we'll have to rely on them for your safety," Belisarius said.

It would be impossible, Theodora thought, for a scant

three thousand to provide security for members of the Imperial household when countless thousands were waiting to storm the walls.

"Mundus and I agree that it isn't possible to send a courier to the corps down the coast. Anyone trying to leave these grounds would be cut down instantly. We're hoping, though, that we might be able to send someone out at night, when most of them will go home. We hope." Belisarius paused, then added grimly, "If my corps were here, we'd restore order fast enough. Over a mountain of corpses. I'd have the chance to show you how effective 25,000 trained men can be!"

"I pray," Justinian said heavily, "that the people will calm down of their own free will, and that we can hold bloodshed to a minimum."

Theodora stared at him, as did the general. Both realized that the rioting would continue—and become worse —until drastic action was taken to curb the excesses and punish the violators of Imperial law who were challenging the nation's supreme authority. The application of stern, unyielding discipline was essential, and until order was restored, it would not be possible to study the roots of the problem and alleviate the causes of unrest. Justinian, ever the scholar, seemed unable to recognize the reality of a violent world in which those who possessed power exercised it or perished.

Belisarius tried to reply, but a lifetime of training that had taught him to respect the man who wore the mantle of Emperor rendered him speechless.

Theodora knew that she alone had the courage to tell her husband the truth. "Either you or the mob will prevail," she said. "This is war, not of your choosing, but war. Either you or your subjects will win, and the loser will be crushed."

Justinian made no attempt to dispute the assertion. Had he listened to her earlier in the day it might have been possible to avert the worst of the tragedy, but it was too late for self-recriminations. "If my abdication would preserve the Empire and salvage the good I'm trying to accomplish," he said quietly, "I would give up the throne right now. But I know of no one more devoted to Rome than I am, and since the question of the succession has never been settled, a civil war might rage for years. No matter what my personal feelings, I am trapped, and must continue to wear the laurel wreath of the Caesars."

Belisarius glanced in the direction of the officials, hoping they had not heard him.

Theodora was too overcome by guilt to be aware of anything but her own remorse. In more than a decade of their life together she had not borne a child. She had continued to hope that, unlike so many who had been harlots and courtesans, she had not become sterile, and until now, by refusing to dwell on the problem, she had not allowed it to engulf her. But she could find only one way to interpret Justinian's remark: he was blaming her because the crisis could not be solved, and she believed his criticism just.

Belisarius looked at the Emperor, then at the Empress, conscious of the undercurrents. Antonina had been urging him to seek the favor of the people, and he had been tempted, knowing the throne might be within his grasp. But, seeing the torment of the couple who reigned over the unsettled land, he was inclined to doubt his willingness to change places with them.

Theodora stood very still, her back straight and chin high, her nails digging into the palms of her hands. The world she had tried to create for herself was crumbling, but she seemed helpless, unable to halt the deterioration or save herself.

Justinian paced up and down the roof, hands clasped behind his back, shutting out the sights and sounds of the tumult beyond the walls of the Imperial compound. The troops of the household guard stood with locked shields, keeping him apart from those who, for his sake and their own, had tried to serve him. He was the source and symbol of power, the living personification of the greatest nation in the history of civilized man.

But his authority, like the very substance of his nation, was crumbling away, and the columns of smoke above burning Constantinople obscured the late afternoon sun, plunging the city into premature darkness.

❀ ❀ ❀

For eight days and nights of terror the mindless, destructive mob ruled the most civilized and sophisticated city on earth, the capital of the Roman Empire. Maddened by loot and carnage, the people of Constantinople burned and killed, pillaged at will and evened scores, real and imaginary. Nothing was sacred and no place was safe. The homes of the wealthy were looted, then torn down. The libraries and lecture halls of the university no longer existed, the shipyards were hacked into kindling, the small factories that made cloth and porcelain and leather goods and a host of other products were razed.

Fires burned incessantly, and although a heavy rain might have extinguished them, there was no rain. No one knew how many were homeless, but at least two-thirds of the city's buildings had been transformed into gutted, charred skeletons. The mob, intoxicated by its own powers of destruction, respected no man and no profession. Merchants, university lecturers, and shipowners were buried alive and left to die in the debris of their homes and workrooms. No inn or tavern was left standing, no lodging house was intact, and the pitiful remains of markets and bazaars were unrecognized even by those who had earned a living in them.

Not even the churches and their guardians were spared. Priests were either crucified by the jeering mob or thrown into the waters of the Bosphorus to drown. And on the eighth night of the terror the great Sancta Sophia was demolished; no one knew who had performed the deed, but it was obvious that hundreds of men had taken part.

The Emperor and Empress, nobles and senators, government officials and their families, were still safe behind the walls of the palace, protected by the unyielding troops of the Imperial guard, but they could do nothing to halt the terror. Twice Justinian had proposed that he go alone beyond the gates of the palace to reason with his subjects, but Belisarius and Mundus had refused to permit such a suicidal excursion.

Repeated efforts had been made to summon the corps of trained troops awaiting embarkation down the coast, but it appeared likely that every courier sent from the Imperial compound had been caught and murdered. The soldiers on the walls had seen at least three messengers being literally torn apart, but had been powerless to intervene. It seemed, too, that no word of the terror had reached the corps from any other source; or, perhaps, rumors had been vague, and Belisarius' subordinate field commanders had decided to make no move for the present, not knowing where their general or the Emperor stood. In any event, the hope that the corps would march on Constantinople and put down the insurrection had virtually died.

On the ninth day of the uprising the observers stationed on the palace roof reported that a large crowd was beginning to gather in the Hippodrome for unknown purposes. Eventually, however, when the few senators who had joined the rebels appeared in ceremonial togas and the leaders of the Blues and Greens arrived in their gold-embroidered capes, it was easy enough to guess that the people intended to go through the form of electing a new Emperor.

A haggard Justinian called a meeting of his senior officials in his audience chamber and, with an exhausted Theodora seated on her own throne beside him, explained the situation. "When someone who will be hailed as Emperor has been elected," he said, "the mobs will storm this compound. Our generals assure us that the Imperial guard can hold off the people for no more than a limited time. Three thousand defenders cannot fight a successful battle against fifty thousand, or one hundred thousand. Our hopes of survival are slender, and we have summoned you for your opinions and advice."

No one spoke.

"If there are any here," the Emperor said, "who believe their security will be greater if they join forces with those who are gathering in the Hippodrome, stand forward and we will release you from your vows of loyalty to us."

No one moved.

"Are there none in our many councils who can offer suggestions?" Justinian demanded.

Again there was a heavy silence, and finally Narses approached the foot of the dais. "If it please the Augustus," he said, "I have made it my business to conduct an intense survey of our situation. A fleet of small ships, some of them pleasure craft, that are the personal property of the Caesar Augustus, lie at their wharves. These vessels are manned by members of the Imperial household, and can carry everyone present to safety, along with many of the troops who have been protecting us. Let me remind the Augustus and my colleagues that the wharves are located at the foot of the hill below the gardens, within the walls of the compound. No one would molest us as we go on board, and I think it unlikely that the people of Constantinople would know we had gone until many hours after we set sail."

There was a murmur in the throng of courtiers, and faces brightened.

The magister of Merchant Marine came forward. "There is much to be said for the Imperial secretary's plan," he said. "Merchant ships in the city's harbor have been either destroyed or driven away by the mobs, and I am convinced that not one ship could give chase to our fleet."

Several ministers of state and an elderly senator laughed in open relief.

John of Cappadocia moved to the base of the dais, fingering the heavy chain of gold that he wore around his neck. He bowed to Justinian, then to Theodora, and flung back his fur-trimmed cloak of silk. "Narses has discussed his idea with me, and I think it sound. The Augustus will be pleased to learn that the Imperial treasure—all of it—can be carried to the ships and stored in their holds. I have already investigated the possibilities in detail. The task can be performed within a short time if every servant in the compound is put to work, and I need not tell the Augustus that the treasure—in gold and precious jewels—will enable him to transfer his capital to any place he wishes."

Narses smiled broadly. "The puppet elected by the people will be discarded fast enough when the mobs discover he is a pauper."

A score of officials began to speak simultaneously, all of them obviously in favor of the scheme.

Only Belisarius and Mundus stood immobile, their faces expressionless.

The Emperor held up a hand for silence. "Do you advise us to accept this plan?"

"Yes, Augustus!" In their anxiety and joy men were shouting, forgetting the etiquette of the court.

Theodora had heard enough and rose slowly to her feet, gathering her mantle of purple wool around her. She faced the courtiers and nobles, and they fell silent again. "You may do what you please, all of you," she said. "If you go, you will depart without me. When I first was clad in the Imperial color, I took an oath that I would wear no other in this life, and I shall be faithful to my promise. I shall remain in Constantinople, and if my subjects wish to deprive me of my purple robes, they shall have to kill me before they divest me of these garments."

They gaped at her as she stood, proudly defiant, wrapped in her mantle of Imperial purple.

Belisarius grinned, and with one accord he and Mundus went to the Empress' side of the dais.

Justinian broke the silence. "You make me ashamed," he said to his wife in a low voice that nevertheless carried to the farthest corner of the audience chamber. "I pray that God will forgive me for my weakness." He turned back to his subjects, his face stern. "Those who wish to leave have our permission to depart in the ships of our personal fleet. You may take your own belongings with you, and we place only one condition on your departure. If we should survive the events of these uncertain days, those who leave our court now will be banned from it for all time.

"We," he added, "shall remain in our beloved Constantinople, with the Augusta beside us to give us strength!"

Everyone watched him as he, too, stood and took Theodora's hand.

"Those who wish to depart may go at once!" he said.

Regardless of their personal desires and obvious fears, no one stirred.

"Clear the chamber," Justinian ordered. "We wish to confer in private with our generals."

He and Theodora sat on their thrones again, and, while the courtiers filed out, Mundus and Belisarius mounted the dais.

"Is there no way to bring the mobs under control?" the Emperor asked. "I've been wondering whether there might be some way to use Orestes' Greek fire—assuming he's still alive."

"I'm certain," Belisarius replied, "that Orestes is safe in his citadel."

"You can rely on it," Mundus added. "He's probably under siege, as we are, but if an attack were made on him, he wouldn't hesitate for an instant, and the flames of the Greek fire would be greater than any blaze the city has yet seen."

Theodora looked at each of the men in turn, her face troubled. "Aside from the difficulty of obtaining Greek fire from the other side of the city, I wonder if you'd be wise to use it. I'm not advocating a soft approach to the rebels. They should die for their disloyalty. But the Greek fire is so terrible that thousands of innocent people who have taken no part in the revolt will suffer, too. And I don't believe that we could ever rely on the support of the survivors."

"Do you really think anyone in Constantinople is innocent?" Justinian asked her.

"I'm sure of it," she replied firmly. "I know the people."

Belisarius stirred impatiently. "The question of whether we should or shouldn't use Greek fire is academic," he said. "We have no way of getting any of the material from Orestes."

"And something must be done before the fools out there elect someone as their new Emperor and attack the Imperial compound," Mundus added.

"You believe, then, that something can be done?"

The generals exchanged glances. "We have some thoughts on the subject," Belisarius said, "but we can make no promises."

"We'll look once more at what's happening in the Hippodrome, and then we'll do what we can." Mundus saluted and walked out of the audience chamber.

"We'll try, Augustus," Belisarius said, and followed his colleague.

Justinian and Theodora were alone. He looked at her for an instant, then averted his gaze. "I scarcely know what to say to you," he murmured.

"Say nothing, my dear. We'll die together—or triumph together."

"If we live, your courage will have been responsible. I've excluded you from too many affairs of state, but I swear to you it won't happen again. From now on, until we die, your power will be equal to mine—"

"Make no promises or speeches," Theodora said. "Let's go up to the roof, and we'll learn our fate soon enough."

❦ ❦ ❦

Only a skeleton force of household guards remained on duty in the Imperial compound, on the walls, and at the gates. Virtually the entire force of three thousand men had vanished from the palace, and the nobles, officials, and courtiers gathered at one side of the roof were justifiably nervous.

Standing apart from them, with only a single centurion stationed near them as a symbol of their authority, were Justinian and Theodora. They were able to see the interior of the Hippodrome below them very clearly, and they watched in silent fascination as a figure was led to the Imperial box. From their vantage point they could hear the blaring of trumpets, they saw a procession form, and Theodora sucked in her breath as a mantle of purple was draped on the man in the Imperial box.

The throng that packed the amphitheater began to cheer, but at that moment the household troops appeared. Belisarius and about half of the command materialized at the top rim of the Hippodrome, and neither then nor later were Justinian and Theodora able to figure out how they had made their way to such heights without attracting attention. Simultaneously the other fifteen hundred, with Mundus in the lead, poured through the passageway that led from the palace into the Imperial box.

The crowd assumed that the young generals were joining the rebellion, bringing the troops with them, and the cheers became louder. But Mundus swiftly dispelled such illusions; a single stroke of his double-edged sword decapitated the foolish nobleman who had allowed himself to be draped in Imperial purple.

By the time the people grasped the reason for the troops' dramatic appearance, it was too late. The soldiers locked shields and, moving in solid lines, hacked mercilessly at the civilians. Belisarius and his men spread out across the top row and started to work their way down while Mundus and his guards, doing the same on the ground level, slowly started up the stone steps.

Had the rebels been organized, properly led and armed, they could have overwhelmed the small military force. But there was a wild panic, men tried to reach the exits, trampling one another in their desperate haste, and succeeded only in blocking every means of escape from the Hippodrome.

The guards, operating with ruthless efficiency, continued to slash and cut, their swords dispensing elementary justice to those who had defied the authority of the Caesar Augustus and had transformed the first city of the Empire into a charred shell. Neither Mundus nor Belisarius showed mercy, ignoring the pleas of those who dropped to their knees and begged the generals to spare them.

Trapped between the lines moving on them from above and below, the rebels had nowhere to go. In their frenzy they clawed each other as they tried to fight their way to the already choked exits, and there were many who either died beneath the feet of their friends or tumbled down the long stone flights. Their screams of fright and shrieks of agony were plainly audible on the roof of the palace.

The troops gave no quarter, even though many whom they were attacking might have been friends or relatives. These soldiers were the elite of the Empire, men whom Belisarius and Mundus had trained and disciplined before their own promotions to higher commands, and the guards knew no loyalty except to their superiors and, through them, to the Emperor. The troops of other units might have felt compassion; certainly less experienced men would have been sickened by the carnage of their own creation. But the lines neither wavered nor halted, and not once did the advancing soldiers slow their pace.

There were tears in Theodòra's eyes, and she tried to look away, but could not. The horror of the grisly spectacle held her in its grip, and she continued to watch. "May God have mercy on their souls," she murmured.

Justinian was pale, too, but his face was set in stern lines. All he had done, all he still wanted to do, had been placed in jeopardy by mindless mobs that had destroyed the city, and he was incapable of forgiveness. "May their souls rot for all eternity in the nethermost regions of Hades!" he replied harshly.

The government officials were too stunned by the carnage to speak, and some, unable to watch the cold-blooded killings, left the roof. Narses, however, was enjoying himself, and his incongruous laugh caused others to peer at him.

Theodora glanced briefly in his direction. She would remember his cowardice in advocating flight and would not forget his pleasure when others mourned. Soon, very soon, she would settle her score with him.

The troops of Belisarius and Mundus met on the slopes of the Hippodrome, and then separated to complete what they had started. Again the double-edged swords went into action, and those who had either escaped the initial attack or been slightly wounded were cut down. The killing was an endless nightmare beyond the capacity of rational, civilized beings to grasp.

At last the slaughter ended, and the brigade of guards formed straight lines on the field at the base of the amphitheater, responding with precision to the commands of the generals. They marched out into the streets beyond the Hippodrome, leaving the dead, dying, and wounded behind them. Not until much later was it estimated that of the more than fifty thousand who had gathered to celebrate the crowning of a new Emperor, at least thirty thousand were dead.

News of the attack spread swiftly through the battered city, and people either watched in silence or fled as the guards marched through Constantinople, the Imperial banner of the Caesar Augustus held high in the vanguard. The display of ruthless might was what was needed to restore order. No one opposed the troops, and citizens who until now had continued to entertain hopes of establishing a new regime hastily abandoned such thoughts.

The guards marched back to the Imperial compound, and the gates were thrown open to receive them. The Emperor and his court no longer had anything to fear.

Dusk blurred the Hippodrome, making it more difficult for the Emperor and Empress to see, and night finally obliterated the tragedy. Theodora realized, however, that the story was not yet ended. She could make out the vague outlines of shapes in the amphitheater and knew that the women of Constantinople were searching for the bodies of their husbands and sons.

❦ ❦ ❦

Justinian spent an entire day, from sundown to sunset, inspecting the still-smoking ruins of his capital. He went on foot from place to place, and even when Theodora joined him on his tour, he refused more than a token escort of guards. "The rebels have been punished," he said, "and I am in no danger. Now my people and I must work together to create a new Constantinople."

That same evening, accompanied by his magisters, he took the architect Anthemius with him to the ruins of the Sancta Sophia. There, the lines of sorrow in his face emphasized by the light of flickering torches, he inaugurated a new era.

"Anthemius," he said, "I want you to build a new Sancta Sophia on this site. I want a church larger and more beautiful than any on earth. I want you to rebuild other churches, too. For each one that was destroyed, let two rise in its place. Build a new library at the university that will dwarf the great library of Alexandria. Build new lecture halls and experimental stations for our scientists. We will build a whole new city."

The architect was eager to accept the challenge, but was troubled. "Where will I find the men for all these projects?"

"No one in the city is employed, and no one will be able to work until Constantinople is restored. Every man capable of doing work, no matter what his vocation, will take part in the creation of a new Constantinople."

The proposal was so revolutionary that the magisters began to murmur.

Justinian immediately turned to them. "There will be new roads and squares, new plazas and resting places, new government buildings and homes. The waterfront hovels of the poor must not reappear, and I want houses built they can enjoy. I want the wharves restored so the merchant fleets of the world can bring their cargoes here, and I want inns and taverns where merchants and sailors can find rest. Where is John?"

The Caesar Praefect stepped forward.

"Open the vaults of the Imperial treasury, and use our gold to pay for the building of a city that will be the glory of Rome and the envy of all mankind."

John of Cappadocia tried to protest.

The Emperor raised a hand. "A prosperous Constantinople, the wonder of the world, will double and redouble the treasures in the vaults. You'll find ways to raise new taxes, I'm sure. Where is the magister of Grains?"

The youngest member of the Council of State approached him.

"Let no one go hungry. Open your warehouses and give food to all who need it. Belisarius?"

The general saluted.

"Your expedition must be postponed for a year. The gold and grain that would have supported you must be used for other purposes, but your troops will not be idle. We have a need for their strong arms and backs."

Belisarius was disappointed, but accepted the command without question.

The Caesar Praefect was not satisfied, however. "Augustus," he complained, "your plans for the future are in ruins."

"No, John, this city is in ruins. What will we accomplish if we build a great nation around a decayed core? First we must make Constantinople worthy of her promise, and the Empire will flourish around her."

EIGHT

❀ ❀ ❀

By Imperial design, accident, or the preoccupation of Justinian with the broader aspects of government, Theodora's seraglio became the headquarters of the campaign to reconstruct and rejuvenate Constantinople. While the Emperor sought ways to increase foreign trade, the Empress approved the architectural plans for new buildings and personally supervised their construction. While the Emperor made strenuous efforts to obtain the closely guarded secret of silk-making from distant Cathay, the Empress made certain that new docks and shipyards, university lecture halls and almshouses for the indigent were constructed.

Justinian concerned himself with the details of only two reconstruction projects. He made daily inspections to check on the progress of the new Sancta Sophia, which, when completed, would boast the largest unsupported dome of any known structure on earth. And he not only donated a substantial sum from his personal fortune for the purchase of books for the new university library, but appointed and himself directed the efforts of special agents who traveled throughout the civilized world acquiring such volumes, scrolls, and manuscripts.

Finally, when the new Constantinople began to emerge, eighteen months after the abortive, catastrophic rebellion, he devoted his full attention to preparations for the long-delayed invasion of Carthage. New problems had arisen, but the Emperor was determined to reunite the Empire of old, and refused to feel discouraged.

John of Cappadocia proved himself a genius in finding new ways to raise money, but Theodora drained off such huge sums for the rebuilding of Constantinople that the funds available for the waging of war remained limited. Thousands of workmen were still being employed in the city, and their food needs, combined with those of the general population, kept the granaries and warehouses half-empty, even though Theodora was offering bonuses to all farmers who would sell to her. So, thanks to her zeal on behalf of the city, virtually no supplies could be spared for the expeditionary corps.

Two additional, severe blows dimmed the Emperor's military hopes. The soldiers' term of enlistment expired, and five thousand of the men, tired of the long wait and heartily sick of being employed as construction workers, returned to civilian life. And a few days later word was received from the Persian frontier that Mundus had been killed while accompanying a party of scouts across the border.

A new commander was appointed to take charge of the defense sector in the East, and Justinian sent for Belisarius. "I can't give you the support you need and deserve," he said. "The best I can offer you is a small war chest, a two-month supply of food—and my prayers. Can you defeat the Vandals with a corps of only twenty thousand men, or would you prefer to train two brigades of replacements before you sail?"

"If I wait," Belisarius replied, "other veterans will retire by the time the recruits are ready for combat. I'm impatient, Augustus, as you are. I'll take the men at hand, with whatever you spare me in supplies and money, and I'll either take Carthage for you or die in the attempt."

The corps departed in secret, and Justinian went to the camp established two years earlier, a day's journey from Constantinople, to bid his commander and troops farewell. Theodora planned to accompany her husband, but a series of sudden crises made it impossible for her to leave the city.

A merchant fleet carrying five shiploads of badly needed Lebanese cedar was reported to have been captured by pirates, and substitute woods had to be found in order to maintain construction schedules. Three thousand additional workmen were hired for various projects, and the Empress purchased several huge blocks of rare Palestinian marble, but the Caesar Praefect, outraged by her unending expenditures, refused to allocate funds to buy the marble or pay the wages of the workmen.

Justinian went alone to see his army corps sail, leaving his wife with full powers to act as she saw fit in all matters. She summoned John of Cappadocia, and after a brief, stormy session that left him shaken, obtained the treasury funds she required. She conferred with the deputy commander of the new Imperial navy, who promptly sent a squadron of warships to search for the pirates and retrieve the lost cedar, and she solved a number of relatively minor problems, giving crisp orders and letting it be known that, as always, she would tolerate no delays.

She worked furiously for the better part of two days, and when she was at last ready to relax, a private visit from Mundus' widow made her realize there was a matter she had neglected for far too long. She changed from her state robes into a simple gown of cream-colored silk, and, after retiring to her private sitting chamber in the seraglio, sent for Narses.

The director of the secretariat, aware of her increased power, did not keep her waiting. He was surprised by the summons, since she usually ignored him, but was pleased when she received him informally. Perhaps, he thought, she realized that he, too, had become a more important personage in recent years.

Theodora greeted him with a cordiality she found difficult to feign, poured him a chalice of wine, and offered him a comfortable chair opposite her own. "I've been wanting to have a private talk with you," she said, "for a very long time. But you and I have never been friends, have we?"

Narses tried to protest.

Her smile was guileless. "Let's not pretend. Years ago, when Justinian and I first met, you were upset when he took me into his house. You had designs on him yourself, and you were disappointed."

Narses found her candor disconcerting. "It's true," he said, "that I was afraid he might not want to keep me on his staff if he became Emperor."

"Instead, you've expanded the secretariat, and you've become someone of consequence. The Emperor tells me you've been making long-range plans for the rule of Italy after our armies conquer it. Do you see yourself as a viceroy there?"

"I hope the Augustus might find use for my talents," he said, carefully modest.

"I'd be far happier if your attitudes were more consistent with mine." She paused for a moment, then waved a slender hand, casually. "However, we'll let that pass for the moment. The Emperor was pleased, you know, when you found a high place in the secretariat for Mundus' orphaned son."

He was troubled by her first comment, but as she had not enlarged on it, decided to stress the values of her later statement. "When I heard the boy had been granted a year's leave from his military studies at the Strategium, it occurred to me that a civilian post in the government might be very useful to him in later life. As the son of a martyred general he's certain to rise to a high rank in the army, and he'll be of even greater value to the Empire if he understands civilian administration."

"The Emperor was pleased. He said you were being very thoughtful and considerate."

Narses gracefully inclined his head.

"I understand he's exceptionally bright for a lad of sixteen." She kept her tone light.

"He's been in the secretariat only a short time, but he seems capable."

"Well," she said with a laugh, "he's handsome enough to make a place for himself in the world on his appearance alone."

"Yes, he's as rugged as his father was."

"Is that why you made advances to him?" Theodora asked the question quietly.

Narses stared at her.

"Mundus' widow came to me only an hour ago to complain."

"She lies!" The secretary suddenly found his voice.

"I believe her," Theodora said flatly.

"I—I've tried to be kind to the boy—and—and perhaps he misunderstood."

"Enough." Theodora scarcely raised her voice, but spoke with the ring of command. "For many years I misjudged Mundus, but now that he's no longer here to protect his family, perhaps I can repay them for my failure to appreciate him."

The cold rage in her violet eyes made Narses squirm.

"For many years I tolerated your hatred of me because you were faithful to Justinian and served him well. But you made your first great mistake when you urged the Emperor and the court to share your cowardice and flee during the riots two years ago. Now, by trying to corrupt the son of a dead hero, you've doubled your infamy."

"Surely you won't take the unsubstantiated word of a callow boy—"

She silenced him with an imperious wave. "I haven't quite decided how to deal with you. Perhaps you've heard rumors of special treatment that's been given to various—ah—guests of mine. No two have been treated alike, as each case is considered on its own merits. But I haven't yet made up my mind whether you can be rehabilitated."

Narses, trembling violently, pulled himself to his feet and looked at one door, then another, as though seeking escape.

"In any event," Theodora told him, "I'm relieving you of duty in the Emperor's service, and employing you in mine." She picked up the jeweled bell from the table beside her and rang it.

Two burly guards in her household livery appeared.

"Remove this person," she told them, and shut out the sounds of Narses' protests.

🏵 🏵 🏵

Justinian was exceptionally busy in the months following his return to Constantinople, and the Council of State held a series of long, grueling meetings. Theodora had been made a member of the council soon after the riots, not as Empress, but as a magistra in her own right, the first woman in the history of the Roman Empire to hold such a high post. She carried her share of responsibility, and her colleagues, who had been deferential to her when she had joined their ranks, now granted her a grudging respect based on her abilities. She, like the others, followed Justinian's example and worked from early in the morning until late at night, sparing herself as little as did the staff who worked with her.

"The Augusta," John of Cappadocia told several of his fellow council members one day, "should have been a man, but—unfortunately for us—she isn't. When she loses an argument to one of us in a meeting, she speaks her own language to the Emperor when they go to bed that night, and he reverses his decision. Whether you realize it or not, milords, the Empire is being ruled by a woman."

Theodora laughed when his words were repeated to her, but she grew thoughtful, and the next day ordered the keeper of her dungeons to send Narses to her sitting room.

The jailer appeared with the barefooted, manacled prisoner, who wore only a long robe that covered him from his neck to the floor.

"Remove the chains," Theodora said, "and leave us alone."

The keeper of the dungeons hesitated. "Is the Augusta armed? I mean, prisoners sometimes become violent, and—"

"I'm sure I can handle this one," she said with a laugh.

The jailer removed Narses' shackles and departed.

Theodora looked at the silent figure before her. "I've meant to give your case consideration before now, but I've been terribly busy. Tribonian is making still another digest of laws, we're opening some new caravan routes to Palestine and Syria, and, well—you may remember how frantically hard everyone works when the Emperor becomes impatient. At least you haven't suffered from your—ah—holiday, and your hair has grown as long as a girl's."

"Perhaps the Augusta doesn't know," Narses said in a low, sulky tone, "that there are no mirrors in the dungeons. One lives like an animal there."

"I've been told the facilities are rather primitive. But help yourself to a mirror." She gestured in the direction of a burnished square of silver on a table, and was amused when Narses involuntarily looked at his reflection.

"Now," she continued, "take off that absurd robe. We use them only for the sake of modesty when prisoners are brought up from the dungeons."

Narses became flustered. "I—they gave me nothing to wear under it."

"I know, but they did bathe you." She paused, then became impatient. "I don't have all day to spend on you! Remove the robe or I'll cut it off myself!"

He reluctantly pulled off the garment, then clutched it.

Theodora snatched it from him, threw it aside, and inspected him with critical, impersonal detachment. "A loss of weight becomes you," she said. "Your legs have always been attractive, and your hips are much improved."

The speechless Narses was scarlet.

"I've considered gelding you," she said calmly.

His nakedness suddenly forgotten, Narses threw himself onto the floor at her feet. "Augusta, I beg you—"

"Stand up," she said, irritated, "and hear me out. As a eunuch you'd have no value to anyone. But if you can be taught new disciplines, new loyalties, and an objectivity you've always lacked, you can be of value to me—and to the Empire."

"Augusta, I'll do anything—"

"When you hear what I have in mind, you may not be too sure of that." Her amused smile vanished. "You've spent your entire life competing with women, envying women, hating women. But the disadvantages of being a woman have never occurred to you. When you've chosen, you've slipped into the privileged role of man. Now you shall learn better. For as long a time as it pleases me— for the rest of your days if you fail to gain an appreciation, or until I think you've learned a new humility, you shall live here, in the seraglio, as a woman."

Narses was too stunned to reply.

"Your teachers are a trifle apprehensive, but they'll soon learn you're harmless. They'll pierce your lobes so you can wear earrings, they'll teach you the secrets of cosmetics and clothes—and, above all else, of feminine service. You see, I've decided that you shall become one of my personal serving maids."

✿ ✿ ✿

The Empress stretched out lazily on her divan, reading government reports while her feet were bathed and oiled, and lacquer was carefully applied to each toenail. Occasionally she glanced at the silent figure kneeling on the floor at the foot of the divan, and thought it remarkable she sometimes forgot that Narses wasn't really a woman. The combination of kohl-rimmed eyes, delicately rouged cheeks, and golden ear hoops that showed beneath a fall of long dark hair, the slender figure in the flimsy garments of a slave girl, the rattle of bracelets, and more than anything else the nimble deftness of slim fingers would have convinced anyone unfamiliar with the truth that the serving maid was truly a woman.

"How do you like your new life?" Theodora asked.

"I have no complaints, Augusta." Narses was careful to speak in a dulcet voice.

"The endless gossip about nothing more important than a bangle or a lady-in-waiting's new gown doesn't drive you mad? Tell me the truth."

Narses sighed. "When one had become accustomed to great affairs of state, the triviality of the seraglio is sometimes frustrating. But I try to be patient."

Theodora wriggled a toe that had just been lacquered. "Patience," she said, "is woman's greatest asset. I hope you're developing a sense of humor, too. I'm told that one of the maids who dresses my hair has a habit of borrowing your skirts without asking permission, and slaps you when you protest."

"She's a brute," Narses admitted.

The Empress averted her face to hide her silent laughter. "Women," she said, "are far more brutal than men. Does the slave mistress still beat you?"

"Not very often, now that I've learned to speak and walk in ways that please her."

"One of these days—or, more probably, one of these nights—you'll see another side of her nature. She's always taken a fancy to her own sex—just as you once did—and I've heard she's intrigued by you. She says you'll be a new experience for her, a new kind of conquest."

Narses' hands shook, forcing him to put the lacquer pot on the tray beside him. "Will you spare me no humiliation, Augusta?"

Theodora felt a twinge of pity for the helpless creature before reminding herself that he had unhesitatingly used his official standing to force the compliance of his lovers. "Surely you can refuse."

"You know I can't, Augusta. The slave mistress is taller than I, and stronger."

"Feminine guile, used with discretion, can be a powerful weapon when a woman wants to avoid an unwelcome suitor." The Empress discovered she was enjoying the situation and realized she was being compensated, in part, for the indignities she had been forced to endure in her early life.

"She'll whip me if I don't give in to anything she demands."

"A woman's weakness can plague her when she doesn't learn how to turn it to her advantage. When one can't avoid a suitor, one submits gracefully. Charm—even submission itself—can win a woman favors, protection, special privileges, if she is clever."

"You mock me, Augusta."

"Perhaps, but I also speak the truth, and I'm helping you, although you don't yet realize it. Real subtlety can be a tremendously potent weapon, as you'll find out if you're a willing pupil." Suddenly she tired of the conversation. "That's enough of the lacquer. You may go."

Narses stood, lowered himself to the floor in a deep curtsy, and backed out of the chamber, every move feminine.

Theodora was elated with his progress. Not until he became thoroughly familiar with the total subjugation of womankind would he be ready for the next step, the granting of little prerogatives that would offer him hope. Eventually he would become her instrument, ready to do her bidding in all things, but she was in no hurry. While still an adolescent, she herself had been taught the cruel lessons of patience.

So she was willing to wait, even if the completion of his education took a year or two, or even longer. Having repeatedly discovered that the efficacy of her agents was limited by their sex, Narses would be able to perform unique services for her—and, of course, for the Empire. He would return to the world of men, but his searing experience would make him a half-woman for the rest of his days, and he would become her most pliable, valuable weapon.

❦ ❦ ❦

Belisarius accomplished a near miracle. Displaying brilliance as a tactician and sound thinking as a strategist, he inflicted a crushing defeat on a Vandal army several times the size of his expeditionary corps. Carthage fell to him, as did its hinterland, and he returned to Constantinople with the treasures of Hannibal and a shipload of royal Vandal prisoners. Not the least of his achievements was the fact that he had accomplished so much at an incredibly low cost. Only twenty of his men had been killed, with a slightly larger number wounded, yet he had restored to Rome a major segment of her ancient Empire.

Constantinople forgot her previous opposition to foreign wars and gave the general the welcome worthy of a conqueror. Triumphal arches were erected in the Mesé, flowers were strewn in the path of the victors, and a service of thanksgiving was held in the not-yet-completed Sancta Sophia.

The Emperor could not do less for the hero than his subjects had done, and in a ceremony that was witnessed by a cheering, overflow crowd in the Hippodrome, awarded the general a gold laurel wreath and promoted him to the rank of consul. Belisarius was the the most popular man in the Empire, throngs followed him whenever he left his palace just beyond the Wall of Constantine, also a gift from Justinian, and people everywhere began to take a renewed interest in the Imperial succession.

Even the most conservative nobles and government officials became Belisarius' supporters, and the Emperor, hoping he could quiet speculation about the future, decided to give a banquet in the general's honor before retiring him to private life. Theodora, anxious to learn whether the universal adulation had turned Belisarius' head, invited the general's wife to pay a private call on her only two days before the holding of the banquet.

Antonina appeared at the seraglio in a gown of pale violet, and her smile was bright as she and her old friend embraced in the sitting room of the Empress' private suite. Naturally, Antonina paid no heed to the serving maid who removed her sandals and bathed her feet in scented water, then hovered discreetly in the background in the event the distinguished guest required additional service.

Theodora chatted lightly with her visitor about the joys of recent days and gradually turned the conversation to the subject of Carthage. "Was the palace there really built by Hannibal?"

"I don't know," Antonina replied. "The Vandals are such liars. All I can tell you is that it was surprisingly comfortable."

"You and Belisarius used the royal suite, of course." Theodora signaled to the serving maid, who refilled their wine cups.

Antonina became defensive. "Belisarius thought it was important to make the Carthaginians realize he was the representative of the Caesar Augustus."

"To be sure. I'd have expected nothing less, and neither

would Justinian." Theodora's voice and manner were soothing.

Antonina relaxed against the cushions of the divan.

"I'm terribly curious about something, probably because it's such a marvelous coincidence. Do you remember, many years ago, that you played the role of Hannibal's wife in the theater on the Mesé?"

"I recall it vaguely." Antonina did not like to think about her previous existence.

"I'll never forget it. You and Hannibal sat on thrones of gold—"

"That was a dramatist's fancy. The thrones in the audience chamber there—which the Carthaginians say were Hannibal's—are very plain. The arms and backs are made of ivory, but the rest is plain wood."

"How disappointing," Theodora murmured. "I suppose they're uncomfortable, too."

"No, the Vandals may be barbarians, but they take their creature comforts seriously. Both thrones were covered with a filled padding of gold cloth."

"At the very least," Theodora said, rising and escorting the visitor to the door, "you should have those cushions as souvenirs. I'll see that they're sent to you."

They exchanged prolonged farewells, and after Antonina had gone, Theodora turned to the serving maid. "Well?"

"She's dangerous," Narses said. "You were very adroit, Augusta, and she didn't quite realize what she was saying when she admitted she had used the throne of the Queen of Carthage. What really surprised me, though, was her gown. Violet is too close to Imperial purple to be an accident."

"We think alike." Although concentrating on the problem at hand, Theodora was pleased by Narses' growing powers of subtle observation. "You think she's ambitious, then?"

"Unquestionably, Augusta." Narses almost forgot to play the role of serving maid in his eagerness to deal with a matter of the sort he had known for so long before being captured and degraded. "She already sees herself on your throne, wearing the purple."

"And Belisarius?"

The slender shoulders rose and fell in a delicate shrug. "I haven't seen him in a long time, so I can only guess. He was always loyal to the Emperor, but there's no way to predict how someone will act when influenced by the woman who goes to bed with him."

Theodora was delighted with him. "You're learning. I'll have your bondage anklet removed today."

Narses' rouged lips curved upward.

"That's right. You'll be free of the slave mistress. However," she added, "you'll stay at the seraglio for the next phase of your rehabilitation, and won't be allowed to leave the premises. You'll rank as a junior lady-in-waiting, and I'm sure there's a great deal you can learn from Lady Daphne, the magister's wife who left him to take up permanent residence here. She's had her eye on you."

Narses sighed tremulously.

"This association will be voluntary—and good for you. And I'll want your advice on how to handle Belisarius and Antonina before they become so popular that the demand to make him the Emperor's heir will become too strong to resist. Discuss the problem with no one, but come to me when you have something specific to contribute."

❧ ❧ ❧

Justinian paused frequently on the stroll through the grove of almond trees in the Imperial garden, making no secret of his distaste for even a mild form of physical exercise. He realized his paunch was growing, his sleeplessness worse, and the occasional numbness in his legs more intense, but he found it far easier to think at his desk, and if Theodora insisted he walk with her daily, it was time she understood that he had to halt in order to concentrate. "You're quite certain Daphne's information is accurate?"

"I've told you all I know, my dear." Theodora tried in vain to resume their walk. "The wives of the other magisters have felt sorry for her since she left her husband, and visit her regularly at the seraglio. And for the past week they've spoken only of Antonina. The woman is more ambitious—and ruthless—than either of us knew, and has been urging each member of the Council of State to support a proposal making Belisarius your formal heir."

"The relationships of women are so complicated," her husband replied, "that I don't necessarily accept the claims of one or another as valid. For all I know, Daphne has been jealous of Antonina, and went to you in the hope of causing trouble for her enemy."

"Daphne hasn't come to me. She's confided in someone else, someone very close to her, and she has no idea everything she says is repeated to me." Theodora could not elaborate, since he had no idea what had become of Narses and would be shocked if he found out. "I swear the reports are true—"

"That must be good enough for me, then."

"And I warn you that if Belisarius stays in Constantinople much longer, the campaign to make him your heir will become impossible to resist. Once you give in, your life will be in danger, and so will mine. I've never forgotten Vitalian."

Justinian glanced over his shoulder at the household guards, who were out of earshot, and began to walk rapidly. "Neither have I, unfortunately."

Theodora tried to match his pace. "The fault in this situation is mine, so it's my place to stifle Antonina."

"How are you to blame?"

"If I'd given you a son, the future of your dynasty would be settled."

He seldom referred to her past, but she was giving him no choice. "The physicians have told us you lost your ability to bear children because of the way you were once forced to live. So it's absurd to call yourself guilty."

"Antonina was a harlot, too, but she's presented Belisarius with two fine sons."

"I've grown tired of hearing that family mentioned in every other breath."

"Then send them away," Theodora said.

"Into exile?" He halted again, surprised.

"Hardly. You're anxious to start your campaign to recapture old Rome and the Italian provinces—"

"Yes, yes," Justinian said impatiently. "Belisarius is the obvious choice as commander of the expedition, but ever since he told me he's reluctant to go into the field again, I've been trying to find another general who can beat the Goths."

"Belisarius loves war as much as you love your books and manuscripts." Theodora was still astonished by his inability to understand even those who had been his closest associates for many years. "It's Antonina who wants to stay in Constantinople. But what difference does it make whether they want to stay or go? Give Belisarius no choice. Order him to capture Rome and the Italian provinces."

Again the Emperor halted, absently plucking a leaf from a pomegranate tree, crushing it in his hand and sniffing it. "I've been tempted, as I'm sure you realize. But a reluctant general wins no victories, and we can't afford defeat."

"Belisarius can afford it even less than you," she said quietly. "If an expedition should fail, you'd still be Emperor, but if Belisarius lost his reputation, he'd be bankrupt."

Justinian shredded the leaf, tearing it into tiny bits and watching as the breeze carried them across the garden.

She knew better than to press. "A merchant fleet from Carthage is putting into port," she said. "Shall we go to the end of the garden and watch the ships sail in?"

❧ ❧ ❧

The news that Belisarius had encountered virtually no opposition when he occupied the island of Sicily sparked one of the noisiest, most joyous celebrations in the memory of Constantinople's oldest citizens. Excitement mounted still higher when he established a base on the Italian mainland, and, leaving his wife there with the troops of his supply corps, marched north to invade old Rome.

After a campaign of only a few months he captured the ancient city, but the exultation of Constantinople was tempered by his sober report, which was copied and posted in prominent public places. A huge force of Goths, among them the most ferocious fighting men on earth, had laid siege to Rome. For the present, Belisarius declared, he was in no danger. His supply lines were open, the Romans had hailed him as their deliverer and would join him in resisting the barbarians.

One section of his report was suppressed on the recommendation of the Council of War. Belisarius wrote that he desperately needed reinforcements, preferably cavalry, as the Goths were inexperienced in opposing mounted troops. He also wanted as much gold as the treasury could spare; he believed that some of the subordinate Goth commanders, accustomed to easy living, might be amenable to bribes.

Justinian immediately sent five thousand cavalrymen to Italy, all he could spare, and, ignoring the anguished protests of John of Cappadocia, filled the holds of three new navy ships with gold. If Rome could be held and the lesser Italian towns taken, the major task of reuniting the Empire of old would be accomplished, and, Justinian felt, his own place in history would be solidified.

During this anxious period, Narses suddenly and unexpectedly returned to duty on the Imperial staff, and on the strong recommendation of the Empress was promoted to magister. He had grown so effeminate during his absence that many of his former colleagues suspected he had been gelded, but no one asked questions. Justinian's security police and Theodora's private army of agents had grown so powerful that even the highest officials knew it was safer to remain in ignorance on delicate subjects. Narses seemed to enjoy the confidence of both the Emperor and Empress, and that was sufficient.

Taxes were raised again to meet the increased war costs, but people of every class quietly accepted the new burden. The Empire was enjoying unprecedented prosperity, and the hope of achieving the permanent recovery of what so long had been the core of the Empire made them willing to endure the sacrifice.

Theodora conferred in private with Narses several times each week, the new magister coming to the seraglio for the purpose. Completely at home in the place where he had been held in servitude, he voluntarily changed into feminine attire before these meetings, asserting that he felt more comfortable, and Theodora knew her gamble had succeeded. His mind was as keen as it had ever been, but he had become her creature, and, watching him as he smoothed his skirt of thin wool, she thought that although she had spared him physical mutilation, he had, for all practical purposes, been gelded.

"The Council of War met early this afternoon," he said, "and the generals agreed with Orestes that it would be wrong to use Greek fire in the Italian campaign. Between them they persuaded the Emperor not to send any to Belisarius."

"What was their reason?"

"The usual. They think Greek fire should be saved for the emergency defense of the Empire."

Theodora shook her head. "Men can be so shortsighted."

Narses nodded, automatically aligning himself with her. "If we used the fire, the Goths would retreat across the Alps and leave the whole Italian peninsula in our hands."

"Perhaps," she said deliberately, "the time will come when someone other than Belisarius will be granted permission to use it. Someone who performs other vital services and earns the right."

His kohl-rimmed eyes brightened. "I'm sure those services can be performed, Augusta."

"I hope so." She paused, then asked abruptly, "Is John of Cappadocia honest?"

"I don't know."

"Neither do I. It disturbs me that he's bought another estate."

"And fifty camels to be used on the caravan routes to Egypt. He claims he's earned the money in his various investments."

"I wonder. Can you find out?"

Narses was silent for several moments, and then his high-pitched giggle filled the room. "He trusts no one, you know, not even his own wife and daughters."

"So I've discovered."

"And he never discusses his personal affairs with anyone else in the government. He's very cautious, but I wouldn't be surprised if he could be persuaded to confide in me, little by little." Narses held a new ring of semiprecious stones up to the light. "We've known each other for many years, and although we've worked together, he's never had much respect for me." He giggled again, still more loudly. "Since I've returned, he thinks I'm completely harmless."

"So much the better."

"Precisely, Augusta. I may need time, but even John must grow weary of carrying the burden of his secrets alone. If he's stealing from the treasury, I think I can trick him into telling me a bit."

"I'm depending on you." Theodora reached out and patted a hand almost as slender as her own. "Meanwhile we have another problem that's more immediate. If Belisarius manages to hold Rome, the demand that he be made heir to the throne will become overwhelming."

Narses' eyes narrowed. "I've been thinking of Belisarius. And Antonina. She was your friend, Augusta. What sort of woman is she?"

Theodora cast aside the discretion she would have used in discussing the problem with a man. "Calculating, and very hard."

"I saw myself that she's vain. Am I right in assuming she's callow?"

"Very." Theodora grew tense. "What have you in mind?"

"Belisarius is a genuine hero. His capture of old Rome establishes him as a military genius, so he's untouchable, beyond reproach. But," Narses continued, a hint of malice in his soft voice, "Antonina may be the weak spot in his armor. Think of her situation, Augusta. She loves adulation and luxury, but she's pining away, neglected and miserable, in a dreary army camp on the Italian coast while Belisarius holds the Goths at bay outside the walls of old Rome."

"I'm beginning to see your point." Theodora smiled.

"I'm not certain there is a point. But I can't help wondering how she spends her days. She needs admiration, but is she getting it? She must demand excitement, but how is she providing it? I find the questions very provocative."

Theodora was convinced that the transformation of Narses was the best investment of effort she had ever made. "How do you propose to find out the answers?"

"I suggest you send Antonina some gifts in the next convoy. Some silk bedding, some new gowns and scents. The usual—that will whet her appetites. I suggest she also be sent a pair of new serving maids. Not as gifts from you, because she'd hold them at arm's length. Let's tell her they're being presented to her by the grateful citizens of Constantinople."

"That's just the sort of gesture she'll love." Theodora laughed admiringly.

"There are two girls right here in the seraglio who are exceptionally clever, and worthy of absolute trust. I can vouch for them without reservation, and if they're promised their freedom, I'm sure they'll send us very full reports."

"Can they read and write?"

"No, but I'll work out a code with them before they sail."

"Take charge of the matter, and do whatever you think best. I wonder what they'll find."

"I don't know," Narses said, "but I can't help suspecting that Antonina is vulnerable, and if she is, there will be no threat to the throne."

NINE

❦ ❦ ❦

"I'm positive," Narses told the Empress, "that John of Cappadocia is stealing government funds, although I can't prove it. He's hinted that he's been clever, so clever no one will ever know how he's taken Imperial treasury gold, but he's too cunning to reveal any details."

Theodora couldn't make up her mind how to proceed. The evidence against the Caesar Praefect was too flimsy for her to go to Justinian with the little she knew, as he would demand specific information. In all probability he would summon John, who would take great precautions to conceal his illegal activities. On the other hand, it also would be a risk to take the treasurer into custody in the hope she could force a confession from him. He ranked second only to Belisarius among the Emperor's subjects, and if she failed to obtain solid evidence, Justinian would have a right to feel she had exceeded her authority.

Eventually she concluded, however, that the chance of arousing her husband's anger was worth the gamble. She alone had the power to take action against the Caesar Praefect, and if she did not intervene, he would continue to amass a fortune at the expense of the state.

She made her plans with care, aware he would escape unless she proved herself his equal. John politely declined an invitation to visit her at the seraglio, suggesting they confer instead, if she wished a meeting with him, at the main palace. Obviously he was apprehensive, having heard rumors, at the very least, that men who called on the Empress at her private court sometimes vanished for long periods.

But Theodora would not accept his refusal and repeated her invitation, blandly, but with an insistence that he could not ignore. Not even a man in his position, one who had enjoyed the lifelong friendship and confidence of Justinian, could reject her thinly veiled command.

Theodora elected to receive him in her audience chamber, with all of her ladies in attendance. She wore her new crown, a triple tier of diamonds and pearls, with a huge emerald topping the other gems, and dressed in her formal robes of state for the occasion. John, immediately realizing this was no ordinary meeting, was wary, as his guarded expression indicated. He bowed low, but made no attempt to converse, and waited for her to indicate why she had summoned him.

For a quarter of an hour the Empress made small talk, watching with satisfaction as he became increasingly tense and irritated. Then, abruptly, she dismissed the members of her court and was alone with him. Smiling graciously, she indicated that she wanted him to mount the dais.

John gathered his fur-trimmed robes around him and climbed the steps.

Theodora knew that as she was seated and he was standing, she possessed the basic advantage, and she took her time, letting him fidget.

"Surely you didn't call me here for a state audience," he said.

She smiled quietly.

"You're busy, Augusta, and so am I!"

"I had hoped to see you many days ago," she replied. "I've chosen to receive you here, in these surroundings, to remind you that I am more than your colleague. I am your Empress."

"I need no reminder of that fact," John, rarely tactful, was blunt.

"I'm not so sure. You see, I've decided to examine all of your records."

His eyes widened for an instant. "With all due respect to your talents, Augusta, do you think you would understand my interminable columns of figures?"

"Probably not." She watched him carefully, knowing that what she revealed would rock him. "But a capable man who has reorganized the finances of the Church has agreed to study the treasury for me. Perhaps you've heard of Peter Barsymes?"

"Yes, and I suppose he's efficient enough on a minor scale, but I'll tolerate no outsider examining my confidential records."

"He'll go to your office tomorrow."

"I'll go to the Emperor today!" John said in a loud, deep voice. "I hold my warrant from him—"

"You'll go to no one, unless you choose to be foolish. I have reason to believe there are irregularities at the treasury. Confess them to me, now and here, and you'll suffer nothing worse than retirement to one of your country estates. Defy me, and you'll pay consequences you'll regret until the end of your days."

"I have nothing to hide, Augusta," he said, striking a defiant pose, "so threats don't frighten me. I'll appeal to Justinian, which is my right as Caesar Praefect!"

She knew the prerogatives of his rank and had taken them into consideration in her planning. "I'll grant you," she said, "that the time at my disposal is very short. By tomorrow, at the latest, the Emperor will wonder what has become of you, and I won't be able to deny him the full story. That gives me a maximum of twenty-four hours to persuade you to tell me the whole truth."

"What is it you want to know?"

"How much you've stolen from the Imperial treasury, and how you took it."

"I deny that I stole a single copper."

"You own eight grand estates and have built palaces on three of them. You have scores of servants, stables of fine horses, and a collection of priceless statues from ancient Greece. Not even you could have earned the money for all these treasures in honorable ways!"

"I say that I did, and unless you can prove otherwise, your charges are false. I'm going to Justinian at once!" He was so angry he turned his back as he descended the dais and headed toward the door that led to the main corridor.

Theodora made no attempt to halt him.

John opened the door, but armed sentries in the Empress' household livery barred his path. "Do you know who I am?" he thundered. "Let me pass!"

The crossed swords of the sentries remained upraised.

The outraged Caesar Praefect turned back to Theodora. "I demand—"

"Be sensible," she interrupted, "and realize you're in no position to make demands. I've already indicated to you that you're forcing me to use methods I dislike. There are men in my employ who are expert in obtaining the truth from those who would prefer to keep their lips sealed, and with only twenty-four hours at my disposal, it will be difficult for everyone. More difficult by far for you than for anyone else."

"The Emperor will be unhappy, Augusta. If you subject someone of my rank to torture, no one in the government will be safe, and men of integrity will leave the Imperial service."

She couldn't help admiring his effrontery and courage. "If I'm mistaken about you," she admitted, "the Emperor may lose faith in me, and the government may suffer. But I must do what I think right for the Empire. For the last time, will you give me your free confession of the truth?"

"You'll regret this, Augusta!"

Far more disturbed than she was willing to let him see, she signaled to a young officer outside the door, then tried to shut out the sound of John's booming voice as he was dragged away.

❀ ❀ ❀

The air in the dungeons beneath the seraglio was cold and stale, the odors of unwashed bodies, rotting food, and other scents, equally disagreeable but unidentified, making it difficult for Theodora to breathe. Clamping her sweet-smelling cloth over her face, she followed the keeper of the dungeons down the long, narrow tunnel, walking slowly on the old cobblestones. The torches held aloft by two guards revealed the damp walls of the individual cells, and it was a consolation to her that few were occupied. The longer she had reigned, the fewer prisoners she had found it necessary to incarcerate here, which was a relief.

The dungeon-keeper opened the door of a large cell, unlocking it with a heavy key and pushing back a bolt of iron-studded oak. The guards entered first, planting the spiked bottom ends of their torches in the damp ground, and the dungeon-keeper followed, then beckoned and bowed to the Empress.

Theodora had thought herself prepared for any sight she might see, but the transformation of John of Cappadocia in a period of a day and a half was so shocking that she gasped. Stark naked and held by ankle and leg chains to the wall, he looked like a grisly caricature of a sleek powerful official.

His back and legs were crisscrossed with ugly, inflamed

welts, and when he raised his head wearily to focus on the woman who gaped at him, there was no sense of shame in his expression. He was defeated, utterly crushed, and no longer cared what happened to him.

Theodora waved the dungeon-keeper and guards from the cell. "I've read your signed confession," she said.

John made no reply.

"I shall take it to the Emperor this morning. It speaks for itself. You were clever, just as you had claimed. Only you would have thought of shaving a small quantity of gold from every coin you took into the treasury, and it's no wonder you became so wealthy."

He remained limp, scarcely hearing her words.

"Were you a lesser man, I'd urge the Emperor to execute you. But you served him well for many years, so I shall take pity on you. Pity of a sort. Before the sun sets today, you will be taken on board a ship that will sail to Alexandria. There you will be given a hair shirt to cover your body, and a beggar's bowl. If you are diligent, you won't starve."

The tormented, chained creature emitted a tortured sound similar to that of a wounded animal surrounded by hunters.

"Your children are married," Theodora said, "and are leading their own lives. They hold high places in the nobility and will not be punished for your transgressions. I'll give your wife a suite of her own here, in the seraglio, and she will lack neither honor nor luxury to the end of her days. She will be free to visit her children when she pleases, or to receive them and her grandchildren here. She will be placed under only one restriction. In all of the Empire, Alexandria is the one place closed to her."

John subsided, his head sinking onto his chest in a broken gesture of acceptance.

Theodora was tempted to tell him his wife would be relieved to be rid of him, but refrained. Even though it was true that his own family would not mourn his departure, he was being made to pay a severe penalty for his crimes, and there was nothing to be gained by adding to his degradation.

In fact, Theodora thought, she was proving she could be compassionate and merciful. She had hoped to wrest from John the admission that she had won their duel, but he had sunk into a lethargy so deep it resembled a stupor, and she found the atmosphere of the dungeon so oppressive that rather than savor her triumph she withdrew. Only by exercising self-control was she able to walk rather than run; the dungeons brought back sharp memories of the miseries she had suffered as Hecebolus' mistress early in her life, and her greatest victory, perhaps, was her ability to conquer the unreasoning fear that rose up in her so suddenly.

♔ ♔ ♔

Ordinarily Justinian could grasp the meaning of any document by glancing through it, but he read John of Cappadocia's signed confession with infinite care, as though memorizing every phrase and word. At last he put it aside, his expression bleak.

"I know every word is the absolute truth," Theodora told him. "The household slaves who shaved the gold coins for him—and who shared in the spoils—have surrendered the special knives they used, and my agents brought them to me. Would you like to see them?"

"No," the Emperor said dully, "it's all written here, and I'll take his admission as final."

"I can imagine how badly you've been hurt. It isn't easy to give someone your trust and then find him wanting."

Justinian made no reply.

She was growing uneasy. "Perhaps I shouldn't have sent

him off to Alexandria until you knew the whole story, but I wanted to spare you as much heartache as I could."

Justinian glanced at her for an instant, heaved himself to his feet and, walking with an unsteady tread, went out to the balcony of their suite that overlooked the Imperial garden.

Theodora knew he was suffering from shock and dis-illusionment, and waited patiently in their bedchamber until he recovered sufficiently to return. But she could see him leaning against the wrought-iron rail, staring out past the mammoth dome of the new Sancta Sophia into the void of a dark sky, and after a time she could tolerate the suspense no longer.

But his stillness, combined with the rigidity of his back and neck, warned her that he would not welcome an in-trusion on his privacy. So, even though she wanted to help and comfort him, she realized that on this one occasion, at least, he would have to suffer alone until he overcame his grief.

She pretended to read, brushed her hair, and occupied herself with trivia. The wait was endless, and she had no idea how much time had passed when he finally returned to the bedchamber.

Justinian was wearing his tunic of Imperial purple, with the sword of Julius Caesar hanging at his side, but never had he looked more like a lumbering, ungainly peasant. "You were wrong," he said bitterly.

Theodora was stunned.

"I don't know what made you so certain that John was stealing from the treasury, and I don't really care. But you were wrong to challenge him and force a confession from him. Once he confessed, of course, you had no choice, and had to punish him, but by then it was too late. You'd al-ready done the damage."

She thought he had taken leave of his senses.

"No one in this world is perfect," Justinian said, "and

an ambitious man sometimes reaches beyond his grasp. Have you forgotten what I did to Vitalian?"

"Is that what's bothering you?"

"I merely wanted to give you an illustration you'd understand," he said, sinking into a chair before removing his sword belt and sandals. "I've guessed for years that John was robbing the treasury. He had become one of the wealthiest men on earth after I took the throne."

"And now all of that wealth reverts to the Crown," she reminded him.

"You're thinking only of today, not the years ahead." The sword dropped to the floor with a thud. "We must raise still another corps of cavalry and infantry for Belisarius, and he'll need additional supplies, uniforms, arms. The fortune you've taken from John of Cappadocia will barely pay for the new expedition to Italy. What then? We'll need funds to send troops from Macedonia across the Danube, and one of these days there will be a new war with the Persians. Chosroes won't remain patient forever while I grow stronger."

"Was John the only man capable of putting money into your treasury? Peter Barsymes is exceptionally able—"

"He is, and I'll be obliged to make him a magister. But there was only one John of Cappadocia. He found the money to rebuild Constantinople and make it the most beautiful city in all of the world. He found the funds to expand the army, create a navy, enlarge our trade, and open hundreds of new business enterprises. He found ways to help the farmers become more prosperous, even though no one ever taxed them so severely. He was unique, a genius, and there will never be another like him. Honest or a robber, I needed him, and because of that need I was willing to overlook his faults."

"How could you lean on a man you knew to be a thief?"

"Perhaps you didn't hear me say I needed him! A dozen like Peter Barsymes won't replace him!" Justinian spoke savagely, his hand pounding the arm of his chair. "Tribonian has tried to create a framework of laws that are reasonable as well as just. Belisarius is using bribes to win some of the Goth leaders in Italy to our cause, and all of those who join us will be treated as honorable men—even though they're traitors. You've crippled me, and the Empire will never recover from this blow!"

The inside of Theodora's mouth felt dry. "I hope you're wrong," she said, "and that you'll find you've exaggerated this calamity."

Justinian made no reply, and stared into space.

ᕯ ᕯ ᕯ

Justinian proved to be an accurate prophet. His new magister of Finances was capable and honest, but funds drained from the Imperial treasury more rapidly than Peter could replace them. On the surface the Empire was enjoying the greatest prosperity in its existence, but Justinian was worried, and Theodora became increasingly concerned when she saw her husband's dire prophecies coming true.

Ironically, the growing crisis was compounded by a military victory that caused victory bonfires to be lighted in every city and town in the Empire. Belisarius again demonstrated that no living man was his equal as a tactician, and drove the Goths from the gates of Rome, forcing them to take refuge in the provincial Italian fortresses to the north.

The ancient city of Rome was restored to the Empire, and Belisarius' popularity soared to new heights. The mere mention of his name caused the people of Constantinople to demonstrate in the streets, and the members of the Council of State agreed that it would be difficult, perhaps impossible, for the Emperor to resist making the general his heir.

A glum Justinian retired to his work sanctum after a long council meeting, and Theodora accompanied him, even though he had made it clear that he sought privacy. He was annoyed by her refusal to take his broad hint, and glowered at her when she sat down opposite the table at which he worked.

"You made my responsibility very plain to me when I rid you of John," she said. "Now I'm prepared to offer amends that will restore your finances and remove Belisarius' threat to the throne."

He shook his head. "Even if you made a pact with demons, you couldn't accomplish all that."

"Hear me out. My plan is very simple, and I'll explain the better part of it. There's only one portion you must accept on faith, and if you trusted John of Cappadocia, you must know that I work only on your behalf."

"True, although you trample on anyone who grows too powerful and threatens your own standing."

Theodora realized he spoke the truth and winced. But this was no time to give in to her own feelings. "First," she said, "I suggest you send Narses to Italy."

Justinian laughed aloud for the first time in months. "I can't see Narses playing the role of a warrior. I don't know what you did to him during those two years he disappeared, but he's more woman than man."

"He is, and therefore he'll be no threat to you when he completes the conquest of the Goths."

"How do you expect him to perform that miracle?"

"Give him your secret weapon. Let him take several shiploads of Greek fire to Italy with him, and he'll burn the barbarians out of their fortresses. But don't send the new corps of cavalry and infantry you've raised. You won't need them in Italy, and you can save a huge sum of money by keeping these troops in their garrisons."

The amused scorn vanished from his eyes, and he considered the idea. "It's possible, you know, that Narses could do it. He's always wanted a taste of military glory, oddly, and he'd remain loyal to me."

"There's no question of it."

"He couldn't deal directly with Belisarius' veterans in Italy, of course." The Emperor continued to think aloud.

"I'm well aware of that particular problem, and suggest you order him to see no one but the senior brigade commanders. Then the troops won't be in a position to laugh at him."

Justinian was silent, drumming with nervous fingers on his worktable.

Theodora gave him time to examine every aspect of her plan.

"What would you do with Belisarius?" he suddenly demanded.

"Order him home as soon as Narses arrives in Italy," she said. "You certainly don't want him to gain credit for using the Greek fire and driving the Goths across the Alps!"

"Hardly. But he's still the man who set old Rome free, and the people will demand a conqueror's reception for him."

"Give him one. You'll probably want to crown him with another gold laurel wreath, and—I'm not certain of this— make him Consul-for-Life."

Justinian blinked in astonishment. "You're virtually guaranteeing that he'll succeed me, and no matter how honorable he is, he'll be under tremendous pressure to assassinate me."

"I think I can promise you that even if you promote him again, even if you give him the greatest reception ever held for any hero, Belisarius will publicly repudiate any suggestion that he be made the official heir to the throne. Within a month of his return to Constantinople you can bring your cousin's sons here from Macedonia, and no one will accuse you of cheating Belisarius of his due."

"Why would Belisarius repudiate the throne?" He was contemptuous. "No sane man—"

"Belisarius is sane, yet he'll reject it. That's the one portion of my idea that I can't explain to you. You'll have to take my word."

"But this is insane."

"You trusted John, even though you were certain he was robbing you. Now I ask you to trust your wife!"

❦ ❦ ❦

"You're offering me the most magnificent opportunity of my life," Narses said. "It hadn't occurred to me that I'd be the first to use Greek fire."

"Your military venture is certain to succeed," Theodora told him, "and if the entire plan works out as it should, you'll be rewarded with the title of Imperial Viceroy for Italy."

The overwhelmed Narses could not reply.

"But if you fail in the most important of your directives, I'll have you gelded, paraded in a yellow gown through the streets of Constantinople, and put to work for the rest of your days as a daughter of Venus."

Narses grew pale. "I've already assured you, Augusta, that I'll do my very best."

"You cannot and must not fail. I hope you understand it's imperative that Belisarius' wings be clipped before he returns to Constantinople.

"How could I forget it, Augusta?"

"Show me the coded message from the slave girls you sent to Antonina. I want to see it again."

He handed her a small, badly smudged scroll. "I've studied it by the hour, and I'm certain they've discovered something, but don't know how to tell me their news."

Theodora scrutinized the paper at length. "I pray that you're right."

"If I am, I'll know what to do." He delicately refrained from adding that he was equally conscious of what would happen to him if the information in the garbled message failed to live up to his hopes.

"We must trust no man in this scheme," Theodora told him. "Take as many women with clever minds and strong muscles from the seraglio as you'll need."

"Thank you, Augusta. Six or eight should be enough."

"I leave the details to you. But until you've followed my orders, take no chances. Concentrate only on your task. There will be ample opportunity later for you to play the bride while one of them acts the role of groom."

Narses flushed. "I should have realized you'd know everything about me, even my diversions."

"The slave girls you sent to Antonina are burly enough for any feminine taste, and they'll probably be so grateful to you for setting them free that they'll want to stay with you, so your private life as viceroy won't be dull. But don't for an instant forget that the throne depends on your cunning!"

※ ※ ※

The strongest squadron in the Imperial navy cast anchor in the inadequate port at Ostia, the ancient Italian town at the mouth of the Tiber River, twenty-one miles from Rome. There a crisply energetic Narses, showing no traces of the femininity that had become second nature to him, stored his supplies of Greek fire in a stone warehouse built around A.D. 46 by the Emperor Claudius, and posted all of the one thousand troops he had brought with him from Constantinople to guard the secret weapon.

Traveling to Rome with an entourage that included almost as many broad-shouldered, Amazonian serving women as it did male soldiers, he discovered that Belisarius and his troops had already marched north and were maneuvering in the field against the Goths. Instead of following at once and relieving the general of his command, Narses tarried briefly in the ancient city, where, contrary to custom, he visited neither the great churches nor the semiruins of great public buildings.

He briefly paid his respects to Antonina, and then went into a conference behind closed doors with the two serving maids who had preceded him to Italy. They talked until midnight; the women who had accompanied him were even busier in the hours that followed, and in the morning Antonina and the officers of the garrison Belisarius had left behind were astonished to discover that the new Imperial representative had hurried back to Ostia. It was generally agreed that he was afraid of active combat, had no taste for the hardships of field living, and was returning to the luxury of the court at Constantinople after losing his appetite for adventure.

Those who decried him would have been surprised had they seen him in the great cabin of the trireme *Maigui*, flagship of the admiral, Desius, who was in command of the squadron that had just arrived at Ostia.

Narses' voice was deep and his manner incisive as he reached into a hidden compartment of his inner belt and drew out the gold seal of the Empress Theodora, which he had been instructed to use only in the event of supreme emergency. "I'm sure you recognize this medallion, milord," he said.

Desius examined it, then handed it back. "Command me in all things," he replied, "and I'll obey."

"I'm afraid you won't like your orders, but it can't be helped. You and your men have been looking forward to a stay in old Rome, but it has become necessary for you to return at once to Constantinople on the *Maigui*."

The admiral grimaced, but made no complaint.

"Take as many naval vessels for convoy purposes as you'll need to make absolutely certain that you can beat off attacks of any strength from pirates or enemies. Use every precaution, as though the Emperor and Empress themselves were sailing on this ship. If you reach Constantinople safely, the Empress will grant you any wish, I know, and I can promise you'll be made Grand Admiral of the entire navy. Failure—and even a delay of a few days at sea would be a failure—will be severely punished."

"I assume I'm expected to take some passengers home," Desius said.

"Yes, a party of seven women. Post a sentry detail over their quarters and let no one approach them on the voyage. They'll remain in isolation, and will even take their meals in private."

Desius was curious. "There were six rather extraordinary serving women in your party on the voyage here."

"You'll be responsible for the safety of seven on your return voyage," Narses said firmly, and did not elaborate.

"I had imagined—that is to say, I'd taken it for granted— that Belisarius would sail home with me."

"Your assignment takes precedence over that of giving passage to Belisarius."

The admiral whistled softly under his breath, finding it impossible to guess what person or persons in the Empire were more important than the great general. As nearly as he could determine, he was being ordered to carry a number of slave women to Constantinople, and the assignment made no sense to him. On the other hand, Narses spoke with the full authority of the Empress Theodora, so his demand could not be disobeyed, evaded, or even questioned.

"How long will you need to take on supplies for this voyage, Desius?"

"Two days, perhaps three."

"Every Imperial granary and warehouse in Ostia will be opened to you, and you may feel free to utilize the services of every cargo handler in the town. Leave no later than the afternoon tide today—"

"Today!"

"—and under no circumstances put into any ports before you reach home. Place the *Maigui* in quarantine when you arrive in Constantinople, and permit no one—I stress, no one—to board or leave the ship. I'll give you a sealed letter to the Empress that you're to guard with your life. Send it to her by messenger the instant you drop anchor there, and the Augusta herself will give you further instructions."

"Have no fear, milord. Everything will be done precisely as you've directed." The admiral was confused. On the voyage to Italy, Narses had been a simpering, mincing eunuch, or worse, but something had happened to transform him into a firm, hard-bitten man who was making it painfully clear that he would tolerate no deviation from the specific orders he had given. Things were happening on the highest levels of Imperial society that were beyond his ability to comprehend, and perhaps it was best that he remain in ignorance. His instinct told him it might be healthier to be ignorant of machinations close to the throne.

TEN

✿ ✿ ✿

Theodora had never been in higher spirits than she demonstrated in the days that followed her receipt of a letter from Narses, brought to her on the trireme *Maigui*, that told her of his safe arrival in Italy. She alone was cheerful, however. The news that Belisarius had sailed for home on board a transport was received with foreboding by the members of the Imperial court loyal to the Emperor, and Justinian himself became increasingly morose.

"There's no need for fear," the Empress told him repeatedly. "Prepare a welcome for Belisarius that Constantinople will remember for one thousand years. Spare him no honor. I give you my sacred word that he'll be no threat to your security."

Forced to accept her word and goaded by her, the Emperor expanded his plans for Belisarius' reception, convincing the magisters and other high-ranking officials that he had decided to make the general his heir, even though his own life might be placed in jeopardy. It was obvious to the court, however, that he took no pleasure in the grandiose plans he was making, and his subordinates shared his apprehension.

A triumphal arch of marble was built in the Forum of Constantine and decorated with sculptures showing the great general's victories over both the Vandals and the Goths. A new building just completed at the Strategium, which would be used as a conference hall by officers of the high military command, was named in his honor, and a statue of him, mounted, was cast in bronze and erected in newly named Belisarius Place on the Mesé.

Several small agile schooners were sent out to sea to keep watch for the ship bringing Belisarius home, and when one of them returned with word that the ship had been sighted no more than a three-hour sail from the city, Constantinople erupted with joy. A naval squadron sailed out to escort the conqueror into the harbor, and when he came ashore, walking on a cloth-of-gold carpet, with Antonina a step behind him in a dazzling lilac-colored gown, he was greeted by a fanfare of rams'-horn trumpets.

Tens of thousands of citizens had crowded the waterfront area, and troops of the Imperial household guard were compelled to use force in order to clear a path for the Emperor and Empress, who broke precedent by coming in person to welcome the hero and his wife rather than wait for them to make a formal call at the palace.

The citizens went wild when Justinian and Belisarius clasped forearms, and another cheer, equally loud, welled up when Theodora embraced Antonina before the general's wife could drop to her knees in the accepted form of greeting to the Empire's first lady.

Justinian tried to sound jovial, but the uneasiness in his voice was apparent. "I'm holding games in your honor at the Hippodrome tomorrow afternoon," he said, "and at that time I'll publicly announce that I'm making you Consul-for-Life." Theodora had insisted, but the idea did not appeal to him.

Belisarius indicated gratitude, but was not surprised. He

had expected a reward that would recognize his achievements, but there was no hint of arrogance in his attitude; he had earned his honors, but was not making undue demands on the Emperor. He took care, however, not to look in the direction of his wife, who was gloating over his forthcoming promotion to a special rank that few men in the history of the Empire had held.

"What progress are we making in Italy?" Justinian had to search for something to say.

"If you'd given me more troops and another two years," the general replied bluntly, "I'd have reduced every Goth fortress by conventional means, but Greek fire should make it possible to complete the task in a much shorter time." Belisarius leaned closer to the Emperor in order to make himself heard as they walked down the cloth-of-gold carpet toward a row of waiting chariots and coaches.

Justinian neither smiled nor waved. His subjects had come to honor Belisarius, and there were few in the dense crush who bothered to glance in the direction of their Emperor. "Do you care to make any special recommendations when the Councils of State and War meet tomorrow morning?"

"Officially, I can offer nothing but praise to every member of the corps. But I don't really know why you sent Narses to replace me."

"I didn't want to dim your glory."

"You're very thoughtful, Augustus. But I spent years creating a machine of fighting men unequaled since the time of Julius Caesar's legions, and I shudder when I think of my men being led by Narses."

"We're going to need a civilian rather than a military administration in the Italian peninsula after the barbarians have been driven out," the Emperor said lamely. "Church problems, particularly some intricate theological questions, are becoming more complicated."

Belisarius' broad-shouldered shrug indicated that he

neither knew nor cared about the long-simmering feud between the bishops of the West and the patriarchs of the East. "All that bothers me is the thought that Narses' appointment as my successor will make it appear that I've accomplished very little."

"You'll have no cause to be dissatisfied with your recognition." Justinian glanced over his shoulder at his wife, deeply annoyed because she had embarrassed him and was doing nothing to relieve the difficulty of dealing with an unhappy general.

Theodora knew the Emperor was not enjoying his conversation, but, walking arm in arm with the radiant Antonina behind the two men, she appeared unconcerned. "My dear," she said to the former actress, "this is one of the great days of your life."

"I gather that tomorrow will be another."

"Tomorrow will be unique," Theodora promised.

Antonina could not resist waving to the throngs crowding behind the lines of household guards on both sides of the walk. Everyone in Constantinople was conscious of her charm and beauty, her successful marriage to a great soldier, and the tiny Empress trudging beside her was forgotten. The triumphs of this moment repaid Antonina for the years of inconvenience she had suffered in far-off Italy.

"Belisarius isn't the only one who'll receive special gifts tomorrow," the Empress said. "When he goes to the combined meeting of the State and War Councils in the morning, come to me at my own court, so I may give you a suitable reward."

Although Antonina had been shrewd in her assessment of the political situation at home, reality exceeded her expectations. Belisarius, with her beside him, enjoyed even greater strength than she had imagined, and it was plain that the Emperor and Empress wanted to placate him and were afraid of her. Perhaps, by taking advantage of the public enthusiasm, Belisarius should press his attack, and

Justinian would be unable to resist his demand that he be designated heir to the throne of the Caesars.

"I want no favors or honors I don't deserve," Antonina said, her manner becomingly modest. "Belisarius is a great conqueror, but I've done nothing extraordinary."

"Oh, I disagree," Theodora said, her smile gentle. "I insist that you be given your due."

❁ ❁ ❁

The Emperor and Empress spent the better part of the night bickering, and both were tired, ill-humored, and hollow-eyed by morning. But on this, of all days, neither could afford the luxury of rest, and when Justinian went off to join Belisarius at a meeting with his senior officials, the exhausted but confident Theodora dressed in her robes of state for an audience with Antonina in her seraglio audience chamber.

The guest of honor arrived and was conducted into an empty throne room, but the festivities began as soon as she was shown to a place at the foot of the dais. The Empress' ladies filed in through doors on both sides, the young, single girls marching at the head of the procession, the higher-ranking matrons following. Each took her designated place, the doors were closed, and female guards in uniform blew a fanfare on their trumpets.

The curtains at the rear of the throne parted, and Theodora entered, her triple crown on her head, her slender body almost completely concealed beneath a gown of gem-encrusted purple silk.

As she seated herself on her throne, the members of her court prostrated themselves, all of them facing her. This gesture of total self-abasement was new since Antonina had last visited the court, and she hesitated, her dignity and self-importance warring with the knowledge that she would be expected to obey the rules.

Theodora intervened, however, holding out a hand. "Join me here, old friend," she said.

Antonina mounted the dais and stood at the Empress' right, certain now that nothing could prevent the appointment of Belisarius as the Emperor-designate.

John of Cappadocia's wife pounded the floor three times with the base of a golden staff, and the whispered conversations in the hall ceased abruptly.

"We have convened our court in formal session," Theodora said in the high soprano she used on such occasions, "to pay special honor to a woman who has sat on the throne of Hannibal in Carthage and that of the Empress Livia in old Rome."

Antonina quickly glanced at her, but saw that her expression was bland.

"It is our pleasure, before her warrior husband receives his just rewards later today, to present her with a gift symbolic of the unique regard in which we hold her." Theodora became remote as she added, "Let all who are present remember this occasion and profit by the lessons it teaches."

The trumpeters blew another fanfare, longer than the first, and the double doors at the rear of the audience chamber opened. Several sturdy slave girls half-pushed, half-carried an opened lacquer screen that stood about seven feet high, and halted in the center of the room.

The screen was whisked away, revealing the presence of an exceptionally rugged and virile young man in a very short tunic of white silk, with golden curls falling almost to his shoulders. Thin chains of gold were attached to his wrists and ankles, but the bonds were merely symbolic, and he could have broken them with ease had he wished. Smiling with boyish delight, he bowed deeply to the Empress, then to Antonina.

The ladies gasped, some of them pleased and some shocked, and then all of them turned to see the reaction of the guest of honor.

Antonina, looking as though she might faint, stared in horror at the young man.

At a signal from the Empress, John of Cappadocia's wife pounded on the floor again with the golden staff, and the ladies of the court filed out. It was so quiet in the audience chamber that there was no sound but the patter of their sandals and the quiet rustle of their silken gowns.

"Perhaps," Theodora said pleasantly to the young man, "you prefer to wait elsewhere."

He bowed and took his leave, surrounded by the slave women who formed his unusual bodyguard.

"Theodosius," the Empress said conversationally, "is one of the most handsome, charming young men I've ever met."

Antonina tried to reply, but almost strangled.

"I'm told he fought with great courage against both the Vandals and Goths when he served as Belisarius' aide-de-camp. Before you had him made the head of your personal bodyguard."

"I was so careful," Antonina muttered. "I could have sworn no one knew."

The Empress pretended she had not heard. "He's grateful to you, naturally. His family is poor, and he appreciated your gifts. A young officer doesn't earn very substantial wages."

The crushed Antonina didn't know what to reply.

"I have no intention of keeping him a prisoner or punishing him," Theodora said. "Our prisons would be overflowing if we sentenced every soldier who has had an affair with a married woman. Besides, it wasn't his fault, you know. The relationship made him uncomfortable from the start, but there was no way he could escape from a situation that no young man in his position could control."

"What—do you—intend to do with him?"

"I've promised him he needn't go back to you, which relieves him. He'll be given an honorable assignment, not in Constantinople, where his presence might be an embarrassment, but sufficiently near so he can be summoned to tell his story. In the unlikely event that it should become necessary."

After another long silence color rose in Antonina's face. "Now I can put all the pieces together. He disappeared from Rome the same morning that Narses vanished. Of course. Theodosius was abducted and brought back here. You found some way to force him to talk—"

"You're quite wrong," the Empress said honestly. "I was prepared to use force, but it wasn't necessary. He was actually eager to tell me the whole story. I'd say he had been troubled by an uneasy conscience for a long time, and was purging it. I can't blame him."

"Have you been so pure and noble?"

"Since the day I moved into Justinian's house," Theodora said, "I haven't as much as looked at another man. I could claim I've never been tempted, but women as experienced as you and I know that's absurd. I simply knew an affair wouldn't be worth the problems I'd cause if I were discovered."

Antonina's rage was as great as her mortification. "You had no right to interfere in my life!'

"As I was saying, I've always remembered Julius Caesar's motto. The wife of Rome's ruler must be above suspicion."

The true significance of the maneuver dawned on Antonina, who clutched her bare throat.

"Would you like to sit for a few minutes?" Theodora stood and with seeming sympathy offered the other woman her throne.

The irony was not lost on Antonina, who refused with a curt gesture.

The Empress sat again, adjusting her cushions of purple silk. "There are some men who simply don't care what their wives do, but Belisarius believes in all the old-fashioned virtues, just as Justinian does. I'm sure you'll find it comforting, after your perspectives have been restored, to realize that the most powerful men in the Empire have rejected licentiousness. By helping them, we'll preserve the standards of monogamy that set civilized people apart from barbarians."

"Stop mocking me, Theodora. You and I have known each other too long."

"Indeed we have, and it's because of our old friendship that I brought Theodosius to you instead of telling the story to Belisarius."

Antonina shuddered, knowing her husband would not hesitate to run her through with his sword if he discovered she had been unfaithful to him.

"Rely on me," Theodora said. "I'll never tell your secret."

"What about all those women who were here?"

"You'd be astonished how many private intrigues they know, and don't mention. We're loyal to each other, all of us."

"You made it your business to spy on me. You and that filthy Narses connived—"

"You're upset, of course," Theodora interrupted, her voice soothing. "Don't say things you'll regret."

Antonina bit her lower lip, aware of her impotence.

"Do you remember the old Syrian woman who owned that little brothel on one of the lanes behind the Mesé many years ago?"

"Vaguely."

"I've never forgotten her," the Empress said. "She never let a day pass without telling us, 'Once a harlot, always a harlot.' You might say she goaded me into leading a different sort of life. I wouldn't be surprised if you'll feel as I do after you've recovered from what must be an unpleasant shock."

The humiliated Antonina blinked back the tears that filled her eyes.

The Empress glanced out of the window at the sun,

which stood almost directly overhead. "It's growing late, isn't it? I mustn't keep you here too long, my dear, because I know you'll want to change for the ceremonies this afternoon. And I hope you'll let me present you with a gold and white gown that will be very attractive on you. When you've seen it, I'm sure you'll agree it does much more for you—than lilac."

🏵 🏵 🏵

The citizens of Constantinople lined the streets to roar with approval as Belisarius, his wife beside him, drove his own chariot to the Hippodrome. There a huge throng gave him a frenzied welcome, and the applause continued unabated as a military parade was staged in his honor. Standing erect on the platform of his chariot, he returned the salute of each unit, and his bearing was so modest, so dignified, that even the magisters loyal to the Emperor muttered to one another that it might be best for the nation if he were named the heir to the throne.

A glum Justinian watched in unmoving silence from the Imperial box, saying nothing to the quiet Theodora beside him. He could not quarrel with her in public, but indicated his disapproval of the advice she had given him by ignoring her, and even when his turn came to participate in the ceremonies, he acted as though she were not present.

Antonina, lovely in her gown of gold and white, was escorted to a place in the Imperial box, and then Belisarius, bare-headed, slowly walked across the grass of the Hippodrome to kneel before the Emperor.

A chamberlain presented Justinian with a double laurel wreath of pure gold, and the Emperor placed it on the head of his victorious general.

Pandemonium broke loose.

After it seemed as though the people would shout all

day, Justinian raised a hand for silence. "It is our joy," he said, looking far from pleased, "to present our beloved Belisarius with a title he has earned. Henceforth let him be known as Consul-for-Life."

The crowd was ecstatic, somewhat hysterical.

Justinian's expression indicated his conviction that he had sealed his own doom.

According to custom the recipients of high Imperial awards accepted their honors in silence, a practice adopted by wise emperors who had wanted to prevent potential successors from haranguing the people. Belisarius indicated, however, that he wanted to reply, and lifted both arms in repeated gestures before the admiring throng became quiet.

The general expressed his gratitude to the Emperor, praised the veterans who had served with him in the field, and acknowledged the help given him by the heads of every government department.

Justinian became even more depressed.

Belisarius did not take his seat to watch the chariot races being given in his honor, but cut off a new round of applause in order to continue his brief address. "Caesar Augustus," he said, "in the presence of your subjects I pledge myself to support you in all of your endeavors. And should I survive you, at some distant time in the years ahead, I offer the same pledge to the next Emperor. I seek no higher rank for myself than that which you have given me, and were the purple offered me, even by you, I would be obliged to refuse it. Now, and until the day I die, I want only the opportunity to be of help to you and your heirs."

His renunciation astonished the crowd, and the government officials looked at each other in wonder.

No one was more surprised than Justinian; Belisarius' unequivocal refusal to accept a designation as the Imperial successor was as unexpected as it was dramatic.

Antonina, pale and shaken, stared straight ahead, her eyes glazed.

Only Theodora remained composed, a small, tight smile playing at the corners of her mouth.

❁ ❁ ❁

"I know you were responsible," Justinian said, "but I can't understand how you managed. Belisarius had so much to lose and very little, at best, to gain. Even if he changes his mind someday, the people would be very reluctant to support any claim to the throne he might make."

"Send for your cousin's sons," Theodora said, "and begin their training. Nothing stands in your way now."

He nodded, but continued to stare at her. "How did you accomplish it? I have some idea of the methods you use, but Belisarius' record is pure. Some of the most able men in the security police have been keeping watch on him for years, and not once have they found him doing anything that could be used against him."

"I agree," Theodora said, "that Belisarius is one of the very few in the whole Empire who leads a blameless life."

He realized she had no intention of enlightening him. "You never fail to astonish me."

"I've kept my word," she said, "and I hope that in the future you'll find it easier to accept my promises."

"I'm positive," Justinian said emphatically, "that I'll never doubt you again."

❁ ❁ ❁

Narses won a series of spectacular victories, his Greek fire dislodging the barbarians from their garrison strongholds and sending them in terrified, headlong flight across the Alps. The word spread quickly that the Imperial army had acquired a new weapon that rendered the defenders of a fort helpless, and Narses took advantage of the momentum he had gained by sending an expedition into Spain.

There the Goths did not wait for a demonstration of his legion's prowess, and evacuated more than forty towns they had occupied for centuries in the former Roman province. It seldom proved necessary for the Imperial troops to use Greek fire; their mere possession of the frightful weapon was enough, and Narses continued to prove himself a clever student of human nature. He sent still another expedition across the Adriatic Sea from Italy into Dalmatia, long ruled by the savage Lombards, and they, too, retreated in haste, refusing to do battle.

Narses acquired a reputation as a conqueror, but the citizens of Constantinople, even while hailing his feats, were somewhat confused. The capital had known him as an efficient but effeminate administrator, and no one would have dreamed of casting him in the role of a warrior. Nevertheless, his achievements spoke for themselves, they were forced to give him his due, and no voices were raised in protest when he was made Imperial viceroy for the West.

One direct result of his endeavors was the diminution of Belisarius' stature. The great general, who was living in quiet retirement, had been cheered whenever he had emerged from his palace beyond the Wall of Constantine to drive his chariot through the streets of the city. Now, however, people questioned his victories. If Narses could defeat the Goths, perhaps the prowess of Belisarius had been exaggerated, and the real credit belonged to the army itself.

Ambitious young generals and colonels offered no explanations that would have clarified the situation for the public, and the Imperial palace was silent, too. Justinian and Theodora received Belisarius courteously whenever he called, but neither of them sought his advice or help in affairs of state. The Consul-for-Life belonged to the Empire's past, not its present.

The stories that veteran soldiers returning from Italy told in the Mesé did nothing to improve Constantinople's opinion of either Narses or Belisarius. It was common knowledge in the West, these troops whispered to their friends, that the Imperial viceroy found relaxation from his responsibilities by dressing as a woman and allowing himself to be abused and degraded by a corps of tall, physically powerful serving women. In fact, subordinates who wanted to gain favor with him sometimes made him gifts of the burliest, strongest barbarian peasant girls for sale in the slave markets.

Therefore, Constantinople reasoned, if Narses was slightly demented, Belisarius could not be sane, either. Adoring crowds stopped gathering outside Belisarius' palace, and eventually he was ignored by the fickle public.

Meanwhile Justinian's young relatives from Macedonia were being subjected to rigorous courses of instruction and training. Theodora made herself the protectress of the most nimble-witted, and when he adopted the name of Justin, it was evident that the question of the Imperial succession had been settled. Neither the nobles nor the political parties offered candidates of their own, and the joint will of Justinian and Theodora prevailed in all things.

Construction work on the new Sancta Sophia was completed, and the Patriarch Anthimus, promoted to the position of Patriarch of Constantinople, officiated at a service of consecration and dedication. The influence of the Empress over the Eastern Church became apparent when a priest who had befriended her in her youth, Severus, was made Patriarch of Antioch. Vigilius, Pope of the Western Church and Bishop of Rome, was also her friend, and the wits who gathered at the splendid new inns and taverns on the Mesé joked that the uncrowned head of the Christian Church was the Empress.

Those who expressed such sentiments, even in jest, were careful to speak softly, however. Never had Theodora's espionage network been more effective, nor Justinian's security police more efficient. It was impossible to determine whether the Empire approved or disliked Imperial policies, since no one discussed the throne or its proclamations. Even ordinary citizens were reluctant to discuss affairs of state at home, since no one knew whether his wife or daughters might be in the secret employ of the Empress.

There was little that critics could condemn, to be sure. Large portions of the ancient Empire had been recovered at relatively small cost, and it seemed inevitable that when fresh legions were sent into the field, they would prevail against any force of barbarians. Greek fire made Justinian almost omnipotent, and only his old foes, the Persians, kept a large standing army on the frontier and refused to be impressed by a weapon that filled lesser people with dread.

Constantinople had become the most dazzling, beautiful city on earth and was a symbol of the prosperity that was greater than any nation in history had enjoyed. Granaries were overflowing, pirates had been driven from the seas by the Imperial navy, and trade flourished. Even Peter Barsymes found it possible to keep the treasury vaults filled with gold by maintaining the policies inaugurated by John of Cappadocia, his gaunt predecessor, who continued to beg for his daily bread in the streets of Alexandria.

Then, suddenly, a series of unexpected crises shook the Empire to its foundations. The first of them directly involved Justinian and Theodora, and those who knew the close relationship of the Emperor and Empress could not believe what they saw and heard.

ELEVEN

❦ ❦ ❦

Justinian was uncommunicative early in the morning, but after a sound sleep, was sometimes inclined to be somewhat more voluble. He sat up in bed, drank some of the hot, sweetened barley water that a serving maid had deposited beside him, and swinging his legs to the floor, groped for his slippers of Bulgar lynx fur. "Pope Vigilius is a remarkable man," he said, scratching an ankle.

Theodora thought she was dreaming, realized her husband had addressed her, and tentatively opened her eyes.

"I said—"

"Yes, my dear," she muttered. "I heard you."

"What's more, he's an exceptionally able theologian." The Emperor took another sip of his barley water.

His disappearance behind the screen at the far end of their bedchamber made it unnecessary for Theodora to reply, which was fortunate. She was still too sleepy for coherent thought, but knew Justinian was spouting nonsense. She had been responsible for Vigilius' elevation to the Papacy of the West, sponsoring him because she knew him to be malleable. On two occasions he had appointed bishops in response to her hints, and she could not picture him as an inspired clergyman. Sighing, she rang the bell that stood on her bedside table.

A quarter of an hour later, while Justinian consumed grilled fish, breast of peahen, and honey cakes, she sipped a chalice of the diluted mead he now accepted as a harmless potion. Her mind clearing, Theodora vigorously brushed her hair and decided she was sufficiently awake to reopen the subject. "You mentioned Pope Vigilius a little while ago."

Justinian concentrated on the immediate task of boning his fish. "Did I? I must have been thinking aloud."

His caution aroused her curiosity. "I'd like your opinion of him."

"Vigilius," he said carefully, "doesn't rank with Bishop Augustine of Hippo, of course. Few clerics do. But I doubt if anyone alive today has a better grasp of theological concepts. In the finest old Greek sense of the word, he's a philosopher."

Knowing her husband, she realized that the Pope had agreed with him on a subject he considered important. But her manner remained deceptively ingenuous, and she smiled blandly. "I suppose he's grown in stature since he became Pope. He confers so frequently with saintly bishops that his mind has expanded, perhaps. I've seen the same sort of thing happen to laymen who have been appointed to high positions. They grow intellectually."

"The Pope has the best mind and the keenest grasp of theological questions in Christendom," he said severely.

He sounded so defensive that Theodora became uneasy. But, knowing he had become aroused, she felt no need to reply. Even if she failed to encourage him, he would tell her everything on his mind.

"We've been corresponding, you know."

"That's natural." She saw no reason to tell him that Narses sent her word every time the Pope wrote the Emperor a letter.

"Vigilius," Justinian said, "feels precisely as I do, that the Monophysites of the East are heretics."

"You go too far."

"The definition is the Pope's, not mine."

"The patriarchs would dispute the point."

"Anthimus and Severus will change their tune." He sounded grim.

"They're men of conviction." Concealing her nervousness, she drained her chalice and poured herself more mead.

"I've been very patient," Justinian said, "because more pressing matters have occupied my attention. But now that the world I've envisioned is taking shape, I'm at last ready to reform the Church. Even the patriarchs are my subjects, remember, and must obey me in all things."

"A priest," Theodora said firmly, "believes that only God guides his conscience."

"The priests in the Empire will learn otherwise. Vigilius and I have been discussing the advisability of summoning the ecumenical council I've kept postponing."

"Don't call the meeting!" she exclaimed, the words slipping out before she could halt herself.

"Our people obey one set of laws. They're taxed everywhere on the same scale. Men from fifty provinces serve together under a single banner, my banner. We're united in all things but our faith, and my work won't be done until we have one theology, one faith."

"I was afraid this was what you meant. You've seldom mentioned the subject in the past few years—"

"I've thought about it. Incessantly!"

"—but I hope you've remembered something I told you long ago. You and I can force our subjects to prostrate themselves before us. They'll pay taxes, obey our laws, and when you send them to war, they'll give their lives for us. But no earthly ruler can force them to change their beliefs about God."

"We hold different opinions." He was becoming irritated and left his fish untouched.

Theodora deliberately waited until he finished his breakfast before speaking again. "I don't know what you believed when you were a boy, before you came to Constantinople."

"Not much of anything. I was almost a pagan."

"Then you came under the influence of the Western priests—"

"I read Augustine of Hippo, and he alone influenced me."

"In my youth, as you know," she said slowly, "I traveled to many places. Everywhere I found people willing to bow to the whims of governors and amenable to the edicts of the Emperor. But their faith—the faith of every sect—remained unalterable."

"The bishops and patriarchs will gather here for a grand council. I'll give them a directive, and they'll draw up new articles of faith which will be obeyed by every one of my subjects. I demand the complete and ultimate unity of all my people."

Clutching her dressing gown, Theodora went to him. "You've studied the works of every great historian, and you know the past of every nation, every people. Your education is far greater than mine, Justinian, and you'd have every right to call me an ignoramus. But there are some things I know, and I can't forget the lessons of the past."

She was so much in earnest that he saw no harm in humoring her. "I'm listening."

"Barbarians are sometimes willing to exchange one set of gods for another. In fact, we've occasionally been amused by stories we've heard from the provinces about them. But those who realize there is only one God are a different breed. It's our faith, I think, that makes us civilized."

"I intend to strengthen that faith, and with it our civilization."

"The Jews," she persisted, "were the first to realize there is only one God, weren't they?"

"Yes, of course." Papers awaited his signature in his workroom, visitors would arrive soon for conferences, and he was anxious to leave.

"The Egyptians tried to force them to change, and so did many others—the Assyrians, the Babylonians—I can't remember all of them. Even the Romans tried in the early days of the Empire, and when they failed, they banned the Jews from Jerusalem. That was five hundred years ago, but the Jews' faith in God remains unshaken. Then it was the turn of the Christians to suffer. The first Emperors persecuted them without mercy, but Christianity gained converts everywhere, even in Rome, even in the palace of the Emperors!"

"I have no intention of persecuting the Jews," Justinian said, losing patience, "and I don't intend to crucify fellow Christians. I merely plan to reconcile the beliefs of the West and East."

"You want to force the East to accept the theology of the West, and you've already told me that those who won't embrace your ideas—which Pope Vigilius will support— are heretics! Has it occurred to you that I accept the Eastern faith, that I'm a heretic?"

"Nonsense! You'll believe whatever your patriarchs and priests tell you."

His offhand dismissal of her convictions infuriated her. "I'm a Monophysite, and nothing will change me as long as I live. No matter how many declarations are signed by the leaders of the Church, I won't give up what I know to be true, and if that makes me a heretic, you'll have to crucify me in the Hippodrome."

Justinian couldn't understand why she insisted on injecting a personal element into every discussion, and he could see no reason for her to become so emotional. "This is a matter for the clergy to study," he said, trying to return the matter to its appropriate level. "It doesn't concern laymen, and I give you my word that no private citizen will be made to suffer because of his religious beliefs. Once the clergy are united, the problem will take care of itself. Future generations will accept the declarations published by the ecumenical council."

"One of your strengths is your genius for simplification, but the individual's faith in God is already simple. It's fundamental to his being, so basic that no one can tamper with it or change it. Can't you see what I'm trying to tell you, Justinian? If you insist on pushing this scheme, you'll ruin everything that has been achieved during your reign!"

He saw only that it was useless to reason with her. "I insist," he said, standing and moving to the door, "that my subjects obey me."

Theodora had the final word. "When we pray, we say, '*Thy* will be done.'"

❦ ❦ ❦

The Patriarch Anthimus was a man of imposing size who dwarfed even the giants, descended from the ancient Hittites, who inhabited the Imperial hinterland of Asia Minor. He had a massive head, piercing eyes, and a full, luxurious beard that gave him great distinction. And he was so tall that one of the Western bishops attributed his rise in the Church hierarchy to his size. "Whenever a vacancy occurred," the bishop declared, "Anthimus was promoted. Even an inferior theologian is certain to be noticed when he stands a full head above everyone else."

Anthimus knew the bishops had little respect for him as a Churchman, but recognized the reasons for their lack of regard. Long before he had become the Patriarch of Constantinople he had assumed the leadership of the clergymen who accepted the Eastern rites, and he had further infuriated two Western popes and at least a score of bishops by conducting religious services in Greek rather than Latin. "Rome," he said, "seems unable to realize that virtually all of the New Testament was written in Greek. I prefer the original to a poor translation."

He made still more enemies by refusing to visit Pope Vigilius in liberated Rome. "I was a patriarch," he announced, "before Vigilius was made a bishop. I don't try to impose my view on him, but if he feels it would be helpful to discuss matters of mutual interest, let him come to me."

Justinian, warned by Theodora and long familiar with the patriarch's fiercely independent spirit, knew it would not be easy to persuade him to alter any of his convictions. But the Emperor could not proceed with his ambitious plan to unify the two branches of the Church until he won the compliance of the primate of the East. Somewhat apprehensive but determined to let nothing stand in his way, he summoned Anthimus to his sanctum for a talk that would settle the issue.

The patriarch appeared more at ease than the Emperor, and after refusing honey-sweetened figs and other delicacies, saw no reason to engage in polite and unnecessary small talk. "I've read the documents you sent me, Augustus," he said. "Your concepts of the Godhead and the divinity of Christ are interesting."

"What's your reaction to them, Patriarch?" Justinian could be blunt, too.

"Your grasp of abstract theology is surprising. I can't imagine how someone as busy as you has found the time for so much study, but you certainly prove that you know more than any other layman. If I hadn't known you'd written it, I'd have sworn that your position had been prepared by a scholar who has spent his whole life in a seminary."

Justinian was pleased.

"In fact, when I showed the treatise to the Patriarch Severus—without telling him who had written it—he assumed it had been prepared by a bishop."

The first warning note had been sounded, and the Emperor became defensive. "Or a patriarch?" he suggested.

Anthimus smiled and stroked his beard. "Never. The orientation of the treatise is exclusively Western. None of my priests believe a word of what you said."

Justinian took a deep breath. "You may have heard from the Empress that I intend to call an ecumenical council. Since I want to attend the meetings myself, we'll convene at the Sancta Sophia here rather than make the long journey to St. Peter's in Rome. I don't have time to leave Constantinople for a long stay abroad."

"I'll be delighted to welcome Vigilius and his bishops at the Sancta Sophia." Anthimus knew precisely what the Emperor had in mind, but remained urbane.

"I'm convinced that the unification of the Church will be the greatest achievement of my reign."

"We already regard the Western clergy as our brothers, and I hope they feel the same way toward us."

"I'm not speaking of a clerical spirit of brotherhood. I refer to theological unity."

"It's unfortunate that we drifted apart during the time Rome was held in bondage by barbarians. The West would have shared our intellectual growth had the popes and bishops been free."

"No theologian stands in a class with Augustine of Hippo, but he wasn't influenced by Rome. He developed his own ideas."

"Augustine had an extraordinary mind," the unyielding patriarch said, "and it wouldn't surprise me in the least if he's remembered for thousands of years as a philosopher. But you must remember he was educated in the Roman tradition—and then actually lived in Rome itself. So it becomes obvious that his ideas grew out of the theology of the West."

"I agree with everything he says. That is," Justinian added, believing it diplomatic to display modesty in dealing with a man who thought of himself as an expert in his exacting vocation, "everything I understand. I'm not sure whether there's an element of mysticism in his philosophy. Let's just say he becomes too pure in his thinking for an earth-bound layman to absorb some of his more esoteric concepts."

Again Anthimus smiled, but made no reply.

"But I digress, as I always do when I discuss theology and theologians. My primary interest, as Emperor, is the healing of the breach that separates East and West."

"It wouldn't surprise me if the bishops gradually move toward our theology," Anthimus said. "Not in your lifetime and mine, probably, but over a long period, a little at a time."

"I have specific goals, and I intend to accomplish them while I'm still on the throne." Justinian showed that he, too, could be firm. "What's more, it would be a disaster if the ideas of the East prevailed."

"That's a matter of opinion, isn't it? Obviously, I think it would be a disaster if the West won."

"The West must win because the theology of the bishops is right."

"We're trying to define absolutes in dealing with the Infinite, Augustus." Anthimus fingered the gold icon suspended on a chain from his neck, and spoke slowly, with great care. "I'm willing to admit that man can become inspired. I readily grant that the Holy Spirit can and does grant us illumination. But I find it highly unlikely that the Holy Spirit will dictate two different sets of theological concepts to two completely different groups of clergymen. One or the other must be mistaken."

"Yes, that's very clear." Justinian's eyes became bleak.

"And it's even more unlikely that a layman supporting one side—it doesn't matter which—would be the primary object of the Holy Spirit's inspiration."

"In this instance, that's precisely what has happened."

It would have been indiscreet for the patriarch to voice his incredulity, but his expression said what he could not put into words.

"I'm sure the Empress also told you I insist the hierarchy of the Eastern Church accept the theology I've summarized. It will be the task of the ecumenical council to fill in the details that I've merely outlined."

"I assume that Pope Vigilius is agreeable?"

"Naturally."

"I'd feel as he does if our positions were reversed. By accepting his theology, I'd also be admitting, tacitly, that he's my superior."

"I'm not demanding that the Eastern Hierarchy admit the primacy of the Western Pope."

"No, that would come within a generation, at the most, if we swallowed the Western views."

"I can't look that far into the future," Justinian said. "My principal concern is achieving theological unity."

"I admire your motives, Augustus."

"Then you accept my request?"

"But I can't admire your thinking on questions that have puzzled Church scholars for several centuries. The interpretation of Scriptures is very difficult."

"Rather than making a request, Patriarch, I'm giving you a command."

"I've long been fascinated by the relationship of the Church and the throne," Anthimus said quietly. "As a man, I'm your subject, and so is Vigilius. He was elected Pope by his bishops, but only after it became known that the Empress favored him. I was made a patriarch by members of the patriarchate, but only after the Emperor Justin indicated he wanted my elevation. My move here from Antioch was more or less automatic when this see became vacant, since I held the second highest place in the East. But it's clear enough that the Crown does exert an influence in Church affairs."

"You clergymen sometimes like to think you're a breed apart, but you're as responsible to the Crown as any other government officials."

"You've cut through to the heart of the matter, Augustus," the patriarch said. "Appointments to posts of prominence in the Church are sometimes made because the palace has used pressure. And bishops—patriarchs, too—wouldn't be human if they forgot their debt. They try, when they can, to return the favor. But a bishop or patriarch, once he takes office, isn't under Imperial jurisdiction in ecclesiastical affairs. He's responsible only to God."

"That's a novel doctrine," Justinian said.

"We become Christ's apostles, regardless of whether we belong to the Church of the East or that of the West. None of us can serve two masters. We've chosen to work for the glory of God, and in the event there's a conflict, we must repudiate all others."

"You would deliberately disobey me?"

"If you directed me to flout God's will, yes."

"God's will—as interpreted by you."

"As interpreted by an apostle of Christ, speaking in His name, with His authority. Not even you, Augustus, claim to be more powerful than God."

"No, but I don't pretend to be His vicar, either."

"We don't challenge your authority, which is secular. But we deny the right of any man, general or governor or even Emperor, to stand between us and God. I speak not only on behalf of the patriarchs, but of the Western bishops. I haven't seen Pope Vigilius in many years and have never corresponded with him. But I'm positive he feels as I do."

"He accepts my theology!"

"Because he finds it similar to his own, and because the Western Church, after being stifled for so long by pagans, needs help from the Crown to become strong again."

"You've given me answers in everything, Patriarch, except on the one subject that's vital to me. Will you support my cause?"

"I must support God."

"I quarrel with stubborn men, not with our Maker," Justinian said. "I want no battle with the Eastern clergy, and I certainly don't intend to make martyrs of you. But if you oppose me, you'll force me to retaliate."

"We read in the Epistle of James, 'Let every man be swift to hear, slow to speak, slow to wrath: for the wrath of man worketh not the righteousness of God.' He also tells us, 'Be ye doers of the word.' He means the word of God, Augustus. Think about these things before you act unwisely, before you defile His tabernacle." The patriarch stood, raised his hand over the Emperor's head in silent blessing, and took his leave.

When a clergyman was losing a battle, Justinian thought, he invariably fell back on a seemingly impregnable line of defense, the special relationship with God that he believed he enjoyed. The patriarch had appeared recalcitrant, but had inadvertently revealed the weakness of his position by quoting Scriptures. There was no power on earth strong enough to oppose the throne, and Justinian felt certain that Anthimus would capitulate, now that he had satisfied his conscience by taking a defiant stand.

❀ ❀ ❀

Ordinarily Theodora took Communion in one of the small churches located in the Imperial compound, going to the new Sancta Sophia only for the most important state functions. She loved the great edifice and knew it was the most impressively beautiful church in Christendom, but the security police and Imperial household guard were reluctant to permit her to attend services there until they had made thorough advance preparations. When they knew she intended to worship there they carefully screened the crowds entering the Sancta Sophia, turning aside the questionable and placing the disreputable under temporary arrest. Several pews were blocked off, with unobtrusively dressed security police corps members surrounding the section and placing themselves at strategic locations throughout the church.

Then the Imperial guard insisted on supplying the Empress with an escort, as it did whenever she left the palace grounds, and thirty or forty soldiers sworn to protect her with their lives formed a tight cordon around her, making it difficult for her to see or be seen.

On the Sunday following the confrontation of Justinian and Anthimus she created consternation at the headquarters of the security police and the office of the Imperial guard command by announcing to them that she planned to attend services at Sancta Sophia and would go there within a quarter of an hour. Since the church was already filling, it was impossible to set aside a block of seats for her party, so, at her suggestion, a throne was hastily set up for her in the nave, between the altar and the front pews. Troops of the guard stood below her on her dais, giving her an unobstructed view of the congregation and allowing the thousands of Constantinople's citizens who were present to see her.

Noblewomen who had come to know her over the years were convinced she had not come to the church on a sudden whim. She was wearing her triple crown of pearls and emeralds, gems blazed at her throat and on her fingers, and she was attired in a long robe of Imperial purple, a gown she saved for the most important state affairs.

Something in the atmosphere added to the tension, although it could not be defined. The Patriarch Severus, who was visiting the city, was present to assist the Patriarch Anthimus, and scores of priests were sitting in a special section set aside for them. Those who dealt with the Church realized that Anthimus' entire staff was on hand.

The choir had been augmented, too, and more than three hundred voices were raised in a hymn of praise to God as the patriarchs, followed by their deacons, came down the center aisle and took their places.

It was the custom of those conducting religious services in the Sancta Sophia to ignore the presence of royalty, but Anthimus bowed deeply to the Empress, and she surprised the congregation by rising from her throne and curtsying, an unprecedented gesture which was a mark of respect to both the office and the man.

Tension continued to rise, although there were few in the congregation who knew of Anthimus' meeting with the Emperor. But the service followed the usual routines until Anthimus arose from his own throne to deliver the sermon.

"No man can serve two masters," he said, quoting the lines from the Book of Matthew that he had used in his argument with the Emperor. "Ye cannot serve God and Mammon."

Noblemen, university lecturers, and others who realized the significance of the quotation knew he was challenging Justinian.

The patriarch wanted to make certain that even the most ignorant townsman and illiterate farmer in the church were aware of the struggle, and quoted Matthew again. "Render therefore unto Caesar the things which are Caesar's, and unto God the things that are God's."

Everyone present knew he was throwing down the gage of battle, and there was undercurrent of excited comment.

Theodora was neither surprised nor upset, but smiled steadily at the patriarch, making it clear to the congregation that she approved of the position he was taking. Her unexpected presence at the Sancta Sophia was no longer a mystery, and even those who knew that she and Justinian held identical public views in all matters realized there was some sort of rift in the Imperial household.

Anthimus quickly sketched his own dispute with the Emperor, and tried to be fair to his opponent as he outlined the two opposing theological views. "I do not say that I am right, that the Augustus and the bishops of the West are wrong," he added. "I say only that my views on solemn ecclesiastical questions have been formed after a lifetime of study and prayer.

"I cannot and will not change those convictions in response to an Imperial command. Nor can I become a hypocrite and bend my knee in public for the sake of surface harmony while privately continuing to harbor my own views.

"The questions involved in this dispute are of importance to the theologians of both East and West. But of even greater importance to all Christians—to all men in the Empire, Christians, Jews, and pagans—is the right of every man to worship God, or to refrain from such worship, according to the dictates of his own conscience.

"I, as a priest and as an individual, can accept the dictates of God alone in matters pertaining to my faith in Him."

The congregation was shocked by the vigor of his refusal to obey the Emperor, as well as by the extraordinary means he was using to make his position clear. No one could remember when any man had dared to quarrel in public with an Emperor or deny the validity of an Imperial order.

Theodora again made it plain that she supported the patriarch. When he descended from the altar after completing his sermon, he went to her, apparently by prearrangement, and she knelt before him to receive his blessing.

The Empress knew without looking that several officials

of the security police had slipped away to give Justinian a full report of all that had taken place.

The service continued to its end, but of all the thousands in the church, only Theodora, Anthimus, and Severus were tranquil. Others were unable to sit quietly or refrain from exchanging excited, whispered speculation.

When the choir sang a hymn of benediction at the conclusion of the service, a company of uniformed security police appeared at the rear of the Sancta Sophia, and it seemed likely that Anthimus and Severus would be placed under arrest when they led the recessional from the church.

But there appeared to be a quiet commotion of some sort behind the altar. No one was certain what was happening, although some who were present later claimed that they saw members of the Empress' household force milling around.

In any event, as the last strains of music died away, the troops guarding Theodora formed a phalanx, and she left by a side door, going straight back to the Imperial compound.

There was no recessional, and the company of security police tried to push forward through the crowd. But the congregation, enjoying its own unusual role in the strange affair, choked the aisles, making it virtually impossible for the Emperor's men to reach the front of the church.

Had the citizens of Constantinople demonstrated such passive resistance in the square outside, or in any of the city's streets, heads would have been cracked and the security police would have taken scores into custody. But even they were afraid to resort to violence in the Sancta Sophia, where hundreds of scented candles were burning beneath an icon of pure gold. The crowds were not defiant or in any way openly disobedient. People merely seemed a trifle stupid, and when they tried to move out of the way, succeeded in making the snarl more complicated. Eventually the officers in command of the company managed to reach the altar, but only a few of the younger priests on the staff of the patriarchate still remained in their seats at one side of the church.

Anthimus and Severus were gone.

🏵 🏵 🏵

"You were in league with him!" Justinian shouted. "You planned the whole spectacle together!"

"No, you go too far," Theodora replied calmly. "I had no idea what Anthimus would say in his sermon, although I had a general notion he would defend his position."

"The mere fact that you were there proves—"

"It proves that my faith is that of the Eastern hierarchy. It proves I'm willing to let the whole Empire know where I stand in this affair. It also proves I meant what I said when you discussed the matter with me."

"I never expected my wife to become a traitor!"

"I'm the most loyal of your subjects, and stand with you in all things, the question of my faith in God excepted. I'm also your wife, Justinian, and I love you. Even though you're making a fool of yourself."

"You mocked me in public!"

"I took Communion at the Sancta Sophia. Was that mocking you? At least four thousand of your subjects— our subjects—were there. Did they mock you? The Patriarch of Constantinople gave me his blessing. Was it a mockery of you—or of God—or of anything in our realm or His—when I bowed my head and fell to my knees to accept the blessing of the primate of the Eastern Church?"

Justinian advanced toward her.

Theodora thought he intended to strike her.

He stopped short, raising his hands above his head. "I ought to know better than to argue with you. You have a fantastic ability to twist everything that's said, to change meanings, to make black into white!"

She was angry, too, but displayed a surface calm. "You wouldn't believe me when I told you that men won't change their faith just because you give them an order '

"And you made sure of it by supporting Anthimus in public," the Emperor said bitterly. "Where is he? The security police have searched everywhere, and both he and Severus have disappeared!"

"I'd be the last to interfere with the work of your security police."

"Every road out of Constantinople is being watched, and security police agents are searching every ship that leaves the harbor." Justinian looked at her, speaking slowly. "Severus isn't particularly distinguished in appearance, so it's possible—barely possible—that he might be able to leave in a disguise of some sort But he's less important to me than Anthimus, and I can imagine no way he could escape. Even if he shaved off his beard, which his pride wouldn't allow. He s taller than any lancer in the elite foot-soldier brigade, and a man of his size would be conspicuous if he tried to join a caravan or board a ship."

Theodora nodded absently, seemingly disinterested in the problem.

"So I assume he's decided to hide somewhere in the city."

"I'm sure there are many devout people in Constantinople who would give him refuge."

"In spite of their basic loyalty to the Crown?"

"I should think so. I'm sure there are thousands who have a greater faith in God than they have in the institution of the monarchy."

"And in spite of their fear of reprisals from the security police if they should be discovered?"

"Even if you haven't chosen to believe me," Theodora said, "surely your reading has taught you that man's love of God is stronger than fear of his fellowman."

"I suppose you realize," the Emperor said after a long silence, "that Anthimus' challenge spoils my plans. At the very least I'll have to postpone my ecumenical conference."

"Oh?" She contrived to look blank.

"It would be a waste of time to hold the meeting when the Patriarch of Constantinople has already made it plain to the whole world that he'll accept no changes in doctrine."

Her expression indicated that such matters were technical and therefore beyond her grasp.

"Of course I intend to depose him. Severus, too. And then I can—"

"I thought," Theodora interrupted, revealing she knew far more than she had shown, "that a patriarch could be deprived of his office only by a council of his fellow clergymen, and then only if they found he had broken his sacred vows."

"I'm going to round up every patriarch and abbot in the Empire," Justinian said grimly. "I'll bring them here, and they'll vote precisely as I tell them."

"I suppose there are some who are less courageous than Anthimus and Severus, so you might be able to frighten them into deposing the patriarchs. But no matter what charges you bring against them, there will be thousands of devout citizens who won't accept the vote of the council."

"I'm well aware of the stubborn blindness of misled laymen who are encouraged by the example of their Empress. I'll probably have to wait a very long time before I call the ecumenical conference of Western and Eastern clergymen. Thanks to you."

"I've made no secret of my position."

For the moment he chose to ignore her reply. "Unless, of course, I can capture Anthimus and Severus—and force them to accept my doctrine. And you needn't smile. The security police may be less subtle than your torturers, but they achieve results for me, and very quickly."

"Oh, they can be very effective, I know. Their methods may be crude, but they're effective."

"Then why are you being so smug?"

"Am I? Oh, dear." She managed to sound contrite.

Justinian rubbed his already bloodshot eyes. "I'll tell you why. You're convinced Anthimus and Severus won't be captured."

"I'd put it another way. I'd say I have confidence their faith will protect them."

"I believe you're hiding them in the seraglio," he said harshly.

She looked shocked.

"I could order the household guard to dispose of your own sentries and search the place."

"You could. But you'd have to place me under arrest. If you publicly indicate such a lack of trust in me, the whole Empire will conclude—and rightly—that our marriage is ended. So I'll take my place beside the defenders of my palace, and the household guard will be compelled to use force before I'll surrender. It will be quite a spectacle."

"You know I can't use force against you."

"The idea was yours, not mine."

"If I did, the Crown itself would be destroyed. Not even an Emperor can batter down the walls of his wife's private house and keep the respect of his people."

"I'm glad you realize it." Theodora's sudden tension eased somewhat.

"I was hoping," Justinian said, "that you'd offer to let the security police make a search of the seraglio."

"Wouldn't that be just as harmful? Wouldn't it be proof to our subjects that you and I have become enemies, that we can no longer go through even the formality of conducting joint audiences?"

"You've always been exceptionally clever," he said bitterly.

"I've always tried to help you because I love you. And

I work for your good, even when you yourself make it difficult for me."

"If I ordered the seraglio stormed," he said, "a civil war would break out everywhere in the Empire. There are thousands of men in the army and navy who belong to the Eastern Church, and they'd follow you. I'm not even sure how many of my generals and magisters would stand beside me. I do know that when Narses heard there was a rebellion being led by the Empress, he'd join your camp, and probably would make Pope Vigilius his prisoner. You have a hold over Narses stronger than his loyalty to me. And it wouldn't surprise me if there were others who'd join you in a civil war."

It occurred to Theodora that he had grown afraid of her, and she immediately realized that even if the problem of the missing clergymen should be solved, her marriage was in jeopardy. "I've never tried to win fealty to me," she said honestly, "but only to you."

"John of Cappadocia was in my camp, but you got rid of him. Belisarius was my general, but when he became a threat to the throne, you neutralized him, and now he's a harmless nonentity. Even Tribonian, who performs miracles in reforming the law, treads warily when he deals with you. I've been isolated."

There was a measure of truth in his charge, but Theodora was aghast. "I'm not competing with you!" she cried.

"Prove it to me. Hand Anthimus and Severus over to me." Justinian wasn't commanding now, and in his anxiety seemed to be begging for a favor.

She knew he had reduced the complex question to a test of her fidelity to him, but she could not accept his over-simplification without abandoning her principles and betraying the patriarch who had saved her life and sanity when she had been a destitute wanderer.

"If I could," she said, not admitting that she was sheltering either fugitive in the seraglio, "I'd gladly surrender them to you."

Justinian stared at her, his eyes became remote, and finally he turned away, leaving the room without speaking another word.

❧ ❧ ❧

It quickly became common knowledge in the Imperial compound, then in the city, and ultimately in the far reaches of the Empire beyond Constantinople that the Emperor and Empress were no longer living together. Justinian ate most of his meals in his work sanctum, Theodora dined with her ladies, and, of far greater importance, slept in the seraglio, too. She continued to attend meetings of the Council of State, where she and her husband maintained a dignified but remote relationship, and it was said by many in a position to know the couple's movements that at no time did they see each other in private.

It was also rumored, without confirmation, that the Patriarch Severus had escaped from Constantinople with the help of the Empress, and that the Patriarch Anthimus had become a permanent guest in the seraglio. If the latter allegation was true, it could not be proved; none of the women close to the Empress was willing to make an admission of the supposed fact.

The security police and the Empress' private espionage service became rivals, and gradually a sense of uneasiness spread through the Empire. If it was true that Justinian and Theodora were at odds, the entire nation would suffer.

The patriarchs and abbots of the Eastern Church met in the capital, and after hearing a brief address by the Emperor in a closed session, promptly deprived both Anthimus and Severus of their posts. But they stopped short of stripping either of his rank, and lacked the courage to elect new patriarchs for Constantinople and Antioch. The faithful in the East resented the obvious interference of the Emperor in Church affairs, and the security police reported that disaffection was growing.

It was reported, too, that Pope Vigilius, perhaps influenced by the Viceroy Narses, was strongly sympathetic to the deposed Eastern prelates. And according to a story that not even the most efficient of Justinian's agents could verify, Vigilius and Anthimus were conducting a private correspondence. All the Emperor himself knew was that the Pope appeared to lose interest in the doctrinal changes in theology that the Emperor himself had written.

Powerful and influential men came to Theodora and offered her their support, but to each she gave the same reply. She was the Emperor's most loyal subject, she declared, and they could serve her by devoting themselves to Justinian's cause. Magisters and generals were confused, but, given no choice, did as they had been bidden. The security police dutifully reported each of these incidents to the Emperor, and Justinian withdrew deeper. Life apparently offered him no pleasures or satisfactions, and he drove himself without mercy, working at least twenty hours out of each twenty-four, yet making himself inaccessible in his work sanctum.

Justinian's vanity was shattered by a report that his young cousin and heir, Justin, paid a long visit to Theodora at the seraglio. The security police, reluctant to question the youth, made a laconic report to the Emperor, preferring to let him deal as he saw fit with his probable successor. Convincing himself that his duty made an interrogation necessary, Justinian summoned the boy.

"The Augusta has been kind to me since I first came here from Macedonia," young Justin said. "So I offered her whatever help I might be able to give her."

"You seek to supplant me on the throne?" Justinian, sounding feverish, found it difficult to control his feelings.

The youth was astonished. "I hope I'm not that stupid, and I pray you'll live for many years. If you were to die today and I was forced to wear your mantle, Augustus, I'd fail. My education has scarcely started, and I'm not capable of ruling a province, much less the Empire."

Justinian's suspicions were not allayed. "If you aren't conspiring against me, why did you go to the Empress?"

"My country, which was your land, too, long ago, has been grieving ever since the patriarchs were deposed, and there has been talk among our hill people of setting up an independent state. I told the Augusta I was willing to make a journey there, if she thought it wise, so I could speak to our old neighbors and quiet their fears."

"And she urged you to go, no doubt."

"She insisted I stay here. She said no one, least of all you, would believe the purpose of my journey."

"Then you prefer to let a revolt develop in Macedonia?"

Justin had been warned of the Emperor's perversity, but nevertheless found it baffling. "There will be no revolt, Augustus. The Augusta knew far more than I about the mood of our hill folk, and her representatives are already there, calming them." Justin's admiration for Theodora was greater than his concern, and he grinned.

"How do they propose to perform this act of magic?"

"I don't know, really." The boy became edgy, recalling Theodora's solemn warning to avoid discussions of religion with the Emperor.

But Justinian was aware of more than he had been willing to admit. "A lifetime has passed since I left home, but Macedonians never change. They don't accept the word of outsiders, so why should they believe that there will be no changes made in their doctrines of faith?"

The blue eyes of the adolescent grew wide. "They know the Empress always keeps her word, and they'll believe her before they'll believe each other."

"Do you accept her promises, too?"

The boy recognized the need for diplomacy. "You've had a quarrel with the Patriarch Anthimus, Augustus. I'm just a student, and I know nothing about theology, so I'm not capable of judging the merits of the arguments. All I know is that I have confidence in you, just as I have in the Augusta. I know you realized, long before I was born, that the Empire is made up of many different people, and that they remain united because they're allowed to keep their own religions and customs. That's what you yourself told me when I first came to Constantinople. I've never forgotten it, and I never will. You called it the secret of Imperial rule, which is just what the Augusta said today. So I'm positive you'll find a way, the right way—whatever it may be—to work out an agreement with the patriarchs that will benefit everyone."

Justinian studied his young relative, who radiated optimism. "You sound very certain of the outcome."

"Oh, I am. The Augusta told me you've been studying the problem, and she promised me you'd find the right solution."

Justinian wondered how long he could avoid falling into the trap Theodora had set for him. The issue at stake was no longer merely his right to dictate theological concepts to the clergy, but had become even more basic: was he the master in his own house?

TWELVE

❦ ❦ ❦

The Persians watched the Roman Empire becoming weaker, and their generals awaited the right moment to strike a mortal blow at their ancient foes. The barbarians who had been driven from the Italian peninsula, Spain, and North Africa took heart, and prepared for the reconquest of the vast territories from which their warriors had fled. And, north of the Danube River, the tribal chieftains of a young and vigorous people, the Lombards, made plans to sweep south through the land of the Bulgars, Macedonia and Greece and, perhaps, capture the most glittering of prizes, Constantinople itself.

Justinian's espionage service reported developments everywhere, and the Emperor knew he might be forced to pay a high price for his stubborn refusal to admit that he might have been wrong in his argument with his wife and the Church hierarchy of the East. But his generals assured him that the borders of the Empire were safe. No other nation, civilized or barbarian, had yet learned the secret of Greek fire, and the terrible weapon would protect the frontiers for centuries to come.

But an unexpected foe struck the first blow, an enemy

that respected neither national boundaries nor weapons invented by man.

No one was certain where the pestilence first appeared. It was rumored that the town of Daras in distant Armenia, near the Persian border, was suffering from the plague. Antioch and Beirut had been swept by an epidemic, but Jerusalem had been mysteriously and providentially spared. Nomads fled from the Sinai Peninsula, but caravans traveling across the desert to Egypt were decimated, and the survivors wearily turned back.

But the plague struck where it pleased, and all three of Egypt's principal cities, Alexandria, Tanis, and Pelusium, suffered staggering losses. Narses wrote from Rome that the Italian towns had been infected, and that the strange disease had leaped across the Alps to attack the Goths.

Justinian conferred with his Council of State and asked the advice of every competent physician he knew, finally deciding to seal off Constantinople from both sea and land. But it was too late. A street vendor who sold meat cakes to visiting seamen came down with a raging fever, as did a daughter of Venus. An attempt was made to isolate the two victims, who were allowed to die untended, but within a day scores of other citizens were stricken, and the plague spread swiftly through the city.

In virtually every case the symptoms were identical. The victims complained of headaches, dizziness, and nausea. Within a few hours they were felled by high fevers, and less than a day later huge boils appeared somewhere on the bodies of the stricken. If a boil broke, a victim sometimes recovered; if it did not, he died, and death was also inevitable when a boil was lanced. Physicians, including the most learned lecturers on medicine at the university, admitted their ignorance of the plague's cause and cure. And the clergy could not claim, as their predecessors had done in past ages, that God spared the saintly and punished the evil. Many virtuous men and women died, and many scoundrels survived. The plague's attack was irrational, lacking any element of human justice.

The Council of State, by a majority vote, petitioned the Emperor to close off the Imperial compound to the outside world, but Justinian refused. Conditions in Constantinople were becoming more chaotic with each passing day, and he insisted that government officials remain at their posts. Farmers were refusing to bring produce into the city. The Imperial granaries were opened to all who wanted food, but the citizens would not visit the warehouses when it was learned that several men had fallen ill just inside the entrance to the main storage building and had died there.

Men, women, and children dropped in the streets, in the churches, and in public buildings. Survivors sometimes fled from their homes, leaving their doors open, but there was a remarkable lack of looting; even the most hardened criminals were afraid to go into houses the plague had visited. The great harbor was deserted, naval and commercial vessels having put out to sea in the vain hope that their masters and crews would be spared. The bazaars were empty, the slave markets had been closed, and no caravans entered or left the city.

There was no need for the university to suspend its classes, since lecturers and students alike absented themselves from public gatherings. The army brigades stationed in the city made a brief, futile attempt to maintain order, but the effort was abandoned when whole battalions fell ill and troops by the hundreds died.

Justinian issued a decree ordering that the bodies of plague victims be buried, but the command was ignored. Gravediggers who were spared could not be persuaded to touch the dead, and slaves, more afraid of the pestilence than of their masters' threats, could not be forced to perform the grisly task.

From the time the plague first struck Constantinople, Theodora went out into the city each day to do what she could to help the victims. Refusing a bodyguard and ignoring a curt, written order from Justinian commanding her to remain inside the Imperial compound, she went everywhere on foot, giving financial help and comfort to survivors and in a number of instances nursing the stricken.

She hoped that others would follow her example, but even the most courageous of her entourage were too terrified. A very few ladies from the seraglio hesitantly followed her into the city, however, and when a bearded giant in the robes of a patriarch suddenly appeared on the Mesé, a number of priests and monks overcame their fright, too.

Belisarius spent two days in his palace with his family, but when he heard of the Empress' activities, he went into the streets, which encouraged some of his veterans to do the same. But the pestilence was so widespread that the small number of volunteers could not stem the tide. Not until many months later did it occur to anyone that those who had exposed themselves to the pestilence had gained immunity from its ravages. Neither physicians nor theologians were able to explain the strange phenomenon.

Theodora worked in the city from dawn until dusk each day, and on the eighth evening, bone-weary and heartsick, she was walking unattended up the hill that led to the Imperial compound when a young officer of the household guard approached her at a run.

Dropping to one knee, he caught his breath. "We've been watching for the Augusta from the walls. The Emperor—." He halted, unable to finish.

A spasm of fear gripped Theodora. "He's ill?"

"He went to his bed an hour or two ago with a violent headache, and now he's suffering from a fever."

It was useless to berate the officer, or his superiors, for that matter. She should have been notified at once, but Constantinople had become a city of cowards, and she needed her breath for the climb to the top of the hill.

The uneasy leader-of-fifty preceded her, but there were no pedestrians to be cleared from her path.

A tall, bearded figure fell in beside Theodora. "I heard," he said. "I'm coming with you."

"You can't, Patriarch." She felt unaccustomed panic welling up in her. "No one has molested you as you've gone back and forth from the seraglio to the city, but you can't expect to be ignored in the Emperor's own palace. If he's still in his right mind he'll recognize you and have you arrested—"

"I'm coming with you, child," Anthimus repeated.

She knew it was useless to argue, and was oddly flattered because he, of all the Empire's citizens, did not address her as Augusta.

The single sentry at the compound gate saluted, as did the household guards at the entrance to the main palace. Theodora, in spite of her anxiety over her husband, noted that not one of the soldiers was surprised to see Anthimus. Obviously the entire staff knew she had been giving him shelter, but in a time of national catastrophe no official would place the fugitive patriarch under arrest without a direct order from the Emperor. Not even the most dedicated of officers wanted to risk Divine retaliation at a time when thousands were falling ill and dying.

Two badly frightened young officers were standing sentry duty outside the entrance to the private Imperial suite, and three uneasy physicians were conferring in an anteroom.

Theodora's sharp gesture halted them when they would have fallen to their knees in greeting. "Who is with the Emperor?" she demanded.

"We're attending him, Augusta. From here." The senior physician knew he had to tell her the truth. "There's nothing we can do for him in the bedchamber, so—"

"So you're staying as far as possible from him in the hope

you'll be spared. I know." There was no rancor in her voice. "Send relays of runners to the mountains for snow. In the meantime I want water from the garden spring— it's the coldest in the compound. And sheets. About ten of them. I'll look after my husband myself."

She opened the door and went into the Emperor's bed-chamber, Anthimus a step behind her.

A single taper was burning on a table, but even in the uncertain, flickering light that it cast, a single glance at the florid-faced man in the bed was enough. Theodora had seen so many cases of the plague in the past eight days that she recognized the symptoms immediately.

As she went to the Emperor's bedside Anthimus used the taper to light several oil lamps.

Justinian saw his wife, recognized her and feebly waved her away. "Don't come near me," he said thickly. "You'll get this accursed plague, too."

She paid no attention and propped several pillows beneath his head and shoulders. "You'll feel a little better when we wrap you in cool, wet cloth."

"Nothing will help," he replied. "I'm going to die, and I beg you, for the sake of the love we bear each other, to leave me."

He had addressed no personal remark to her for more months than she could recall, much less confessed that he still loved her, and tears came to her eyes. But her voice was firm as she said, "Because of our love, I'm staying."

Anthimus came forward to place a lamp on the bedside table. "Don't speak of death, Augustus. If it's possible to save you, we shall."

Theodora caught her breath as her husband focused on the tall figure.

"I'd have known your voice anywhere, Patriarch," Justinian said, and managed a short, gasping laugh. "I've heard rumors these past days that you've appeared out of no-where, but I've been too busy to look into the story."

Anthimus expertly stripped away several silken covers. "I've noticed," he told Theodora, "that the patients who are bundled too tightly have the most difficult time."

Justinian continued to peer at him. "If you've come to gloat, I don't blame you."

The observation was unworthy of him, and even though he was desperately ill, Theodora felt ashamed.

But Anthimus took no offense. "I don't know if my prayers will help, but I intend to pray for you. And I'll give the Augusta any practical help she needs."

"If I've sinned," the Emperor muttered, "God has chosen His own way to punish me. In my extremity, only the wife I cast out and the priest whose life I sought have come to attend me. Are there demons in Hades, Patriarch, or are they part of our superstitious folklore? If they're real, how they must be laughing at me now!"

Theodora bent over him, and, paying no attention to her own safety, placed a cool hand on his forehead. "Save your strength," she said. "There's a long, hard battle ahead, and you'll need all of your energy."

Justinian was startled by her intensity. "I can't believe the life of any one man is important."

"The Empire needs you," she said, speaking very slowly and distinctly. "Only you can rebuild it after the pestilence has passed. The Church needs you, too. Only you, with your knowledge of doctrine, can reconcile the East and West. When you're better, we'll tell you of the patriarch's correspondence with Pope Vigilius, and of their inability to find a common ground for their beliefs. You can help them, Justinian. Only you have the power and the knowledge to guide them toward each other and undo the harm you caused when you widened the breach between East and West."

The Emperor was too tired to reply, but his faint smile indicated he had known there had been correspondence.

Theodora leaned still closer to him. "I need you, too,

Justinian," she said. "I'd willingly give up my power, even my throne, if you wished. I'm a woman who needs your love. So fight, please fight—for the Empire, the Church, and for me."

For a moment or two he returned her steady gaze.

Theodora believed he had understood, and intended to battle for his life against the dark forces of the pestilence. That belief would sustain her in the long, terrible days that lay ahead.

※ ※ ※

Theodora and Anthimus remained in Justinian's sickroom, nursing him day and night. Occasionally one or the other slept, and sometimes they remembered to send for food, but all of their energies were devoted to the care of their patient. They wrapped him in sheets that had been soaked in cold well water, and when runners brought snow from the mountains, they immersed him in it for periods long enough to bring down his raging fever. They watched a boil appear on his body and grow steadily, but when they discovered that the snow temporarily reduced its size, they gave up their attempts to hold down his fever and let the plague take its course.

Not wanting word to spread that the Emperor was near death, a situation that might cause the already panicky citizens of Constantinople to riot, Theodora allowed no one else to enter the bedchamber, and found it easy to enforce her ruling. Government officials, household guards, and personal servants all demonstrated a desire to stay as far as possible from the Emperor. One day blended into the next, and as heavy drapes were drawn across the windows to protect the patient's sensitive eyes from sunlight, the Empress and the patriarch frequently did not know or care whether it was day or night.

Throughout his illness, Justinian was out of his mind

most of the time, emerging from his delirium only briefly. At such moments Theodora encouraged him to take nourishment, and he was too weak, too confused, to realize that she splashed distilled grape wine into the cups of goats' milk that she held to his lips.

After several days of slow deterioration the Emperor fell into a coma, and there appeared to be little that either of his dedicated attendants could do to help him. Anthimus went to the far side of the chamber to pray in a loud, firm voice that fatigue had made hoarse, and Theodora dropped to her knees at her husband's bedside, aware that the crisis was at hand. Justinian's breathing was labored and shallow, and she had seen others slip away quietly, never regaining consciousness before they died.

If Justinian lost his life, she knew her own reign would come to a sudden end, too. To the best of her knowledge, young Justin had not been stricken by the plague, and would become Emperor the moment his cousin expired. The boy was as yet incapable of ruling in his own right, of course, particularly when conditions throughout the Empire were chaotic, and therefore would, in all probability, ask for her help in the dangerous months ahead. But he would acquire his own advisers as time passed, and she would make no overt attempt to retain her influence over him.

She would remain Dowager-Empress until the end of her life, to be sure, and would enjoy the privileges of wealth and rank. But she was startled by the realization that, with Justinian gone, she would have no desire to retain power, no desire to share in the rule of the Empire. In fact, she thought as a wave of desolate loneliness swept over her, she would want to retire from the world, perhaps to a remote place where she could meditate, keeping her distance from the problems and struggles of the power-seekers.

What she had told Justinian when trying to prepare him for his struggle was true: her need for him was great, far greater than she had ever been able to admit to herself, and without him her position would lose its savor. Although she had always hated weakness in her own sex, she told herself she was a despicably weak woman, and loathed herself because of it.

Justinian stirred slightly, and emitted a sound that was part moan, part scream.

Theodora became rigid. "The boil has burst!" she said.

Anthimus joined her, and in silence they watched the poison drain from the Emperor's body. Then the patriarch began to pray again, and Theodora was reminded that the crisis was not yet ended. The next few hours would be decisive: either Justinian would succumb after ridding himself of the fatal poison, or would have a fair chance of survival.

✿ ✿ ✿

His eyes slightly glazed, Justinian lay on the clean bedclothes, his head and shoulders propped on pillows as he slowly sipped a chalice of goat's milk that had been fortified with distilled wine. "I can remember nothing since you told me to fight for my life," he muttered.

"That was many days ago," Theodora told him. "But don't try to talk now. You're weaker than you know."

"You also told me," he continued, ignoring her advice, "that you need me."

"I do. I knew it then, and I've learned how very much I need you. When I came so close to losing you, I was—in despair."

He could not see her too clearly, but tried to study her face. "You look tired."

She made no reply.

His mind functioning slowly, Justinian made a shrewd guess. "I've seen no one except you since I've come to my senses. Did you look after me—alone?"

"No, Anthimus was with me." She wished she didn't sound so defensive.

"Anthimus. Now I remember."

"You owe your life to him as much as to me."

Justinian tried to smile, but the effort was too great. "You've won a different sort of battle, haven't you?"

She looked at him.

"I'd be an ungrateful wretch if I arrested him for treason. What's treason? A man who saves the life of the Emperor can't be a traitor."

"We'll talk of all these things another time."

"No. Where is Anthimus now?"

"In the next room, sleeping."

"I'd like—to thank him."

"He wants no thanks."

"All the more reason for me to tell him I'm grateful." Justinian lowered his arm, the chalice suddenly becoming too heavy for him to hold.

Theodora took it from him.

"What did the physicians say after they examined me this afternoon?"

"That you'll recover."

"They told me that much themselves. But then they talked privately with you beyond the closed door. I want to know."

"They were afraid you'd become discouraged, and I'm frightened, too. But you have a right to know. If you were younger and stronger, you might recover quickly. But you suffered badly, after abusing your body for many years by working so hard. Someone in your condition needs a long period of recuperation. If you try to work again too soon, you'll collapse—and kill yourself. You need complete rest."

"For how long?"

Theodora was afraid to tell him, and hesitated.

Justinian's eyes burned in his gaunt face.

"Many months," she said reluctantly. "They can't

really predict yet. Remember, this was the first time they've examined you in all these days."

"Tell me."

"They spoke in terms of—at least a year."

He leaned back against the pillows and closed his eyes.

"I'm sorry," Theodora murmured.

"I thank God I'm alive." He was silent for some moments. "Are any members of the Secretariat alive and on duty?"

"Of course."

"Send for someone. Let him bring a tablet and stylus, and my seal. And send for a few magisters and ministers who can act as witnesses."

"What—"

"Do as I ask, Theodora. Please. I'm growing drowsy again and can't stay awake much longer."

Afraid he intended to issue an order for the arrest of Anthimus, yet unable to disobey his direct request, she did as she had been bidden.

The government officials arrived, and even though assured that the Emperor was on the mend, clustered nervously at the far side of the chamber, plainly unwilling to approach someone who had suffered from the plague. The secretary would have kept his distance, too, but Theodora beckoned, and he reluctantly approached the bed.

"Write these words," the Emperor said. "We, Justinian, Caesar Augustus, being temporarily unfit to rule in our own right, hereby appoint our beloved Empress, Theodora Augusta, to act as Regent in our stead, granting her the total authority vested in our person."

The secretary wrote rapidly on the clay tablet.

Justinian, exhausted by the effort, was unable to speak again, but gestured feebly, indicating he wanted the Imperial seal.

The secretary gave it to him, and with a trembling hand

the tired man pressed it into the clay before closing his eyes and dropping off to sleep.

Theodora had been so concerned about his health that the problems of ruling the Empire had not crossed her mind. But now, suddenly, she realized she would reign alone until Justinian recovered. In the most practical of terms he had demonstrated that he needed and trusted her, too, and as she felt the weight of the burden he had thrust on her, she hoped she would have the wisdom, strength, and stamina to sit alone on the throne.

THIRTEEN

❦❦❦

The wives and mistresses, daughters and mothers of prominent men had influenced the policies of the most powerful nation in the civilized world, but never before had a woman been the sole ruler of the Roman Empire. Governors of provinces and generals, magisters and the judges who sat on the bench of the highest courts, would have objected, feeling themselves denigrated by subservience to a mere woman, but the turmoil everywhere, in the wake of the plague, was so great that they were relieved to let someone else assume the final responsibility.

No one knew or would ever know how many had died, although the Council of State estimated that at least 500,000 persons had been killed and an equal number invalided. Whole towns and villages were inhabited only by ghosts, farms were untended, and military garrisons reduced from one-half to one-third of their previous strength. Noble families were destroyed, leaving no heirs, the contents of warehouses rotted, and caravan routes became deserted trails.

Patience, effort, and money were needed to repair the ravages of the plague, and Theodora went to work with a vengeance, promoting men of promise to replace high-ranking officials who had died, relying on the lieutenants of Justinian who had survived. Making her husband's work sanctum her headquarters, she labored from dawn until long after midnight each day, conferring with subordinates and making the decisions which initiated the rebuilding. The first task was that of feeding and clothing the living, burying the dead, and finding homes for orphans. Children, strangely, had been relatively immune to the plague, and in them lay the Empire's future. The Empress, setting an example, converted her seraglio into a home for boys and girls who had lost their parents. And the Patriarch Anthimus, who quietly resumed his place as the head of the Eastern Church, transformed most of the monasteries under his jurisdiction into orphanages.

The drain on the Imperial treasury was heavy, and Theodora began to understand the limitations of Peter Barsymes, who tried to meet her demands for money, but could not. The Empress was tempted to recall John of Cappadocia from his cruel exile in Alexandria, but refused to give in to the urge. There was a principle at stake, and no matter how great the financial need, she felt compelled to prove that the Empire would not rely on the services of a dishonest man.

Slowly, almost imperceptibly, living conditions began to improve. The surviving farmers grew new crops and sent their produce to the cities. Tanneries and mills reopened, ships reappeared in the Empire's ports, and caravans again moved on the long-deserted trade routes. The battle was not yet won, but as Theodora told the convalescing Justinian, she finally had reason to believe that the Empire would recover.

But the enemies of Rome had no intention of allowing the once-powerful nation to regain her strength, and a new crisis erupted. Chosroes of Persia sent his legions against Edessa, and other Persian columns, augmented by hordes of barbarians, were marching on Constantinople itself. Narses sent an urgent appeal for help from Italy, saying the Goths were gathering their forces in the Alps, and word from Carthage indicated that the Vandals were forming a new assault force in the North African interior.

Officers of the Imperial military staff who had survived the plague inundated Theodora with advice. She presided at three long meetings of the Council of War, and the generals, furiously competing for the vacant post of chief field commander, contradicted one another, each claiming that only his plan could prevent the dissolution of the Empire.

Theodora knew she was too ignorant of military affairs to make the right decision, and after asking the generals to leave outlines of their plans with her, retired to Justinian's work sanctum to reflect on the dilemma. There was only one solution, she decided, and sent for Belisarius.

The Consul-for-Life arrived at the Imperial palace in civilian attire, and not until Theodora saw how old he looked did she realize how much his enforced retirement from the army had sapped his spirit. Never had a situation required her to use a more delicate blend of candor and guile.

"You have no cause to love me," she said. "I'm sure Antonina blames me for the years you've spent in idleness."

"A wise man," Belisarius replied diplomatically, "doesn't always listen to his wife."

"And a wise woman knows better than to come between husband and wife." Under no circumstances could she tell him of his wife's affair and its effect on his career. "I'm not important, and your opinion of me is irrelevant. You've proved your love for the Empire and your loyalty to Justinian, and they need your advice." She told him of the many threats from the Empire's foes, and handed him the latest reports from the frontiers, which were written in a terse, military style, almost a language of its own, that made little sense to her.

Belisarius glanced through the documents, quickly absorbing their contents, but made no comment.

"For the past three days," Theodora said, "I've been meeting with the Council of War. Would you care to see the generals' recommendations?"

Belisarius managed to look less haggard, almost handsome when he smiled. "That won't be necessary. All of them served under me at one time or another, and I know their minds."

It was apparent that he held none of them in high regard, and Theodora drew a deep breath. "I've managed to cope with civilian problems of food and health and transportation, but I'm no soldier. What should I do?"

"The plague," Belisarius said, "did what no human enemy could accomplish. It destroyed our finest brigades. If there were time, I'd urge you to recruit new forces. But the Persians are already in the field, the barbarians are ready to strike the moment they believe they can beat us, and Constantinople itself will fall long before any new regiments would be ready for combat."

None of the generals had given her such a pessimistic prediction, but she felt instinctively that Belisarius was not exaggerating.

"Chosroes has chosen the perfect time to strike," he said, "and the barbarians are vultures waiting to pick the bones of the Empire after he defeats us."

Theodora's heart sank. "Then you think I should make peace with him and accept whatever terms he may dictate?"

"Under no circumstances!"

For the first time in many days Theodora laughed. "I know it's what he expects a woman Regent to do, and for that reason alone I'd like to confound him." Her smile faded. "But I don't see how it's possible for a weakened Empire to defeat so many enemies."

"I'm not saying it can be done. But it's possible."

Belisarius shuffled through the reports until he found the one he was seeking. "Edessa can hold out for months. Her garrison is strong, she has ample supplies of food, and there's time to send enough Greek fire there to hold her besiegers at bay. Chosroes made a mistake, you see, and we can take advantage of his error. He should have sent an overwhelming force against Edessa to crush her quickly, sweep through Armenia, and capture all of Syria and Palestine before sending a force against Constantinople. Well, he hasn't, so we should let the Edessa garrison take care of itself, with the aid of Greek fire, and concentrate our forces on the more important front."

She felt herself becoming confused. "What forces?"

"I'm sorry, Augusta. I see I take too much for granted. Our only hope lies in making an appeal to our retired veterans to enlist for this one campaign."

The idea seemed so obvious and simple that she wondered why she hadn't thought of it herself, but she knew she was incapable of dealing in such concepts. "That's brilliant," she said.

"No, but it's our only hope. The barbarians will wait to see whether we're beaten before they act, and I can promise you that if we should win, the peace won't be broken in Italy, Spain, and Carthage."

"Will the veterans reenlist?"

"If you make a personal appeal to them, yes. If you'll call them to rallies in the Hippodrome, on the Mesé—in all parts of the city."

"I'll do it on one condition. I insist that the most famous of veterans come out of retirement, too, and take command of the army."

Belisarius could not resist the temptation to let her see he was less ingenuous than she had supposed. "Aren't you afraid I'll turn against you and steal the throne? With Justinian spending his days sleeping and strolling in the garden, it would be easy to drive a woman Regent into exile."

"I deserve that." She met his gaze. "I never doubted *your* loyalty, and I have complete confidence in you now. These aren't empty words, Belisarius. I offer you the complete command of the entire army and navy, and disposal of all three arsenals of Greek fire. Do what you will, on your own initiative. You'll have my automatic approval, and I ask only that you keep me informed. My offer isn't limited to the one campaign, either. Keep the command as long as you live. I'll put the terms in writing, and I'll seal the bargain before the Council of War. Does that satisfy you?"

The man who had been the dashing conqueror of Carthage and Rome stood and ran a hand through his short, graying hair. "You wouldn't know this, but I was in love with you many years ago."

"I suspected it."

"If you had become my wife, I imagine I'd be Emperor now." His smile was forced. "That doesn't bother me. I never wanted the Empire. But I sometimes can't help thinking of the life we'd have had together." Suddenly he held himself erect and his voice became crisp. "I accept your offer, Augusta, but for the sake of what might have been, don't put it in writing."

Theodora couldn't remember when she had felt more like a woman and less like an Empress.

🏵🏵🏵

Peter Barsymes owed his position as magister and director of Imperial finances to Theodora, but never felt at ease when dealing with her. He had always found Justinian reasonable, logical, and amenable to the dictates of common sense, no matter how pressing a claim on the treasury. But the Empress demanded the impossible, and whenever Peter felt her piercing eyes looking through him, he couldn't help remembering the fate of John of Cappadocia. Even though he himself was honest, the Empress' opinion of him was all that mattered, and if she became sufficiently displeased with him, he might be tortured, sent into exile, or, for all he knew, murdered.

Spreading papers on her worktable, he made one more effort to convince her that he could not perform miracles at her bidding. "Augusta," he said in his clipped, controlled voice, "these figures on our expenditures and income will tell you their own story. Tax collections dropped to almost nothing during and after the plague, but you spent large sums—very large sums—to restore our trade and commerce." His tone hinted that he believed she had spent more than circumstances had warranted.

Justinian had been right, Theodora told herself wearily, when he had called Peter a man of limited imagination. The magister believed it was his duty to keep the treasury filled, and begrudged expenditures of money for any purpose. Other government officials had complained to her of their difficulties with him, and now it was her turn to suffer.

"I'm sure you've heard," she said, "even in the depths of your precious vaults, that a corps of Persian troops and a huge horde of barbarian Huns recruited by Chosroes' agents in the land of the Volga are approaching Constantinople."

Peter carefully ignored her sarcasm. Only the deaf, dumb, and blind were unaware of the city's peril. Veterans arrived from the countryside each day to join the defense corps that had marched off to meet the advancing foe, and every able-bodied citizen in Constantinople was being recruited to build the city's walls higher. "I know our situation is rather dangerous, Augusta," he said, "but I have great confidence in the talents of General Belisarius."

"So have I, but he can't perform miracles. His army needs food, and we emptied the warehouses when the survivors of the plague were starving. If he takes meat and grain from the farmers without paying them, he—and the

Crown—will earn their enmity. His veterans are making great personal sacrifices by returning to the army and risking their lives for the Empire. Most of them have wives and children at home, and even the families of veterans need food and clothing and shelter."

"To be sure, Augusta." The magister remained stiff-necked, unyielding.

"You may recall that in the recruiting speeches I made in various parts of the city, I promised every veteran he'd be paid his wages in full, each month, from the day he enlisted until the campaign ended."

"I have no intention of criticizing the Augusta's high motives, which were splendid. But I'm afraid your zeal wasn't practical."

"I cannot and will not break my word to men who will decide the fate of the Empire," she said coldly.

Peter could feel an invisible rope tightening around his neck, but had to hold firm. "I beg you, Augusta, spend a moment or two looking at the figures I've prepared for you."

"They mean nothing to me!"

He choked back the retort that her attitude made it obvious she didn't understand them. "In the past six months," he said patiently, "we've spent all that we had accumulated in the three preceding years."

Theodora glanced down at the financial tables, which usually bored and confused her, but now, combined with what Peter Barsymes had just said, a pattern was beginning to emerge. "Are you trying to tell me we're short of funds?"

"The treasury is almost empty, Augusta. Tax receipts will start coming in by next month, of course, and there will be enough to pay the routine expenses of the government, but—"

"By next month," she cut in, "I may be marched through the cities of Persia in chains, and you could well become a slave in Chosroes' household. Or they may give you to the Huns, who are even more brutal in their treatment of people they defeat. We can't wait until next month for money!"

It didn't matter, Peter thought, if the Empress sentenced him to death now or if the agony was postponed. "If you wish, Augusta, come with me to the vaults yourself, and you'll see there isn't enough gold there to pay more than a small fraction of what you want for the army."

"If you'd made yourself clear in the first place, we wouldn't have wasted all this time." Sniffing angrily, Theodora rang a bell and then hurried to the door to confer in low tones with the lady-in-waiting who answered her summons.

It still disturbed Peter to see women occupying the Imperial suite, but his face remained blank.

The Empress returned to the worktable and pointed at his papers. "Remove those documents! I refuse to admit failure!"

"Yes, Augusta." The real tragedy of the Empire's fall, he thought, was the inability of Justinian to take charge of affairs before his realm collapsed.

Theodora watched him as he gathered the papers.

Aware of her steady gaze, he dropped a scroll onto the floor and hastily stooped to pick it up.

The lady-in-waiting returned, followed by several serving maids, each of them carrying a large cloth-of-gold bag.

At a sign from the Empress the containers were placed on her worktable, and the women withdrew.

Theodora opened a bag and emptied it onto the table.

Peter immediately recognized her Imperial crown of pearls, diamonds, and emeralds.

She continued to turn the bags upside down.

The magister blinked at the rings, bracelets, and necklaces, all of them blazing with precious stones.

"These," she said, "are my personal and official gifts from

the Emperor. What would you estimate their worth to be?"

"I—I couldn't say, Augusta, but they've cost a vast fortune."

"Are they the equal of the gold that would fill your main vaults?" she demanded.

"Easily."

"Then sell them, and send every copper you get to Belisarius!"

The magnitude of her sacrifice was overwhelming, and Peter felt compelled to protest. "No other woman on earth has a collection of gems that can equal this, Augusta!"

She swept the jewels back into the bags. "Take them! I'd rather lose a few colored stones than the Empire itself. And Peter, if you value your life, tell no one what I've done!"

❀ ❀ ❀

Each day a fresh crop of rumors sprang up in Constantinople and spread through the city. Belisarius' corps of outnumbered veterans had been defeated in a pitched battle and had suffered heavy losses; the defenders had been scattered, and the host of Persians and Huns would soon reach the gates of the Imperial capital. The Roman legions were using Greek fire, but the foe was continuing to advance. Belisarius had been decapitated. Belisarius had been captured and taken off to Persia as a prisoner; his fate was certain castration and employment in the harem of Chosroes as a slave-eunuch. The conquerors of Italy and Carthage had demonstrated their good sense by selling out to the enemy.

All of the rumors were pessimistic, and none were true. "*I am maneuvering*," Belisarius wrote in a brief dispatch to the Regent Theodora, "*and since I lack the men to challenge the foe, I am awaiting the opportunity to take him by surprise on ground of my own selection favorable to our cavalry and light infantry. Only in the event of the most dire circumstances will I fall back on Constantinople and make a stand there with Greek fire catapults. Be of good cheer.”*

Theodora announced that Belisarius had not yet fought the enemy, but her official proclamation failed to calm the fearful residents of the city. She realized that only by keeping them busily and usefully employed would it be possible to avoid a major panic, so she ordered citizens, slaves, and even foreigners of every class, from young boys to elderly men, to participate in the continuing task of strengthening Constantinople's walls.

Huge boulders from the Asia Minor hinterland were ferried across the straits, and were broken into smaller rocks by men armed with heavy mallets. Long lines were formed, the rocks were passed from hand to hand and finally set in place on the thick, towering walls. No halt was called at dusk, the work was pressed by night as well as by day, and the women of the city were conscripted to prepare and serve meals, funds for the purchase of food coming from Peter Barsymes' sale of the Empress' jewels. Men who were relieved for a few hours were not permitted to leave the scene of their labors, but threw themselves to the ground in the shadow of the wall for some sleep.

People worked sullenly, without spirit, and Theodora concluded that only her own presence in their midst might arouse them. Realizing it was impossible for her to make her way along the top of the wall in trailing robes with full sleeves, she removed the sleeves of a purple gown, chopped off the long skirt, and climbed to the top of the city's defense bastion. Rough stones just set in place made it difficult for her to walk, so she removed her gold, gem-encrusted sandals, too, and the people of Constantinople were treated to the spectacle of seeing the Empress, barefooted and looking like a peasant woman, taking an active role in the extraordinary civilian effort.

Frequently she helped lower a rock into place, and even

more often she filled chinks with mortar. When someone wearily dropped out of line, she took his place before a substitute could be sent forward. And when she went to the inner base of the wall to see how the women fared, she unhesitatingly served food to the workers, including obvious ruffians and even slaves. Her attitude made it evident that she did not believe she was demeaning herself, and soon every noblewoman and lady of breeding were following her example.

Expending her energies recklessly, she worked from early morning until late at night, and would have slept in the open, too, had the security police and Imperial household guard command not intervened. The Empress-Regent, they politely informed her, was carrying more than her share of the burden, but her unique position made it impossible for her to take personal risks beyond their ability to control. There were Persian espionage agents in Constantinople, they said, dangerous men who had not yet been identified and captured, and if the Empress slept at the foot of the wall, not even a strong detail of bodyguards could assure her safety.

Regardless of her own indifference, her life was precious. And since they were charged with her protection, they insisted she return to the Imperial compound to sleep. She obeyed reluctantly, realizing their concern was sensible. If an enemy agent's knife killed her, the terror of the people would become uncontrollable, and riots might break out all over the city.

She knew, too, that she owed it to the convalescing Justinian to preserve his tranquillity and prevent him from suffering a physical setback. So, aware that he would worry if she did not sleep in the chamber adjoining his, she returned to the palace for a few hours each night.

Justinian, she believed, knew nothing of the crisis that threatened the Empire. The servants who attended him had been instructed to tell him nothing of events beyond the palace gates, and the nobles, staff members, and others who lived and worked in the compound had been warned that the Empress-Regent would deal with them in person if they as much as hinted to him that his capital was in danger of capture and destruction.

He seemed calm and in good spirits each morning, when Theodora spent a short time with him before going off into the city. So she was surprised, one evening soon after sundown, about three weeks after Belisarius and his veterans had left to meet the enemy, when a messenger came to her at the wall.

"The Caesar Augustus," the courier said, "hopes you'll join him whenever the Augusta finds it convenient."

Worried by the unusual request, Theodora returned at once to the Imperial compound, and not taking time to change her clothes, merely washed in a bowl of unscented water before going to his quarters. There she was informed he had gone for a stroll, and eventually she found him in the garden, where he seemed to be enjoying the song of an unusually talkative bird.

"I was just told you were looking for me, Justinian," she said, trying to speak casually.

"Thank you for coming. You have far more important things to do than keep the company of a useless old man."

She started to tell him he was neither useless nor old, but he gave her no chance.

"How soon will you be finished building up the city's walls?"

He asked the question so quietly that she was stunned.

"There are bits of mortar on your gown and legs."

Uncertain how much he had learned or guessed, she hesitated before replying.

Justinian rose from the bench on which he had been sitting and, taking her hand, led her across the garden. "By climbing the pedestal of my uncle's statue," he said, "I've been able to watch the construction work every day and on clear evenings. I haven't been able to make out the features of individuals from this distance, of course, but I couldn't help recognizing your purple gown. After all, you and I are the only two people in the Empire who wear the color. At first I thought I might be mistaken, but I've been noticing the scratches on your arms and legs, and the blisters on your hands."

She immediately thrust her hands behind her back.

"I've found it fascinating that the Empress-Regent should be doing the work of an untutored laborer. You're probably the only ruler in history who has erected stone walls with her own hands. It's a rather extraordinary way to win a place in the annals of the Empire."

"I've done it to encourage the people."

He silenced her with an awkward wave. "Oh, I understand. Far more than you think. And don't blame the servants who were assigned to keep me protected from things you didn't want me to know. Everyone from magisters to slaves realizes I'll resume my place one of these months, and no one wants my ill will. So, when I've said I wanted to be left alone here, who has had the courage to deny me?"

"How long have you—"

"Since the trouble began. In your anxiety, you've sometimes forgotten, I think, that you and I can find out anything we really want to know."

She nodded cautiously, still hoping to feel her way.

"You'll also become known as the Empress who sold her jewels to save the country. That's a great distinction."

Theodora became furious. "Did Peter Barsymes—"

"He's told me nothing, but I have my sources of information. All of your jewels are intact, I'm delighted to say, and will be returned to you after the threat is ended. They've been hidden away for the present."

Again she was astonished.

"It was the least I could do for you, and you'll need them. An Empress must stand apart from even the wealthiest of her subjects, and jewels are symbols everyone immediately understands." He smiled at her. "It was a complicated transaction, if I do say so. I sold some estates and other private property, which it was my duty to do in a time of great financial need, and my agents were instructed to pay the price Peter was asking for the jewels. There was no quibbling, no haggling."

Tears came to Theodora's eyes.

He put a hand on her arm. "Your gesture was magnificent, all the same, and I'll see that it isn't forgotten."

"I've had no idea—"

"Of course not, my dear. What you haven't quite realized is that a man who has worked hard all his life can't be content to dawdle away his days. I've tried to do what you and the physicians have wanted, and I've recognized the need for rest if I'm to regain my strength. But a life of complete idleness would have driven me mad. So it may be I've made a personal contribution to the Empire, as well as giving you tangible proof of my affection for you."

She allowed herself to weep freely, and felt a great relief. For the first time since she had assumed the burden of Regent she knew she didn't really stand alone.

"Now," Justinian said, "I've told you many things, and I think it's your turn."

"What do you want to know?"

"How goes the battle?"

Only a few hours had passed since she received a message from Belisarius telling her that he had finally engaged the foe, and she stared at her husband in wonder. "Who told you—"

"No one." He led her to a clearing near the end of the garden and pointed toward the east. In the far distance, where the earth and night sky blended, they could see a bright, steady glow of light. "That's Greek fire," Justinian said, "and could be nothing else. I first saw it early this afternoon, and knew at once that Belisarius had engaged the enemy. No other fire on earth gives off that kind of light, and after seeing it just once, anyone could identify it." He gave her a moment to absorb what he had said, then asked, "Well?"

"I know only that he's met the enemy. He said in his report that he lured the Persians and Huns into terrain best suited for his kind of warfare, and he expected to defeat them. Or perish."

Justinian was not surprised. "Shall we wait together for his next report?"

"Of course."

"Here, rather than indoors, if you don't mind." He went to the bench for his short mantle of purple and draped it around her shoulders.

There was so much Theodora wanted to say, but found herself unable to express her thoughts.

"If Belisarius is beaten," Justinian told her, "I'll go with you to the wall. I may be too weak to fight effectively when the barbarians reach the gates, but I'll stay there until we drive them back—or die together."

She found it comforting to lean against him.

"You taught me a lesson, long ago, and I won't run away from my people, I can promise you," he said.

"I know." Afraid he had taxed his strength by standing too long, she insisted they go to the bench and sit.

In the hours that followed, they spoke infrequently, and occasionally one or the other wandered to the end of the garden to stare at the fires that still burned fiercely in the distance. They had no way of knowing, as yet, whether the battle had been won or lost, whether it still raged, but neither was willing to admit the possibility that a calamity had occurred.

"I had several talks with Anthimus before we were invaded," Justinian said, "and I've read a long treatise he wrote on the divinity of Christ. His thinking is muddled, but he's no worse than some of the Western bishops, who parrot the beliefs of others and have no real convictions of their own."

"I'm not qualified to discuss these things," Theodora murmured.

"Neither am I, really, and that's where I made my mistake. I shouldn't have planned to call an ecumenical council until both sides had the opportunity to exchange opinions. The correspondence of Anthimus and Vigilius, which I stupidly would have stopped, had I been able to intercept their letters, should be encouraged. It may be that the bishops and patriarchs will find their own solutions to the problems of theology that have been perplexing us, so I intend to wait a few more years before I call an ecumenical conference. The Western position is so sensible that, by then, it should prevail."

She realized he was telling her in his own way that he had abandoned his attempt to force the Eastern Church to accept his doctrines.

"I wouldn't be surprised," he added calmly, "if the patriarchs restore Anthimus to the see of Constantinople once the war ends and they're free to travel where they please. Until then, of course, he's acting as primate again, which is proper, since he knows more about the post than anyone else."

Theodora hadn't known that her husband and the patriarch had reached an understanding, and another burden was lifted from her shoulders.

"He's admitted he was as wrong to defy me as I was to impose my doctrines on him. I don't know why it is that men of authority feel the need to challenge each other. It's strange that only you women always seek compromises that grant equal honor and justice to everyone."

Theodora smiled, but suspected that when he completely recovered his health he would become less generous to those who did not share his views. Nevertheless he had mellowed, and it was unlikely that he would ever again express the virulent intolerance that had driven the leaders of the Eastern Church to seek her protection from his wrath.

A servant approached the couple on the garden bench, aware of the Empress' order to shield the Caesar Augustus. "I have been instructed to inform the Augusta," he said carefully, "that business of state awaits her."

"Has a military courier arrived?" Theodora demanded.

The servant was surprised that she spoke so freely in the presence of the convalescing Emperor. "Yes, Augusta," he admitted. "He—"

"Send him to me, here."

A few moments later a smoke-blackened officer with a battered helmet came into the garden, saluted, and handed the Empress a scroll.

She unrolled it and showed it to Justinian, so they could read the message simultaneously.

Belisarius had scribbled a brief report in his own hand. He had won the greatest victory achieved by Imperial troops in centuries, he declared. Thousands of Huns had been killed or captured, and those who had escaped were in disorganized flight. The retreat of the Persians had been more orderly, but he and his veterans were pursuing them, and would not rest until the enemy had been driven across the borders of the Empire.

A peaceful, secure future was assured at last, and Theodora felt numb.

"The people will go wild," Justinian said. "They'll celebrate until daybreak."

She realized he was reminding her, gently, that it was her duty as Regent to prepare and publish a victory proclamation. Even when supposedly replacing him she needed his help, but was grateful for it.

Justinian stood, smiled, and yawned. "It's been a long day."

"Very long." Theodora took his arm and, half-guiding, half-leaning, walked with him through the garden to the palace.

Author's Note

☙ ☙ ☙

The story of Theodora and Justinian, told here in fiction form, is true. Few characters in human history are more remarkable than the great Emperor and Empress who rejuvenated and reformed a dying empire, and their personal backgrounds are as astonishing as their accomplishments.

The scholarly Justinian, who allegedly spent eighteen to twenty hours at his desk each day for more than forty years, was a Macedonian-born peasant, the only member of his family who became literate. His uncle, Justin, paved the way for him by preceding him as Emperor, but this help in no way makes Justinian's achievements less magnificent. He was responsible for the legal reforms instituted by his deputy, Tribonian, and their influence is felt down to the present day. He expanded the borders of the moribund, dying Roman Empire, and his tax reforms, widely copied for centuries thereafter, were unique.

Only in his attempts to reorganize Christian thinking did he fail, in part because of his own intellectual prejudices. He recognized the need to heal the breach between the Churches of East and West, and although he did not succeed, his concept of ecumenism was astonishingly far-sighted.

Theodora, his partner in all things except his dispute with the patriarchs, was extraordinary. To the best of my knowledge and belief, the basic outlines of her story, as presented in these pages, are accurate. A circus performer and prostitute in her youth, she learned to read and write with the help of the patriarchs, became Justinian's mistress and eventually his Empress, co-ruler of the most powerful nation of its age.

Possibly the world's first active suffragette, she was courageous, farsighted, and a brilliant administrator. Her example saved her husband's throne when a revolution threatened to topple him, and she voluntarily sacrificed her jewels, her only fortune, to save the Empire.

At the same time she was inordinately ambitious, jealous of Justinian's lieutenants, and, a product of a despotic age, cruel in her treatment of those who stood in her path. The trick she employed to prevent the military hero, Belisarius, from becoming the heir to the throne, is accurately presented in this book. So is her vicious punishment of John of Cappadocia; limitations of space prevented me from recounting her treatment of many lesser figures who were held as captives in her private dungeons. Few stories in history are as dramatic as the technique she employed in dealing with the homosexual, Narses, whose superior talents as an administrator she preserved while bending him to her own will by "privately transforming him into a woman," as a contemporary historian wrote.

Like Justinian, she was a genius, but it cannot be denied there was evil as well as good in her complex nature, an ability to recognize the weaknesses of others, which she unhesitatingly used to enhance her own power—and strengthen the Empire. Only Tribonian escaped her wrath, and I suspect he made it his business to stay at arm's length from her.

Romantic legends to the contrary, I can find no evidence substantiating the claim that Theodora gave birth to an illegitimate daughter while a courtesan, supported the child from afar, and, long after becoming Empress, brought her grandson to Constantinople for a few years before the boy mysteriously "disappeared." It is also impossible to support the charming tale that she bore Justinian a daughter, who supposedly married a "wealthy, noble merchant" and vanished into the mists of legend. Theodora was unique, and her story needs no gilding.

Samuel Edwards